THE BREEDING CAVE

EMILIA ROSE

Copyright © 2024 by Emilia Rose LLC
All rights reserved.

Visit my website at emiliarose.com
Cover Designer: The Book Brander
Editor: Jovana Shirley, Unforeseen Editing, www.unforeseenediting.com

No part of this book may be reproduced or transmitted in any form or by any means, electronic or mechanical, including photocopying, recording, or by any information storage and retrieval system without the written permission of the author, except for the use of brief quotations in a book review.

This book is a work of fiction. Names, characters, places, and incidents either are products of the author's imagination or are used fictitiously. Any resemblance to actual persons, living or dead, events, or locales is entirely coincidental.

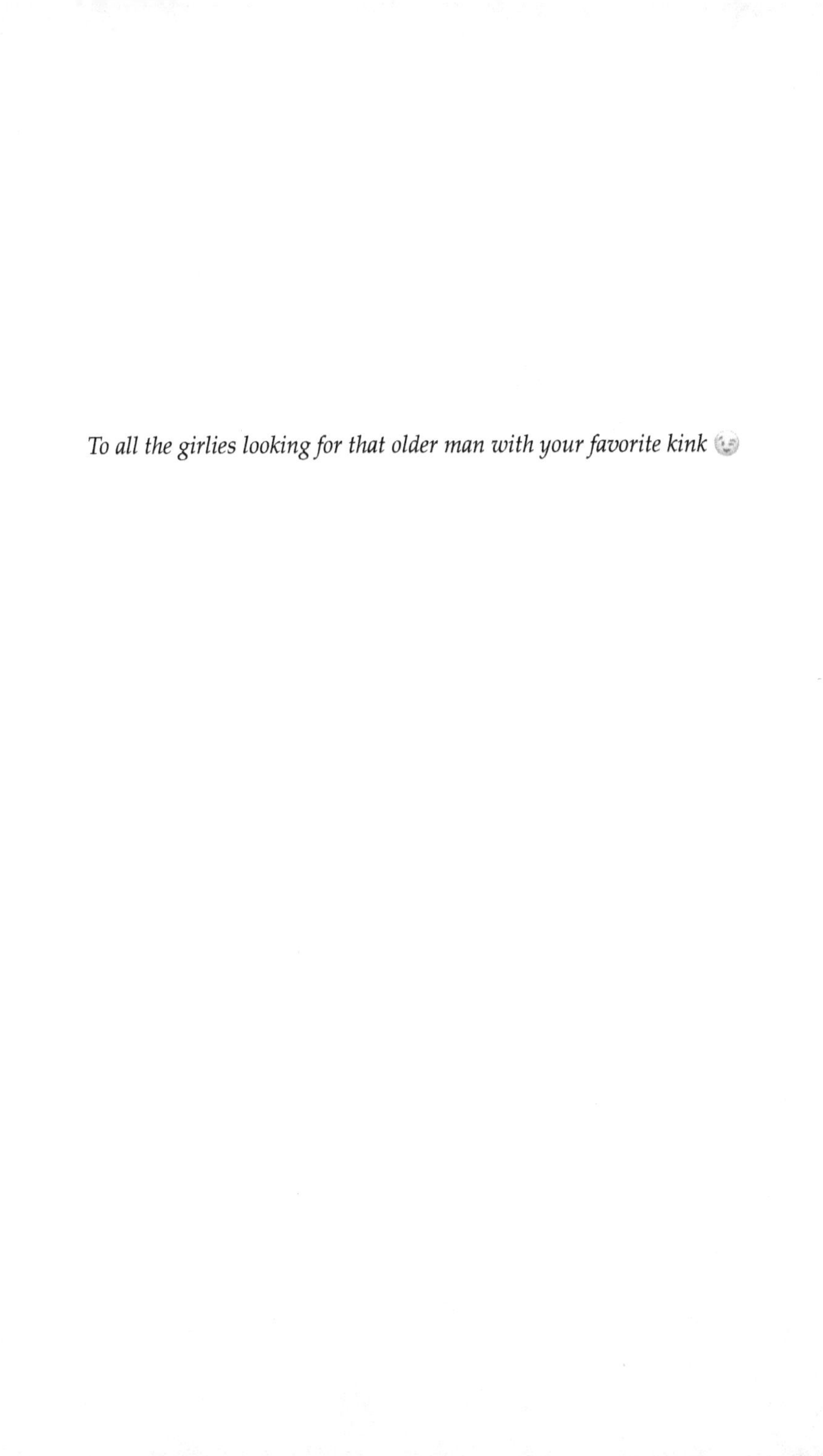

To all the girlies looking for that older man with your favorite kink 🌝

CHAPTER
ONE

YEOSIN

I GRIPPED the matte-black invitation until my fingers turned white and stared down at the words written in crimson red. Rain splattered down on the sidewalk around me from a car that raced down the city street, splashing on my black heels.

You've been selected to attend a night of lust. Along with eight other lucky participants, you'll fulfill the desires of one of nine billionaires. For your willing participation, you'll receive ten million dollars … that is, if you survive the night.

My mouth dried, and I swallowed the little spit left in it and turned over the invitation.

Halloween Night | 9 p.m. | Corner of Ninth and Waltz Street

Rain pattered down around me, smudging my mascara … or the lack thereof.

"You don't need to do this," Alvin, my boyfriend—*ex-boyfriend*—had said.

His words were still ringing in my ears from this morning, after a group of gangsters smashed all my windows in my apartment, cut all the electrical wires, then slashed my tires.

It was his fault we were living in that dump. He had spent all our savings—all *my* savings—on his business without consulting me, only for me to find out that this *business* was him gambling with the Dragon Clan.

My lips quivered. I hated him.

For what he had done to me and for what I now had to do.

I wouldn't survive another night in that neighborhood, so might as well *try* to earn some money. Besides, I still had Mom to take care of. That debt had exceeded five hundred thousand the last time I checked.

Not even a moment more passed before a black SUV with tinted windows drove up to the corner of Ninth and Waltz Street. He rolled down his window, a white mask covering his face. "Ms. Yeosin. Please get in. You're the last to arrive."

Heart pounding inside my chest, I gripped the invitation and slipped into the back seat of the car. I didn't know why the hell I had ever gotten mixed up with Alvin. If I hadn't, I wouldn't be sitting in a stranger's car, hoping he didn't kill me.

Instead of driving, he looked in the rearview mirror. "There's a blindfold to your right."

I looked over at the seat beside me to see a silky red blindfold laid out for me.

"Once you put it on, then I will take you to The Breeding Cave."

My mouth dried. "The … The what?"

"The Breeding Cave. It's where you'll meet the beast you've been paired with tonight."

While I opened and closed my mouth a handful of times, no words would come out. I took the silky blindfold into my hands and glanced back up at the driver, unable to see any of his features, as they were covered with that mask.

"What happens at The Breeding Cave?" I finally whispered.

"Put on your blindfold, Ms. Yeosin."

And so, with shaky hands, I put on the blindfold.

———

After driving for what must've been two hours down a bumpy road, the car slowed to a stop. I listened to the driver open his car door, and then a moment later, a breeze blew onto my legs to my left. He took my hand and helped me out of the car.

"You may take off your blindfold, Ms. Yeosin."

When he released my hand, I inhaled the scent of fresh rain and peeled off my blindfold. I stood in the middle of the dark woods, the only light coming from the full moon above. Behind me, a car door shut.

"Wait." I turned around and tried to reopen my door, but it was locked.

"There's a path to your right that will lead to your designated cave."

"My what?" I whispered, yanking on the door. "Let me back in."

"Good luck."

Without another word, he drove off and left me stranded.

After looking between the path and the dirt road, I chewed on my inner cheek. If I tried to walk back to the city, it would take me days, and I didn't even know which way to go. I didn't know where I was, or if some wild animal would eat me by the time I escaped this place..

"Fuck," I whispered, starting up the path.

Even if I made it back to the city, I didn't think I'd survive the night. Rumor had it that the Dragon Clan took payment in the form of loved ones, and by the way that Alvin had begged me not to come here tonight, I'd say that he still loved me.

Which meant that … I needed the money.

Desperately.

Moans and screams echoed through the forest like howls as I walked up the path. Branches snapped around me. I pressed my lips together and kept my head down, hoping that whatever kind of creatures lurked in the shadows tonight wouldn't see me.

Like the driver had said, the forest cleared out into a cave.

I stared at it for a few moments, heart pounding in my throat.

What am I doing? Dumb people do shit like this and get themselves killed!

"You've finally arrived," a deep voice said from within the cave. "Come closer, little bird."

With my heart thumping against my chest, I stepped further into the shadows. The cave walls and ceiling glowed a deep purple from the faint light that flooded in through the cracks in the rock.

"Come to me," he purred.

The scent of woods and a tinge of cinnamon drifted through my nostrils.

A shiver rolled down my spine. I wrapped my arms around my body and pulled my top over my cleavage in an attempt to hide myself. The thought of someone watching me but me not being able to see them made my skin crawl.

Another step, and then I saw him—a huge monster, probably three times my size, with glowing orange-yellow eyes and hands big enough to wrap around my entire waist. He stalked closer to me. I opened my mouth to scream at the top of my lungs, but my gaze dropped down to his cock swinging between his legs and nearly hitting his knees.

"Oh my God," I whispered. "I'm going to die here."

There was no point in running because I wouldn't be able to make it out of this cave.

When he reached me, he grunted, which sounded more like a hungry growl. "Yeosin."

"H-how do you know my name?" I whispered, craning my head to look up at him.

"I paid a lot of money to be with you," he said, walking around me and taking my hair in his hand. "I know everything about you, Yeosin. The reasons why you're here. What you like to do in your free time. How, tonight, you're the most fertile you've been all month."

My eyes widened. "Wh-what?"

He slipped one of his hands around the front of my throat,

then dipped the other between my legs to cup my now-clenching pussy. "Between your wide hips, which are perfect for bearing children, to all the breeding porn I discovered in your search history, I handpicked you to carry my children."

"What?" I whispered, my mouth dry. "To carry your … your children?"

He moved his fingers around my clit and pulled me toward him, my back against his chest and his huge cock stiffening between my legs. His mouth met my neck, and he kissed me gently at first … but the more his fingers circled my clit, the more I tightened, and the more desperate his lips became.

"Did you read the fine print on your invitation, Yeosin? By coming here, you've agreed to be my little"—he moved his finger across my clit again—"breeding"—his fingers moved faster, pushing me closer to the edge—"bitch."

Pleasure gushed between my thighs, and suddenly, I collapsed against a rock in front of me, my legs completely giving out as wave after wave of pleasure rushed through my body. My head lolled, and I moaned.

The monster grasped my hips from behind and nestled himself between my legs, the head of his cock pushing against my entrance. I dug my fingertips into the rock and cried out in pain as he plunged himself into me.

He pulled my hips toward him with every thrust. "I don't care how long it takes. I'm going to breed you until you give me children. You'll live in my penthouse, walking around with your belly and tits round … all for my enjoyment."

I tightened around him, the pleasure building up inside me again.

But how? How was I finding this enjoyable? A monster was thrusting himself inside me, telling me that … that I would be his, no matter what. That he was going to breed me over and over and over, all night, all day, as long as it took to get me pregnant.

"Are you a man or a monster?" I asked between thrusts.

"A man in the day. A monster at night," he growled. "But I will only ever fuck you in this form. My cock is bigger, can reach deeper. And my balls hold more cum inside them as a monster—better chance of getting you pregnant."

A moan escaped my lips, and I threw my head back. "Oh my God!"

"That's it," he growled. "Tell me how much you want to be bred."

"But it's wrong," I cried, the pressure rising inside me. "So wrong."

He pumped into me faster and faster. "Tell me, Yeosin. Beg for my cum."

Pussy pulsing, I dug my fingers harder against the rock. "P-please!" I cried, the pressure too much to handle. "Please, give me your cum! I want you to get me preg—"

He slammed into me as hard as he could and stilled deep in my pussy, grunting. "Let's see how many times it takes for my cum to catch and for you to start carrying my child."

CHAPTER
TWO

YEOSIN

I SQUINTED my eyes and tried to adjust to the sunlight flooding in through the floor-to-ceiling glass windows. What had happened? The last thing that I remembered was falling asleep in that cave and—

After shooting up in the Alaskan king-size bed, I looked around the huge master bedroom, furnished with plush couches and golden decor with a dash of wooden accents. A silk night-gown brushed against my skin—one that I definitely could never afford.

Where the hell was I?

Once I slipped out of the bed, I headed toward the large windows to take in the sight of the entire city. Soft pinks and oranges danced across the sky, just above the skyscrapers. I couldn't even see the streets from here.

A hint of cologne—woodsy with a hint of cinnamon—drifted through my nostrils from the master bathroom, the scent somehow … familiar. I walked across the handwoven rug that covered the marble floor toward the smell.

Was he here? Had he taken me home with him? What was his name?

Last night, I had barely questioned a goddamn thing. My body had seemed to react to him on its own, moaning and moving to the sound of his words, begging and pleading for him to … for him to …

Breed me.

I gulped and placed a hand over my stomach. Surely, he couldn't have done that in one night, right? Plus, I had strictly been on birth control for the past few years, and I had never ever, ever had one type of slipup.

Right?

My heart pounded in my ears as I approached the bathroom door. But after peering into the room and not finding him, I gently closed the door and leaned back against it with flushed cheeks. Even if I had found a man in the bathroom, preparing for the day, how would I have known if it was him? I had only seen him in beast form.

What did he look like as a human? Normal?

The aroma of freshly baked cinnamon rolls wafted through the air from the bedroom door. I pulled on my top from last night that I had found draped over a couch and peeked my head out of the room in an attempt to find an escape before bumping into someone. But a woman in the kitchen glanced over at me almost immediately and smiled.

"You're finally awake," she hummed, pulling the cinnamon rolls out of the oven.

"Um," I whispered, inching out of the room.

Come on, Yeosin. Ask her something useful! Where am I? How did I get here?

"What's that minty aroma?" I walked closer to her and inhaled deeply, spotting a vintage teapot, the type I used to marvel at while window-shopping with Mom when I was just a child. "It smells so good."

She pulled out a chair at the large table for me, then filled one

of the teacups with the minty tea. "Make sure to drink all of it."
She offered me a small smile and pushed my chair in once I sat. "I
made it specifically for you."

"Oh, um, thank you."

My gaze flickered to the end of the table toward an empty
plate. Was that from ... *him*?

Once she set a platter of cinnamon rolls on the table, she
placed one on the plate in front of me. "If I had known you were
awake, I would've started cooking breakfast for you sooner. My
apologies. The food should be ready soon."

I opened and closed my mouth a handful of times. Should I let
this happen? I didn't know this woman, why I was here, or how
the hell I'd even gotten here. What time was it anyway? Did I ever
get the ten million dollars that I had been promised?

After I sipped all the tea in my cup, she refilled it quickly.
"Have some more, Yeosin."

"You can call me Alana," I said with a half smile, taking one of
the cinnamon rolls. Since I had moved here as a child, nobody
could ever pronounce my name correctly, except *him*. An English
name was always easiest for people.

"I was told to only refer to you as Yeosin."

"By him?" I asked, taking a bite of the roll. When she nodded,
I shuffled in my seat and took another sip of my tea. I had tasted
so many types of mint tea, but nothing as good as this before.
"Where is ... *he*? Do you work for him?"

"He'll return later, but he asked me to give you this."

She handed me a sleek black card.

"What's this card for?" I asked, finishing off the sweet quickly.

"It's your payment for last night," she said.

While I didn't want to sound like an ungrateful bitch, I needed
cash to pay off the debt. Not a card. I didn't care how much
money was on it if it was a credit card. Was it even in my name? It
was completely black, only with numbers.

"Is there any way that I can get it in cash?" I whispered. "I
need it in cash."

"It's dangerous for someone like you to carry around that much money," she said.

"What do you mean, someone like me?"

"If you're going to carry the beast's child, then you need to stay safe," she said, her words coming out like whoever that beast was last night had actually wanted to breed me. "And a frail young woman like you carrying duffel bags of cash will be an easy target."

"An easy target for who?" I asked.

She paused while refilling my cup. "Enemies."

After placing the teapot down, she walked to the oven and continued making breakfast. I stared at her for a few moments, hoping she would elaborate, but she stayed silent. My gaze drifted to the steel-and-walnut dial clock hanging on the wall, and I jumped up.

"Shit, I'm going to be late!" I cursed under my breath, running back into the master bedroom to find my bottoms. I spotted them sitting on the edge of the bed and yanked them over the silky nightgown that someone had dressed me in last night.

"Where are you going?" the maid asked from the kitchen, brows drawn together. "Breakfast isn't—"

"I'm going to be late for work!" I exclaimed.

I might've had ten million dollars on this credit card, but I had debts to repay, and they didn't want a plastic card. The Dragon Clan couldn't use that. They only used cash. Anything else was way too risky.

Deciding that I didn't have time to explain—nor did I want to —I rushed out of the penthouse in a jiffy and slammed the door behind me. I glanced down the foyer at the elevator and hurried toward it.

Once I pressed the button, I bounced up and down and waited quite impatiently for it to open. I'd had an entire cinnamon roll in this guy's penthouse, and I hadn't found out a goddamn thing about him.

Come on, Yeosin. You have to do better than that next time. Not that there will be a ne—

Suddenly, someone pressed me into the wall from behind, one hand grasping my hip and the other posted on the wall beside my head. His suit jacket glided up his arm, revealing a shiny black-and-silver watch.

The scent of cologne, mixed with cinnamon rolls, drifted through my nostrils.

"Why do you need the money in cash?" the beast, dressed as a human, asked in my ear.

Warmth spread through my body, all the memories of last night crashing through me. I shifted under his touch, my body aching to surrender to him again. But I had to stay focused. I had work, and I needed to get my mind right.

Because this life of luxury was *not* me!

"I-I just prefer cash."

He drew his nose up the column of my neck. "I want to see you at The Breeding Cave tonight," he finally murmured.

"B-but I …"

"Promise me you'll be there so I don't have to hunt you down myself," he purred.

My nipples hardened, and I gulped down a moan as he pressed his hardness against my ass. I didn't want to be hunted, but the mischievousness in his voice told me that he *loved* being the hunter. And to say that I didn't want to be chased *by him* would be a lie.

He growled into my ear, "I have no problem hunting you down these city streets."

"I … I don't know how to get there," I whispered.

"There will be a car outside your apartment three minutes before midnight."

And with that, he was gone.

CHAPTER
THREE

"ALANA, I'M TAKING MY BREAK," Henry called from the front of Pink Ivory Coffee Bar. "You're on register!"

After wrapping a pink apron around my waist, I pushed some hair off my forehead, needing to ring out the next customer. Henry had a bad habit of taking his break when he didn't want to chat with guests.

As I stepped out from the back, I lifted my gaze to meet the one and only Luciano. I bit back a grunt because he wasn't the *nicest* guy around and headed to the front with a forced smile on my face.

"Would you like your usual?" I asked, trying to keep eye contact with his intense brown eyes.

With a gruff nod, he pulled out his black card and tapped it on our card reader.

"Oh, actually, one second," I said, typing on the machine as quickly as I could to get his order in before the card reader could shut down on me again today. So much for going home and relaxing after getting my money.

I tucked some hair behind my ear, heart pounding hard inside my chest, and inhaled the scent of cinnamon. Warmth suddenly gathered between my thighs at the aroma from the coffee machine behind me, and I cursed myself because ever since last night, my body had been acting fucking crazy.

The screen turned black, and I reached for the plug to restart it.

"Sorry," I mumbled to him, not daring to peek up.

Luciano was the grumpiest regular that I had ever met. Not mean per se, but I didn't think that I had ever seen him smile once. All he did was grab his coffee, find an empty table in the corner of the shop, and leave after I closed up.

Heat crawled up my torso from that sinful place between my thighs and curled around my nipples from the cinnamon aroma, making them stick right up against my shirt and command full freaking attention from underneath my pink apron.

My cheeks burned, and I tapped on the screen furiously to start it up for the fourth time today. God, why hadn't I at least *searched* for my bra back at that house before I ran away with a card that I couldn't even use and the thoughts that I might actually be pregnant plaguing me?!

"S-sorry," I stuttered. "We need a new machine."

When I peered back up at him again, he stared back with the blankest look of all looks, his dark hair tousled slightly.

The screen finally lit back up, and I quickly typed in his total.

"Okay, you can tap your card now."

"Are you sure?"

My eyes widened because those were the first words that I had heard him speak in a long time. I had almost forgotten the sound of his deep voice drifting through my ears. Except right now, there was a bit of mischief accompanying it.

Was he cracking a joke?

"Yes," I said, tucking some more hair behind my ear and playing with the end of my sleeve, which had a small hole in it. Maybe later, I could visit some shops downtown and pick out some new clothes with the card that beast had given me. "It's working now."

When Luciano tapped the card on the card reader, a loading circle popped up on my screen. I chewed on the inside of my cheek and nervously drew my fingers across the counter, just wanting this interaction with him to be over already.

The circle swirled and swirled and swirled and swirled until the screen finally turned off.

"No. No. No. No. No. No. No," I mumbled.

God, out of all customers that this could happen to, it had to be Luciano!

"I'm sorry," I said, forgoing the machine entirely and running to grab him a black coffee so I didn't piss him off any more. I didn't want him to hate me more than he did.

It was bad enough that Henry had left me during rush hour. There was already a line forming behind Luciano.

After grabbing a cup, I filled it to the top and hurriedly clasped on the lid.

This would have to do. I'd take it out of my paycheck if I needed to. I mean, I had the money now. Well, sorta. I still didn't have the cash to pay back the Dragon Clan, but I had enough for coffee. It was cheap here anyway.

Just as I was about to hand it to him, some hot coffee sloshed over the side of the cup and burned my hand. Pain shot up and down my fingers, making them shake. I set the coffee cup on the counter in front of him and grabbed a rag to my right, placing it over the wound and grinding my teeth.

"Fuck!" I hissed, squeezing my eyes shut. "That stings."

Almost immediately, Luciano reached for my burned palm, but I pulled it back.

"No, no. It's okay," I reassured him, biting back all the pain. "I'm fine. I'm fine!"

Even though I wanted to literally burst out into tears …

Once my hand stopped shaking uncontrollably, I grabbed the coffee cup, refilled it, and made sure the cap was on tight so it wouldn't spill on me again. I balled my burned hand into a fist, holding it behind my back while handing him the cup.

"Have a great day," I said with a trying smile.

Because his day sure had to be better than mine.

Luciano stared at me for a couple of moments, lingering longer than he normally did. Then he clenched his sharp jaw, his eyes blazing the way they did when he was angry, and he walked to his usual table.

What is wrong with him now?! Is it because I spilled his coffee? Did I stain his suit?

The next customer walked up to the register, and I pulled my gaze away from Mr. Grumpy to see my favorite regular here to save the day. Brent Haines, a brilliant software engineer who worked at Midnight Security Headquarters down the block, and he wasn't too bad on the eyes either.

"Don't let him freak you out," Brent said. "He can be a big ole softy."

"Who?"

Brent nodded over to Luciano.

"Luciano?" I asked, my brows shooting up. "A softy?"

Brent leaned in close and lowered his voice. "Just kidding. He scares me too."

The aroma of his cologne drifted through my nostrils, and I gently pressed my thighs together, letting out a small giggle. It was the same smell of cologne from earlier at that beast's penthouse.

Is Brent secretly the beast? If he is, then why didn't I smell that cologne last night? And that musky scent wasn't what was making my pussy ache earlier. No, it was that scent of cinnamon that was doing all sorts of things to me.

"So, do you have any plans for tonight?" I asked, trying to get as much information out of him as possible. I didn't think that Brent was a billionaire or could afford a ten-million-dollar night of sin with me, but … maybe?

At least, if he thought I was onto him, then maybe he would come clean.

He cracked a smirk and placed his forearm on the counter. "Why? You wanna do something?"

"Oh, um," I said, cheeks burning, "no."

"I'm free tonight, if you wanna grab a couple of drinks."

Fuck, why did I have to get myself into trouble?! Tell him no, Yeosin, because you have—

"Sure," I found myself saying because I was a damn people pleaser, which was how I had gotten in trouble with the Dragon Clan in the first place. But I mean, drinks with Brent couldn't be that bad, right?

Plus, I needed something before deciding whether or not to meet that beast again. I wasn't required to do anything more. He'd only paid for one night. But a deep, primal part of me might've wanted to see him again.

"Sure." I smiled. "I'd love to."

CHAPTER
FOUR

LUCIANO

IF HE TOUCHES HER, *I'll kill him.*

I glared at Brent Haines from across the crowded upscale bar in the center of the city and gritted my teeth.

After he had returned to the office, I had given him an unaccomplishable number of tasks to complete before the day's end so he would stand Yeosin up.

But that asshole had returned all the assignments back to me in record time.

With her bandaged hand, Yeosin tucked some black hair behind her ear and blushed at something that he'd said. I tightened my hand around the glass of whiskey that I hadn't even sipped yet and bit back a growl so I wouldn't cause suspicion.

They had been sitting at the bar for thirty minutes, chatting, and I couldn't stand it.

After sipping from his beer, Brent pushed out his stool, said a couple of words to her, and then headed toward the restroom. I followed him and waited right outside the restroom doors. This way, I could catch him on the way out and keep watch of Yeosin.

The door opened, and the stench of piss seeped out into the

hallway. While walking toward me, Brent straightened out his suit jacket that he had worn to work today. I stepped in front of him and placed a hand on the center of his chest.

"Mr. Bates," he started.

"Leave," I snarled at him, attempting to keep my cool in front of everyone.

He had been one of my star employees since I'd started Midnight Security years and years ago. I didn't want to lose him, but I would sacrifice him for Yeosin, who would be my wife, my mate, and the mother of my children before long.

"Oh, come on." Brent laughed. "Lighten up. I'm here with Alana. You know, that girl from Pink Ivory, who you always scare—"

"I know who she is," I hissed out. "And I ordered you to leave."

"We're not at work now. You can—"

"Out."

"Let me say goodbye to Alana first."

"No," I growled. "She's mine." Those two words left my mouth before I could stop them.

After what had happened to my pack decades ago, I vowed to never say those words and mean it. I vowed to only ever mate to extend my line, not for fate.

And then I'd had to walk into Pink Ivory.

Cursed place.

"If you want to keep your job, you'll leave," I said. "Now."

"Fine," Brent said, his happy expression gone—*as it should be*—and his hands up. "I'll go."

I waited for him to turn around and leave, but he lingered by the door, as if he wished that Yeosin would turn around and see him so he could give her a grimace and a goodbye. The longer he waited, the more possessiveness built up inside me.

"I'm not—"

"You should know that I invited her to apply to be my assistant," Brent said suddenly. "I didn't know you had a thing for her or else I wouldn't have said anything to her. But she was telling me that she needed a second job, and I need an—"

Why did she tell Brent that she needed a job? Has she spent ten million already?

It didn't matter how many questions I asked myself; I couldn't wrap my head around her. It had been less than twenty-four hours since she had met me in The Breeding Cave, and she already had me questioning everything.

Why didn't she quit her job today after I gave her the money?

"What do you mean, she needed a job?" I asked. "She has money."

And if she didn't have enough, then I'd give it to her.

My gaze traveled to the bar, where she sat with her back facing me while sipping on a Cherry Coke. Soon enough, she'd be locked away in my penthouse, walking around in a robe made from the finest of silks and her belly rounder than it ever had been.

She wouldn't need to work. She wouldn't need to go out on dates with anyone.

Except with me.

"She said—"

"Fine," I growled. "She's hired."

Besides, it would help me keep tabs on her while I worked. She wouldn't have to be at Pink Ivory, burning her hands any longer. Her desk would be in view of my office so I could see her through the windows.

"Now, go before I change my mind."

After peering into the bar once more at Yeosin, Brent blew out a breath and headed in the opposite direction toward the exit. I tilted my head to watch him leave, and then I followed a few moments later and waited quite impatiently for her to realize that he wasn't coming back.

Thirty minutes passed, and she finally walked out of the bar with a coat draped over her shoulders and a frown on her face. I kicked myself off the building and followed her through the shadows toward the bus stop a few blocks down.

Before she made it to the brightly lit bus stop booth, I wrapped one hand around her waist from behind and slapped my opposite hand over her mouth, pulling her into a dark alleyway and pressing her up against the brick wall.

She screamed into my palm and flailed her limbs everywhere.

"What are you doing at a bar with *him*?" I growled into her ear.

A moment passed, and her body relaxed. She reached up with her smaller hands and peeled away my fingers from her mouth, breathing heavily against me, almost the same way she had done last night after she came for the tenth time.

"With who?" she asked.

"Don't fucking play around with me, Yeosin."

She shuddered when I said her name, her cunt beginning to salivate. I breathed in the pumpkin scent, wanting nothing more than to savor it on my tongue. I hadn't had much of a taste of her yet, but that would change. Soon.

"You were out. On a date." I placed my hand on the brick wall and scratched my claws into it so I wouldn't punch a hole right through it. "You were out on a date when you should be back in my penthouse—or our cave—ready to give me a child."

After swallowing hard, she pressed her thighs even closer together. "Why does it matter if I go out on a date with someone or not?" She crossed her arms, but she wasn't stiff. Oh, no, just by peering over her shoulder, I could see her *trying* to discreetly play with her nipples. "Besides, it wasn't a date."

"You're about to make me lose control," I growled into her ear. "Compose yourself."

Yeosin sucked in a sharp little breath, still facing away from me. "Or what?"

I wrapped my hand around the front of her throat and pulled back on it so she stared up at the moon above us. My canines met her neck, and I ached to sink my teeth into her to show her what would happen.

"Or else I'll breed you here," I murmured against her neck.

"And everyone at your bus stop will watch as you get a pussy full of my cum. Over"—I dipped my fingers between her thighs—"and over"—I pressed them against her clit, making her inhale—"and over again."

A small whine left her mouth, and my dick hardened in my suit pants.

"You'll never go out on a date with *anyone* again. Do you understand me?" I asked, drawing my lips up the column of her throat and to her ear. "You know the pleasure that I can give you, and I can take it all away."

"You would do that to someone who's supposed to be carrying your child?"

"Yeosin," I growled, shoving my claws so harshly against the brick that it crumbled.

Where had all this brattiness come from? Had she been thinking about how she'd react to me tonight? Was she comfortable with me after one night? Was it that she had the money now and didn't care about the consequences? Or maybe it was that cursed thing called fate.

"Fine. Fine," she said, glancing toward the street where the bus pulled up. "I won't go on any more dates with Brent." She pushed back against me and headed toward the bus. "But I have to go. I'll see you tonight."

CHAPTER
FIVE

"COME ON," I murmured to myself after I missed my bus and ran down the street, away from the billionaire beast man, like that was exactly what I had meant to do. I tapped my shoe and anxiously looked behind me at the ATM. "Work, please!"

Two members of the Dragon Clan sat in a blacked-out SUV to my right, watching me.

I drummed my finger on the screen, hoping that this damn credit card would actually let me withdraw cash. Since I had left home, I tried hard not to even own a credit card—I didn't like debt, which made this situation even stickier—so I wasn't sure if this would work.

But if I tried to use my debit card, it would decline and spit my card back out.

"Can't this stupid machine go any faster?!" I whispered to myself, hitting it with the palm of my burned hand and giving myself flashbacks from earlier today when the card machine wouldn't work for me in front of Grumpy Pants himself.

Once the screen gave me the option to withdraw cash, I typed in three thousand dollars. The loading circle on the screen spun and spun and spun, until it finally started to spit out cash in hundred-dollar bills onto the ground and into a puddle.

"God-fucking-dammit," I whispered, trying to pick up the wet bills but also grab the bills before they could drop into the puddle.

I glanced behind me at the car, hoping they'd accept wet bills.

They knew Alvin wouldn't pay because he didn't care about anyone—that was apparent. But I would because, despite not really talking to my family anymore, I cared so much for them, and I never wanted to see them hurt. Or worse, killed.

When the last hundred-dollar bill left the machine, I gathered them all in my hands and counted it three times. Three thousand. It wasn't nearly enough to pay the debt back, and at this rate, I would have to pull out three thousand dollars from the ATM every day for multiple years.

It could work, but … the banks might get suspicious. After all, it wasn't my card.

Pushing my shoulders back to feign confidence, I walked over to the blacked-out SUV and to the driver's side. The driver rolled down the window, and I spotted the leader of the Dragon Clan in the passenger seat.

"You have it?" he asked.

"Only three thousand," I said. "It's as much as the ATM would let me withdraw."

A low grunt exited his mouth, and I handed him the money. He counted it, stopping at the wet bills at the bottom of the stack and raising his brow at me. I grimaced and shuffled my feet, hoping he'd take them.

He counted the money two more times, then nodded. "Ten thousand next time."

Ten thousand?!

"When's next time?" I asked, calculating how much time I had.

"Whenever we find you."

With that, the driver rolled up his window and drove off into the night. The red taillights disappeared down the road, and I swallowed hard. Maybe I could convince that billionaire beast man to give me the ten million in cash.

But that maid was right earlier.

If the Dragon Clan found out I had ten million dollars, they'd take it all.

Maybe that was for the best—get them out of my hair for good.

Rain sprinkled down around me. I pulled out my phone to see if I had enough time to run home to get dressed a bit better for tonight at The Breeding Cave. Somehow, that man had convinced me to come back to a place with such a horrid name.

Who wanted to be bred by a beast, his face masked by the darkness?

Maybe those crazy book girls.

The bright white numbers on my phone glowed up at me— *12:01 a.m.*

"Fuck," I whispered to myself, hurrying down the city streets, dressed in the same clothes that I had on since my date with Brent. *Can I even call it that if he walked out on me? How is it already past midnight?!* "I'm going to be so late!"

I hadn't even had a chance to go shopping for clothes this afternoon!

Fifteen minutes later, when I made it back to my street, a car sat outside my apartment with its lights on, just like *he* had promised.

Before I could make it to the car, the man from last night with a white mask exited the driver's seat and opened the back door for me. I slowed to a walk until I made it to the car, and then I leaned against it to catch my breath.

"You're late," the driver said.

"Sorry," I whispered. "Being late is a normal thing for me."

Especially lately.

"You don't need to apologize to me," the driver said. "But our *friend* is another story."

After slipping into the car, I placed my purse beside me on the seat and buckled my seat belt. I stared at him through the rearview mirror, trying *desperately* to see through the eye holes in his mask, wanting to see if I recognized him.

"Do you perhaps know our *friend's* name?" I asked, wanting to get as much information out of this driver as possible.

I mean, he worked for him, didn't he? He had to know at least a nickname. Or *any* information about him, right?

"I do."

"What is it?"

"I am forbidden to tell you."

"I'll buy you dinner."

He tensed. "I don't believe our friend would like that. He's protective of you."

"I know," I whispered. "Which is exactly why I need to know his name."

My driver met my gaze in the rearview mirror, and for a moment, I thought he would spill everything to me, but instead, he nodded to the seat beside me.

"You need to put on your blindfold. I can't start driving until you do."

Lips curled into a frown, I picked up the silky red blindfold from the leather seat and tied it around my head. Then I pulled it down over my eyes and sat back in the seat. The car moved forward.

"Can you tell me anything about him?" I asked.

"No."

"What's *your* name?"

"Joseph."

"Well, Joseph, who's his maid?"

A long pause.

"What's her name?" I pushed.

"Molly."

"How long has she worked for him?"

"Five years."

"Five years," I repeated, pursing my lips. "Is she—"

"If I didn't know any better, Ms. Cho, I'd think your tone sounded quite *jealous*."

"Jealous?!" I exclaimed, waving my arms all over in an attempt to convince him that I really, really wasn't envious. *My questions didn't sound* that *jealous, did they?* "I just want to know more about him."

Joseph hummed from his seat. "If you want to know more about him, you'll have to ask him when I drop you off. Now, sit back and enjoy the ride." A small snicker left his mouth. "But I'm sure it's nothing compared to the ride you'll get in a couple of hours."

CHAPTER
SIX

LUCIANO

YEOSIN'S PUMPKIN scent drifted through my nose before I even heard the car door open. I leaned against a rock toward the back of the cave, so my face was hidden behind the shadows, my canines aching to be inside her and my claws desperate to run up and down her curves.

The sound of her feet against the forest floor echoed through the cave, until she appeared at the entrance, dressed in the same clothes I had found her in the bar with Brent. She hadn't gone home.

"You're late."

She paused. "I was just out with some friends ..."

"Friends you give three thousand dollars to?"

Of course, I had followed her from the alley. I'd needed to make sure she was safe. She'd be carrying my children soon. It was the least I could do.

"It's none of your business what I do with the money you gave me, especially if you won't tell me anything about yourself." She crossed her arms and stared up at me through her dark brows. "I earned that last night, and I had no obligation to come here tonight."

"But you are here."

"Because you said you'd hunt me down if I didn't show up."

"If *you* remember"—I moved closer to her and grasped her chin, the light hitting me from behind and my face still covered—"your little pussy was salivating at the thought when I told you in the alleyway. I'm actually surprised you didn't make me hunt you down."

The scent of her wet pussy drifted through my nose, and my dick hardened between my legs. I grunted and held myself back from twirling her around, bending her over, and fucking her senseless all night, like I had last night.

She was right. She'd had no obligation to come back—I knew that. But here she was.

"Give me your burned hand," I ordered.

Her eyes widened underneath the dim light. "H-how do you know about that?"

"Your hand," I repeated.

When she placed her hand in mine, I brought her burned hand to my mouth and licked her wound. I had meant to do this earlier in the alleyway, but she slipped away too quickly. It wasn't because I had been too distracted by her scent.

Either way, I didn't know if it would work, but it was the least I could do. Healing saliva was only supposed to work on pack-mates and mates. But almost all of my packmates were dead, and I had cursed the Moon Goddess to hell *that* night so she would never give me a mate.

Especially not with my curse.

When the wound began healing before my eyes, I froze.

"Wh—how is it doing that?" she whispered.

It ... can't be.

"Tell me," she said. "What's your name?"

Still mesmerized and in shock, I stared at her hand. *This is impossible.*

"If you won't tell me your name, can I at least see your face?" she whispered.

A single flame flickered behind me in a vintage lantern, casting a shadow over my face. I didn't want her to see me, not like this. Nobody had seen me this way for twenty years—since *that night.* And I wasn't about to scare her off now.

It was bad enough she already didn't like me.

"No."

"Please," she pleaded.

"Turn around, lean over the rock over there, and arch your back." I paused. "*For me.*"

"And if I say no?" she hummed, almost amused. She rocked back on her heels, stared up at me through those huge brown eyes, and gave me the smallest of smirks. "What will you do if I take off through the woods?"

My lips curled into a smirk. "You're welcome to try."

She sucked in a sharp breath, and I watched her nipples harden underneath her shirt. And then, suddenly, to my surprise, she twirled around, sprinted out of the cave, and ran through the woods.

Tree branches snapped underneath her feet. Her ragged breaths echoed through the darkness. A low growl escaped my mouth, and my beast took over my body. I had been promising all fun and games as my logical human self, but my beast couldn't tell the difference.

He thought she was running from us. *Really* running from us.

I was on her heels before she made it a quarter mile into the woods. She squealed and pumped her legs faster, making it a game that she knew she would lose. She never had a chance, and she had known it from the moment she took off.

When I had bought a night with her, I'd never expected she'd like it.

Never mind want to play with me—or my beast.

So, I let her run while I nipped at her ankles every thirty yards, ripping off some of her pant legs. She moved even more quickly, carelessly hitting branches that ripped her thin shirt and tore through it.

The deeper into the woods she ran, the more clothes slipped off her body, either from me or from the tree branches that her clothing got caught on, until her pants tore all the way up her thigh and her top was pulled off.

Another growl escaped my throat, and I pushed faster, her scent becoming stronger. Moans from another Breeding Cave about half a mile to our left drifted through the woods, and Yeosin slowed down, gazing over toward it.

I took the opportunity to catch up to her, scoop her half-naked body into my arms, and throw her over my shoulder. She shrieked and glanced over her shoulder toward me, but I wasn't going to let her see my face. Not yet.

Even in my beast form, there was a chance she'd recognize me.

After I dragged her ass all the way back to our cave, I pulled her to the back of the cave, where chains hung from the ceiling. I fastened cuffs around her wrists, then some around her ankles to chain her to the spot. She wrapped her hands around the chains to hold herself up and stared at me.

With my claws, I ripped through the straps and the front fasten of her bra. It popped off and fell to the ground as her tits bounced out of it. I drew my claws up her bare abdomen and walked around her, grasping her hips.

She inhaled deeply and arched her back, almost instinctively.

"You'll learn not to run away from me again," I growled against the back of her neck, sprawling one hand across her stomach and pulling her ass back toward me with the other, her skirt riding up her thighs. "I'm going to fill this belly up with my cum."

When I positioned myself at her entrance, she clenched. My balls tightened, and I pushed the head of my cock into her. She stiffened, but I continued to push and push and push until the base of my cock was pressing against her pelvis.

Once I was completely inside her, I dropped my hand to her

pussy and pushed two fingers between her lips. When I began rubbing circles around her sensitive clit, she cried out and threw her head back against my shoulder.

I pumped into her slowly at first, but the more I teased myself in her pussy, the more desperate and feral I became. Not wanting, but *needing* to give her my cum. Like before, my beast took control and slammed into her repeatedly.

I gripped her waist and thrust my cock against her cervix, cum spilling out of my balls.

"Take" — *thrust* — "my" — *thrust* — "fucking" — *thrust* — "cum."

She threw her head back and screamed, grasping at the chains like her life depended on it. Her pussy exploded all over my cock, clenching and unclenching repeatedly. The first of many orgasms for her tonight.

"Beg for your belly to be round, for my pups to grow inside you."

"Please," she cried, thrusting her hips back as if one orgasm wasn't enough. "Please!"

"Louder."

"I want to carry your pups!" she screamed so loudly that I'd bet the other couple in the cave a mile north had heard it, which only made me want to fuck her harder. "Give me your pups! Get me pregnant!"

Usually, after I came, it took at least twenty minutes for me to come again. But my dick throbbed inside her, and my balls grew as warm as they usually did before I spilled my load inside her.

"To be bred by a monster is my fucking dream!" she cried, her grip slipping on the chains. "Please, fill my pussy up with all of your cum tonight." More and more moans escaped her lips. "I need it so badly."

A ferocious growl left my throat, and I slammed her body down on my dick a second time, spilling deep into her and giving her every chance for my cum to catch. Thoroughly breeding her.

CHAPTER
SEVEN

"JOSEPH WON'T RETURN for another half hour," the beast said once he finally pulled out of me. "Let me wash you up. There's a hot spring deeper in the cave. Molly set out some soaps for us this afternoon."

"Molly," I repeated, her name like poison on my tongue. "Who is she?"

In our car ride earlier, Joseph had said that she was *apparently* his maid. I balled my hands into fists and glared at the rock underneath my feet. If she was anything more than that to him, I would rip her head off her—

My eyes widened as I realized the thought drifting through my mind.

Rip off her head?! I could do no such thing to anyone.

And yet I couldn't stop the feelings of possessiveness and jealousy rushing through my entire body. I hadn't known this man for even two days yet, and somehow, I felt like I had known him my entire life.

"She's my maid," he answered once we started down a path that led deeper into the cave. "There's no reason to be jealous over her."

"I'm not jealous," I hummed, crossing my arms.

"Yes, you are."

"No, I'm not."

"Mmhmm."

"What?!" I exclaimed, throwing my hands up and twirling around to face him. "I'm not!"

While a shadow of darkness covered his face like a blanket, I could see the faintest outline of a smirk on his lips. He placed his large hands on my shoulders and turned me back around to continue deeper into the cave, where a shimmer of light glowed against the ground further up.

"She's mat—married," he said. "And I have no feelings toward her."

"You'd better not," I hissed before I could stop myself.

Where is this coming from?! Why am I so jealous?

He chuckled softly—a first taste at something more vulnerable in the beast.

"How do I know you're telling the truth?" I asked. "I don't know anything about you."

When we made it to the shimmer of light, the tunnel opened up into the prettiest hot spring that I had ever seen. Deposits of marble stone surrounded a crystal-clear body of water. I left the beast at the entrance and walked farther into the room, admiring the moonlight glimmering off the water from an opening above.

To my left, a variety of soaps, shampoos, and lotions sat in clear bottles. Molly must've left it, like the beast had said. I picked up a bar of strawberry-scented soap, sat down on a rock, and dipped my feet into the warm water.

After a moment, I slipped into the hot spring and moaned in delight, my muscles relaxing. All the stress from earlier tonight, when the Dragon Clan had paid me a visit, seemed to drift away, and I could finally find some peace.

I closed my eyes and suddenly felt *him* behind me, sitting on the rock with his legs in the water. He grabbed the bar of soap from my hand and dipped it in the water. While I wanted to turn around, I knew he didn't want me to, so I moved between his legs to let him wash me.

"What do you want to know?" he asked.

"Hmm?" I asked, relaxing into the hot spring.

"You said you don't know anything about me, so what do you want to know?"

"Will you really answer my questions?"

"Depends on what it is."

"What's your name?"

"Next question."

"You're not going to answer anything, are you?" When he didn't respond, I flared my nostrils and decided to continue in an attempt to *try* to get something out of this man. "Where do you work?"

"Next question."

"Come on," I drew out. "Give me something."

"Ask me a question that doesn't reveal my identity."

"Why can't I know who you are?"

"I can't risk anyone finding out about my kind," he said.

I pressed my lips together. "Why?"

"Because there are packs of wild animals after me, and if you know, then they'll be after you too." He scooped up some water in his huge hand and wet my hair. "I don't want you snooping in my affairs. It'll only end up putting you in danger."

"Then why did you involve me at all?" I asked. "Why'd you choose me?"

"Because you have birthing hips and a breeding kink. Perfect to extend my line."

My chest tightened, and I stared down at the ripples around my smaller breasts. "So, only for my body?" I asked, just disappointing myself. I didn't know *why* I had even gotten my hopes up for him.

After a day and a half, I'd thought this beast wanted me for more than just my body.

He drew his fingers through my hair and shifted the conversation. "Someone offered you a job today."

"How do you know about that?" I asked, raising my brows and deciding to forget all about how disappointed I was after thinking someone actually loved me and wanted to protect me from the cruel, cruel world.

"You should take it," he urged, almost as if he wanted me there.

"Do you work for Midnight Security Headquarters? Is that why you want me around?" I hummed as a gush of warmth exploded through my chest at the mere thought of how possessive and obsessed he was over me. Even if he didn't like me like that. "So you can keep an eye on me?"

"No, I don't work for Midnight."

"Are you Brent?"

He growled. "No."

"Oh." *Not that I care that much about Brent.*

After Brent had completely walked out on our date—*Was it actually a date?*—I had decided against taking him up on that job offer to be his assistant. Besides, I didn't have any experience being an assistant. That ten million should hold over the Dragon Clan.

I could continue working my job at Pink Ivory Coffee Bar until I figured out a way to actually take all the money out in cash, and then I'd quit and never have to embarrass myself in front of Mr. Grumpy ever again.

"You either take the job or I will lock you in my penthouse all day until I come home."

"So, you're giving me an ultimatum?"

"Yes."

"What if I ignore it?"

"You can't ignore it, Pumpkin."

Pumpkin?! Warmth gushed between my thighs. *God, what is this man doing to me?!*

"So, what's it going to be?" he asked.

I nodded in a haze and placed a hand over my mouth to hide my smile—because had this beast really just given me the cutest pet name ever?! I didn't know squat about him, and I was all giggly over him calling me Pumpkin! Nobody had ever given me a name like that before.

"What's it going to be?" he repeated.

"Oh, what?" I asked, snapping out of my daze.

"What's it going to be? The job or my penthouse?"

My lips formed an O, and I sucked in my inner cheek.

"Maybe I'll take the job. I don't want to be inside all day. Besides, I mean, it can't be that bad to get out of Pink Ivory. There's this one regular who intimidates me there," I admitted, chewing on the inside of my cheek. "He orders the same thing every day, he barely says two words to me, and he's always in a grumpy mood."

"What's his name? I'll take care of him."

"Luciano."

A low growl escaped his mouth.

My eyes widened at the growl, and I wanted to look back at him, but he ran his claws so smoothly over my head that I could do nothing but relax in the hot spring against his legs and close my eyes.

"Do you know him?" I giggled. His growl had surely seemed like he did. "Isn't he grumpy?"

Instead of responding, he stood up and walked to the exit of the hot spring. "It's late. Joseph is here to bring you back home. There's a towel beside the soaps. Use it and get dressed. Don't keep him waiting."

Then, without another word, he walked out of the cave, and I didn't see him for the rest of the night.

CHAPTER
EIGHT

"LUCA," Ella purred, stepping into the elevator with me the next day.

She worked with the marketing team three floors down, yet somehow, we always seemed to catch the elevator at the same time and she was always on my floor. I nodded to her and hit the Close Door button because I was late for getting my coffee at Pink Ivory.

I wanted to make sure that Yeosin actually quit today or else I'd pay her boss to fire her.

As the elevator descended, floor after floor, Ella moved closer to me. I side-eyed her and clenched my jaw, impatiently waiting to hit the bottom floor. She snatched the bottom of my tie and curled her fingers around it.

The doors opened, and I yanked myself away from her.

"Don't touch me," I hissed through my teeth, stepping out of the elevator.

Ella had a bad habit of thinking that I needed her to continue my bloodline, as she was one of a handful of packmates that I had left. But my beast had never once wanted her in any way other than a pack member.

Besides, she knew I hated being touched.

"But, Luca—"

Before she could finish her sentence, I headed down the street toward Pink Ivory Coffee Bar. The scent of pumpkin drifted through my nose. I rounded the corner and pulled open the door to Pink Ivory.

"It's my last day today," Yeosin said to the customer at the counter.

"Well, we'll miss you around here, Alana," the older woman said, adjusting her glasses.

I drew my tongue over my canines. *Alana.* Why couldn't people learn her real name?

A pink apron was wrapped around Yeosin's wide hips, and I gritted my teeth to keep myself in control. If I wasn't careful, I would lose it in the middle of this coffee bar. I had been playing a dangerous game lately whenever she was around.

After that first taste of her, I wanted her whenever I saw her.

When I lifted my gaze to her eyes, she pulled hers away from mine, which meant that she had caught me staring. It was one of the many reasons I always acted so coldly to her and avoided looking at her altogether while I was here.

Last night, I'd led her to believe that I wanted her for her body, even though it wasn't true.

I didn't want her to depend on me. I didn't want her to love me.

Everyone who had done that in the past had gotten killed. *I* had gotten them killed. *I* hadn't done my duties as I should've. *I* had lived with that anguish for twenty years now, and I couldn't let Yeosin suffer the same fate.

Once the customer headed to the pickup area, I pulled my wallet out of my suit pocket.

"Last day?" I said.

She raised her brows, as if surprised I would ever offer conversation. "Oh, yeah."

"Where are you going?" I asked, as if I didn't know that she'd be working for me soon.

"Midnight Security Headquarters," she said, tapping on the register screen. "Black coffee?"

"What's your favorite drink with pumpkin?"

"Pumpkin," she repeated, her cheeks reddening for a moment as her eyes glazed over. Then she shook her head and looked back at the menu hanging on the wall above her head. "My favorite is our pumpkin spice tea. It has a hint of cinnamon in it."

"Cinnamon," I hummed. "That's your favorite, huh?"

Does she like cinnamon?

All this time, I'd thought she enjoyed Brent's musky scent of cologne. I had a whole fucking bottle of it back at my place, which I definitely hadn't bought because I thought that was why she was always friendly with him.

But apparently, it was because *I* intimidated her.

When she smiled, her cheeks rounded. "I love cinnamon."

"I'll take one."

"Switching it up on my last day," she said, twirling around and grabbing a cup. Her hair drifted over her shoulders, and her pumpkin scent flowed through the air and wrapped around every last bit of my body. "You'll love it."

After writing my drink order on the side with a Sharpie, she tapped the register, which seemed to be functional today, and took my payment. I stepped to the side near the older lady and watched her as she poured our drinks.

We should've never stayed late at the cave last night. Joseph had been outside the entire time. He never truly left the forest. But I had wanted more time with her, especially after how jealous she was when I mentioned Molly.

I clenched my jaw to suppress a smirk at the thought.

So jealous. So possessive. So feral *over me.*

"Any new boys I should know about, Alana?" the older woman said.

She giggled. "You love my drama, don't you, Ms. Wilson?"

Ms. Wilson placed her wrinkly hand over Yeosin's. "I don't get enough anymore."

"I've been seeing this guy for the past couple of days," she said. "But it's nothing serious."

"Just a hookup?" Ms. Wilson said. "Is that what you kids call it these days?"

Yeosin's face turned bright red. "Ms. Wilson, you can't say that out loud! But, yes, something like that. I don't think he's interested in something serious."

My gaze snapped up to hers, and I clenched my jaw at the words that had left her mouth. *Fuck.* Of course she would fucking think that because I had told her that I had chosen her for her body and couldn't tell her the truth.

"Well, that's his loss." Ms. Wilson grabbed her hand. "I'm going to miss seeing you."

"I'll miss seeing you too," Yeosin said. "But I'll be back in the afternoons for tea."

Once Ms. Wilson gave a final squeeze, she walked to the exit and disappeared in the bustling city streets. I stuffed my hands into my pockets and stared pointedly down at the counter. I didn't want her to think that I wasn't interested.

It had barely been two days, but nobody had ever been so possessive toward me before, and I fucking loved it. I wanted to see her like that again, wanted to see how far a sweet girl like her would go for me. The alpha of a pack needed an equally strong mate.

I had stayed away from her for so long because I didn't think she could fill those shoes.

But last night—I growled underneath my breath, my dick hardening inside my pants—had proven that my sweet girl had something deep and feral inside her. She would lose control to protect me … not that I would ever let it get that far.

"Your pumpkin spice tea," she squeaked from behind the counter.

When I looked at her, she was chewing on the inside of her cheek and stared at me with huge, fearful eyes. I realized that *this* was probably why I intimidated her. So, after relaxing my jaw, I grimaced, grabbed the tea, and took my usual spot in the corner of the shop.

I shouldn't feel anything toward her. It was dangerous for both of us.

But I couldn't stop now.

CHAPTER
NINE

WITH A HOT CINNAMON tea in my hand, I stepped into Midnight Security Headquarters. Nerves zipped through me, and I replayed my conversation with the Dragon Clan last night. After work, one member had shown up at my apartment and demanded money by next week.

I shouldn't even need to be here.

I had ten million sitting in some bank account that I hadn't bribed the beast to give me in cash yet. Apparently, he had enemies that would take advantage of the fact that I had cash. But he didn't know that I had enemies too.

And those enemies were becoming less forgiving by the day.

Maybe tonight, I would show up at his cave and plead for him to give me *at least* five hundred in cash. After work, I had tried going to the bank to withdraw more money, but the teller had asked for information that I didn't know.

Account number. Account name. PIN.

All I had was a damn credit card that didn't even have a name etched on it!

Security guards eyed me from their stand near the front. "Looking for something?"

"The elevators?" I asked. "It's my first day."

"Name?" one asked, glancing down at a paper with names.

"It's either under Yeosin Cho or Alana Cho."

"Okay, Alana, you're all set to head upstairs." He flashed me a smile and nodded toward the hallway beside him. "Swing around the hallway to your right, and the elevators will be right there. Head all the way to the top floor."

Once I thanked them, I scurried down the hallway to the elevators. My phone read *9:28 a.m.* on the screen, and I picked up my pace because if I didn't make it up the elevator in two minutes flat, then I'd officially be late on my first day.

When I made it to the elevators, I noticed one closing.

"Hold the elevator!" I shouted, running as quickly as I could in heels that I really couldn't even walk in. I had never been a heel girlie, but I'd thought these would be nice for my first corporate job—if I could even call it that.

Someone placed a large hand between the elevator doors right before they closed, and I stopped in front of them as they slowly reopened, trying to catch my breath. When the doors opened all the way, my eyes widened at Mr. Grumpy from Pink Ivory standing inside.

He stared emptily at me like he wasn't surprised to see me here.

"Oh, um, hi," I said, still trying to catch my breath.

I stepped into the elevator and moved beside him.

As the doors closed, I slid my eyes to the side and looked over at him. What was he doing here? Did he work here? I glanced at the button to see the top one lit up. And on the same floor that I did?

"I didn't know you worked for Midnight," I said in an attempt to converse with him.

"I don't work for Midnight. I own Midnight, Yeosin."

A rush of heat coursed through my body at the sound of my name on his lips, and I pressed my legs together. I hadn't known my name on a man's lips could give me this much pleasure, but … the way he had said it did something to me.

I hadn't even thought he knew my real name. At the café, I had gone by Alana.

Alana was even the name I had on my name tag.

"You own this company," I whispered, my nipples hardening against my thin bra—why?! I had no idea! I crossed my arms over my chest and stared at the elevator doors. "I didn't know you owned a company."

When he didn't respond, I peeked over at him. His jaw was clenched hard, and he was now glaring at the same elevator doors.

Fuck, I'm working for him now, and I already pissed him off. I shuffled beside him.

"S-sorry for asking," I said, gulping in an attempt to control myself. "I just …"

The scent of his woodsy cologne became stronger, or maybe it was just the cinnamon tea trembling in my hand. But it was all I could smell, all I could inhale, and it was driving me mad with pleasure.

"Control yourself," he hissed. "Now."

My cheeks warmed, and I gripped my left wrist with my right hand to stop it from trembling. *God, I haven't even started my first day of work yet, and it already looks like I'm going to be fired.*

As soon as the elevator doors opened on the top floor, Mr. Grumpy stormed off the lift and down the short hallway past the front desk. Then a moment later, a door slammed, the sound echoing through the top floor. My stomach tightened, and I suppressed the urge to hurl.

Fuck. Fuck. Fuck. Fuck. Fuck. Fuck. Fuck. Fuck.

"Can I help you?" a pretty girl said with a smile at the front desk with a nameplate that said *Iris.*

"Hi. It's my first day."

"Are you Yeosin Cho?" she asked, pronouncing my name wrong.

"Yes, but you can call me Alana." I tucked some hair behind my ear. "It's easier."

After clicking away on her computer for a couple more moments, she smiled. "So, what'd you say to make the big bad boss mad?"

I furrowed my brows and stared at the long hallway that led from the front desk to—what I guessed was—the main office area, where Luciano had disappeared moments ago. After tugging on my sleeve with my thumb, I peered back at Iris. "I'm not sure."

"Well, don't piss him off too badly." She shot me a small smile. "The only person he hates who he's kept around is Ella."

"Ella?" I repeated, already not liking her.

She stood, handed me a folder, and guided me down the hallway to the main office area, where about twenty people were working at desks and another several were gossiping by the coffee maker. After leaning closer to me, Iris nodded to two girls who were giggling to themselves.

"The girl in red is Ella," Iris said.

"Cool," I said in an attempt to sound interested.

Iris let out another low laugh. "You don't have to pretend to like her. Not many people do, but Luciano keeps her around for whatever reason. Rumor has it—at least the rumors that Ella has spread herself—that they're sleeping together."

My chest twisted, and I gritted my teeth. "Oh?"

While Mr. Grumpy hated me—I thought he always had—that one little good moment that I'd had with him the other day at Pink Ivory made me feel some kind of way about him. It'd made me … possessive, jealous.

But I had to be professional. It wasn't my business who he slept with.

He didn't even like me.

"Alana, over here!" Brent called from the opposite side of the room.

"Well, have a good day," Iris said, offering me a smile. "You'll do great."

I glanced toward the closed office door that I assumed was Luciano's since Ella was eyeing it and sucked in a breath. "I sure hope so."

CHAPTER
TEN

LUCIANO

THREE MINUTES before five in the afternoon, I stepped out of my office for the first time since my encounter with Yeosin in the elevator. Something I had said aroused her because her scent was so strong in that small lift that I didn't think I'd be able to control myself.

From across the office, I could feel Yeosin's gaze on me.

Earlier, her smell had followed me all the way into my office, and I foolishly thought that rubbing one out during the day would hold off my beast. My dick twitched inside my pants. I had jerked one out—not once today, but twice.

When I made it to the elevator, I hit the Down button and glared at the doors. Ella's scent drifted into my nose, and I winced.

She stepped up next to me, holding her laptop to her chest and rocking on her heels. "Leaving early?"

"Mmhmm."

"Wanna get coffee with me at Pink Ivory? That's the place you go, rig—"

"No."

"Where do you go then? I swear you change these—"

"I'm not getting coffee with you," I growled.

Once the doors opened, I stepped into the elevator and smashed the bottom floor button. Ella walked in behind me and stood awfully close—as close as I wished that Yeosin had stood this morning.

I had thought having her here would calm my beast. It'd be easier to keep an eye on her.

But I was so fucking wrong. I couldn't even peer out my office window at her without my beast wanting to trap her in the break room, smash her sexy body up against the floor-to-ceiling windows, and dump load after load of my cum deep into her hole.

"Do you have dinner plans?" Ella said, typing on her phone. "I made a reservation for u—"

"I'm not hungry."

Ella curled her claws around my elbow. "I know you can always eat puss—"

Before she could finish her sentence, the elevator doors opened, and I threw her out of the lift. She landed on the ground with a thud, her eyes wide with fear.

I ground my teeth and took a menacing step toward her. "Stop."

Once she recollected herself, she scrambled to her feet and dusted herself off. "All you had to say was no. Goddess, men like you don't know the first thing about how to be gentlemanly. Maybe that's why—"

I growled and stepped toward her, "I said no multiple fucking times, Ella. Now get out."

After huffing at me, Ella twirled on her heel and marched out of the building like she did every night that I rejected her advances. This had been going on for years now, and she didn't know when to stop. How many rejections would it take?

As soon as she disappeared from view, the elevator dinged behind me, and I slipped into a nearby hallway. Yeosin's sweet scent of pumpkin drifted past the doorway, and then a moment later, she walked out of the elevator by herself.

When she headed for the doors on the opposite side of the building, I stepped out from the hallway and followed quietly behind her. My dick was throbbing, the vein in my neck twitching. My canines extended past my lips. And as we passed an empty office, I snatched her.

One hand on her mouth, the other arm wrapping around her waist.

It was a bad idea. A fucking terrible idea.

HR would have a fucking field day if they found out about it.

"Don't make a sound," I said, pulling her into the room and locking it behind us.

"What are you doing?!" she exclaimed, her back against my chest. "You can't be here!"

"Don't move," I hissed into her ear, reaching between us to pull down my zipper. "I need to be inside you. I need to fucking *breed* you, Yeosin. I told you that I wouldn't stop until you're pregnant with my child."

"It's my first day here," she said nervously, looking around the office to make sure there wasn't anyone else here. "My boss already hates me. If he finds me in here with you, then he'll fire me on the spot!"

I pulled my dick out of my suit pants and dipped it underneath her skirt. "No, he won't."

"Yes, he wi—oh my God," she moaned when I pushed into her. "You're so big."

"My balls have been so heavy all day," I grunted into her ear.

She sucked in a breath. "Heavy with cum that you want to fill my tight little pussy with?" She tightened, her tits bouncing more and more out of her shirt the faster I fucked her. "So much of it that it'll be dripping down my thighs until I get home."

"It's not going to drip down your thighs at all," I snarled into her ear. "I don't want *any* of it dripping out of your cunt. You're going to hold it inside you, plug up your pussy with whatever you need to. Every drop of my cum stays in your cunt. Better chance of it catching and you getting pregnant."

She bit down on her bottom lip to hold back the moans leaving her mouth.

"Tell me you won't let any drip down your legs," I said.

She threw her head back against my shoulder. "I won't let any drip down my legs."

"I don't believe you."

"I won't let any drip out of my pussy," she said again, this time louder and more desperately.

She gripped onto the table tighter and arched her back so my balls slapped against her clit with every thrust.

I wrapped my hand around the front of her throat and pulled her closer to me, sucking on her skin at the crook of her neck. My canines ached down to the gum, desperate to sink into her pretty little neck.

All I wanted—needed—was to claim her.

Right here. Right now.

"Please!" she pleaded, small whimpers leaving her mouth.

After sliding my hand up her throat, I shoved four fingers past her lips and into her mouth. She sucked on them like a desperate, needy little slut.

"I can't come inside you until you convince me you're not going to waste a drop."

"I promise I won't!" she mumbled on my fingers, spit and drool running down her chin. I pushed my fingers deeper into her mouth, and Yeosin flicked her tongue around them. "I'll use every last drop."

As those words stumbled out of her mouth, I pulled my fingers from it, seized her waist, and slammed as deep as I could get. I exploded inside her and tried pushing myself even deeper, shoving as much of myself, my cock, and my balls as I could into her tight pussy.

"Deeper," she cried, spreading her legs wider. "Get deeper inside me!"

I picked her legs up off the ground, taking her knees in my hands and spreading them as wide as they would go, and then I drove further into her until my cock pressed far past her cervix. She cried out—but I couldn't tell if it was in pleasure or pain because her pussy began pulsing wildly around me, milking more of my cum out of my balls.

Once I finally pulled out of her, Yeosin doubled over the table and sank a hand between her thighs, pressing her palm flat against her cunt, then dipping some fingers into it to stuff my cum deeper inside her.

I readjusted myself inside my pants and stayed behind her so she wouldn't dare peek back and see that it was me—her boss and the guy who had been fucking obsessed with her since the moment I'd laid eyes on her.

"Yeosin …" I groaned against her neck. "What are you doing to me?"

CHAPTER
ELEVEN

YEOSIN

BREATHING HEAVILY, I lay belly-first on the desk in the empty office and stared at the blank wall to my right. What was wrong with me?! It was my first day at my new job, and this beast had almost ruined it.

No, *I* had almost ruined it.

I had slipped into the office with him, and I had let him take me. I could've stopped it.

"I need the money in cash," I said, gathering up enough courage. "Just a bit of it."

I squeezed my eyes closed and nervously waited for a response. When the beast didn't say anything, I peered behind myself and noticed that he was nowhere to be found. My eyes widened, and I stood up.

Maybe he is hiding in the shadows.

"Hello?" I called.

Nothing. *Damn it!*

"Of course," I muttered under my breath.

He'd had to leave right after he dumped his load inside me.

No aftercare or anything—not that I actually expected it from a man. Alvin hadn't done it. Why would I expect a beast to?

But I did need that money.

After sighing softly, I readjusted my clothes so I wouldn't look like I had just fucked a wild animal at my new job and gathered my belongings. I hoped to a god that I didn't believe in that they didn't have cameras in this room.

Or else I'd be fucked. And this time, not literally.

Once I smoothed out my top, I grabbed the door handle and took a deep breath. I would need to pay him a visit at The Breeding Cave tonight, and instead of letting him entice me, I would stand my ground and demand my money.

If I didn't, the Dragon Clan would kill me. Or worse … kill my family.

When I finally pushed the door open, it slammed into someone.

"Sorry!" I shouted, leaping out from the room and spotting Luciano.

Oh my God! He is here to scold me. He found out what I did and probably has been looking for an excuse to fire me since this morning in the elevator. And this will be a goddamn perfect reason!

"Ms. Cho, what were you doing in there?" he asked.

"Oh!" I exclaimed, a bead of sweat forming on the back of my neck. "I just … got lost!"

"Lost?" Luciano repeated, his eyes a bit softer than usual. "In here?"

"Yeah, um …" I gulped and looked around. "This place is so big."

"Your cheeks are all red," he noted, as if he didn't believe my excuse.

"Sometimes, they get like that"—my mouth dried—"when I'm nervous."

He stepped closer, his dress shoes on the tiles echoing through the spacious foyer and his voice dropping. "Do I make you nervous, Yeosin?"

Heat raced to my core, just like it had this morning on the elevator when he spoke my name. I teetered from foot to foot and played with the end of my sleeve. Between him and that beast, I didn't know what I was feeling with who anymore.

His eyes darkened, and I pressed my thighs together discreetly so he wouldn't notice, like he had earlier. My nipples tightened, and I wanted to tug on them, but I had to restrain myself or else … I would really get fired.

Luciano cocked his head to the side. "Hmm?"

Stay professional, Yeosin!

I giggled nervously and placed a hand over my chest. "Aren't all bosses intimidating?"

After shoving his hands into his suit pockets, he stopped. "What makes me intimidating?"

Oh, I don't know, Luciano … maybe it's that you're grumpy all the time, my new boss, or one of the most attractive men I've met. Just to name a few!

"Um, you know—"

Luciano chuckled. "Attractive, huh?"

It took me a second to register what he had said, but when I did, my eyes shot open. "Oh my God! I-I didn't just say that out loud, did I?!"

I swore that I hadn't said that aloud to him. I wouldn't have. I *couldn't* have! Not on my first day of work at his company.

"I didn't mean that," I said. "I mean, you are attractive, but I'm not … I mean …" My heart thudded so loudly that I could hear it in my ears. I waved my arms all over. "It's been a long day. I haven't had my afternoon tea. I don't know what I'm saying! I need to—"

Before I could twirl around and run back home, crawl underneath my bedsheets, and scream into my pillow for actually saying that to my boss, he grabbed my wrist. A jolt shot up my arm. He felt so … familiar.

"Haven't had your afternoon tea? Let's get some and … *talk*."

Talk … or scold?!

"No, no …" I stepped out of the building. "Really, it's okay. I—"

My gaze landed on the Dragon Clan's car parked on the corner of the street, and I tensed.

What the hell are they doing here?! How did they find out that I was working here now? It was my first day! Were they even here for me?

Luciano stepped to the side and followed my gaze to the car. I inched behind him so his bigger body would cover up my smaller one and shield me completely from the driver, who had definitely spotted me in the rearview mirror.

"Who are they?" Luciano asked.

"That tea doesn't sound so bad," I said, twirling around in the direction of Pink Ivory and heading down the sidewalk before he could ask any more questions. I glanced nervously behind me to see the car peeling off the curb.

Fuck. I can't go home now.

After his pause, Luciano caught up to me, looking calm, collected, and as grumpy as ever. But maybe he wasn't as grumpy as I thought he was. He had asked me to grab coffee after my first day at work. Maybe his grumpy face was a … resting bitch face.

Luciano with an RBF!

When I bit back a giggle to get my mind off the Dragon Clan, some of the beast's cum dribbled out of my pussy. The wetness covered my thighs, and I clenched in an attempt to keep it plugged inside me. How embarrassing would it be if Luciano spotted it running down my legs?!

From my right, I listened to a feral sound—almost a growl— escape Luciano's throat. I pressed my lips together to stay quiet and practically ran to Pink Ivory when I spotted it. I would grab some tea with him and leave, give him an excuse that I had a date tonight or something.

I needed to wipe this cum out of my pussy before anyone noticed.

Once I ordered and—*unwillingly*—let him pay for my drink, I rocked back on my heels at the pickup section. Luciano stood inches from me, his scent drifting through my nose and making me hot all over.

Damn cologne.

"Alana, your tea," a worker said from the counter.

I grabbed the cup and took a sip, my gaze drifting toward the window. I spotted Alvin, my douchebag ex, parked on the curb. My eyes widened, and I tightened my grip on my piping hot tea.

"Thank you for the tea," I said, heart pounding hard in my chest. "But I have to go."

"So soon?"

"Yes …" I glanced over my shoulder at Alvin stepping out of his car. *Fuck!* "I have a date."

"A date?" he repeated harshly.

When I looked over at him, his jaw was clenched hard. I squirmed underneath his strong gaze and glanced toward the windows, shuffling my feet against the black and white tiles. Forget what I had said about his RBF earlier. He was as grumpy as ever.

I still can't believe I called him attractive—and to his face too!

What the hell has gotten into me lately? First, it was me accepting that invitation to be fucked in a random cave by a billionaire beast man. Next, I switched jobs and let that same beast have me in one of the offices. Then I called my new boss attractive and went out to tea with him.

Alvin, that scrawny blond bastard, shut the driver's door of the hundred-thousand-dollar car that he had used our money on and put his phone to his ear. I gritted my teeth and tightened my grip on the cup, some hot tea spilling over the edge.

If I stayed here any longer, I feared that I'd march right out of here and throw my hot tea in his face, burn that handsome man, and make him cry. And while that was exactly what I wanted to do, I was with Luciano, it was my first day, and I already was on his bad side.

"I have to go," I said to Luciano, heading toward the second entrance. "See you tomorrow … maybe."

Because if I went home now, then I would definitely see the Dragon Clan. And maybe, this time, they wouldn't let me live another day.

CHAPTER
TWELVE

LUCIANO

"A DATE," I muttered to myself on the way to Pine Grove Forest.

Who the hell did she have a date with tonight? Maybe she had just used that as an excuse to leave because she didn't like me. I was too grumpy for her, *apparently.*

Joseph glanced back at me through the rearview mirror, but didn't say a word.

I gritted my teeth. But what if she really did have a date tonight?

It had better not be with Brent. I swore I would choke him straight to death if it was. I had already told him to stay away from her, but what if he had smooth-talked her into going out with him again?

Tonight, she should be at The Breeding Cave, on all fours, desperate to take my cum.

Not out.

A low growl left my throat, and I redirected my attention to the forest that surrounded us. Years ago, this place had nearly burned to ash from our war with the Dragon Clan. Now, it was finally prospering again, which meant that it was time to rebuild our pack too.

But I couldn't do that without Yeosin.

"Get me information on a black SUV. License plate JWGSH89." I stared out the window and gritted my teeth at the forest. "I want to know the name of the owner, their address, pack or clan affiliations, and why Yeosin's afraid of them."

"Yeosin?" Joseph repeated, glancing in the rearview mirror.

As soon as she had seen that car this afternoon, she had gone off in the opposite direction.

"She was fucking terrified," I growled, my canines extended. "Get me everything on them."

"You were out with Yeosin in your human form?"

"She's a new employee," I said. "Nothing more."

She couldn't be anything more. Not after what had happened. I couldn't protect her. That was obvious. But if she really was only my employee and a surrogate, then ...

How'd I hear her thoughts earlier?

Wolves could only hear thoughts of their packmates or their mates. My pack had been destroyed years ago, and my curse prevented me from having a mate the way everyone else could. Plus, I hadn't marked Yeosin.

I wanted to ... badly. But I hadn't.

Joseph hummed from the front seat, a smirk creeping onto his face. "Is that so?"

"Yes."

"Did you ask her to be an employee?"

"No, but it's convenient."

"If she had not agreed, what would you have done?"

Lifting my hard gaze, I stared at him in the mirror. "Not agreed to be my employee? I—"

"If she hadn't agreed to The Breeding Cave," Joseph said. "Would you've found another?"

A vicious growl left my throat. He didn't break a sweat, but I was having none of this. How fucking dare he even ask that? He knew what would've happened.

My lineage surviving was the most important thing.

Joseph smirked even harder. "I'm sure your answer is something like, *You know I would've, Joseph.* But I've known you since you were a boy, *Alpha.* If she's your mate, you can tell me. There's no harm in you being possessive and protective over her—"

"She's not my mate," I snarled. "You know I can't have one."

"You don't think the Moon Goddess spared you?"

"Spared me? She cursed me." I balled my hands into fists, my claws slicing right through the skin on my palms. "None of the alphas can mate anymore. It was our punishment. We should be glad that she didn't take away our ability to have children at all."

Joseph pulled up in front of the house I had been rebuilding deep in the woods ... my old packhouse. "I've never seen you get so ... angry before over this question. Seems like, even if Yeosin isn't your mate, you still have feelings for her."

"She's nothing more than a fertile human woman who can bear my pups," I said, shoving my door open and storming out of the car. "I've known her for a handful of days. I don't have feelings for any woman. Especially not one who's human."

After offering me a, "Mmm," which meant that he didn't believe me, Joseph nodded and drove off back toward the city to retrieve Yeosin herself.

I slid my tongue across my canines and walked into the house, fuming in annoyance.

Yeosin was out on a date. *A date!*

And Joseph had had the nerve to piss me off.

Once I yanked the wooden door open, I stepped into the house, the air thick with the scent of charred wood. It had been years, and that scent still haunted me to this day. No matter how much Molly cleaned it, it would never leave.

Memories flooded through my mind—the crackling fireplace on winter nights with my parents when I had been a boy, the scent of my sister's cooking lingering in the air, the echoes of my father's belly laughter. And then the thought of Yeosin sitting here with me seemed to creep in.

I breathed through my teeth and walked further into the house toward the stairs, now just a frame that led to the second floor. The scent of musty old books from the library lingered in the air. Another growl left my mouth, and I raced to the bathroom to splash some water on my face, the cold snapping me out of my delusions.

When I peered into the mirror, I glared at the man from twenty years ago. The man who had lost everything. Whose body was decorated with scars that would never heal, not even with the powers of a beast. Whose packmates had called out, pleading for someone to come save them. The man who was too much of a coward to do anything, but wished things had been different.

Before they had all burned away by dragon fire, I had promised my pack that their deaths wouldn't be for nothing. I promised that we would rebuild and remember their memory forever. I had promised not to indulge in pretty things or heavenly women until we had a pack back.

Yeosin would do that for me. That was all I cared about.

My chest tightened, and the feeling made me want to hit something.

Joseph was wrong. I wouldn't have cared if she hadn't accepted my invitation. I would've found someone else. I would've stalked them until I knew they were the right one and dragged them to the cave with me.

But Yeosin had accepted. And so she would push out pup after pup for me with those wide birthing hips.

That was all I needed her for.

That was all I *fucking* needed her for.

I didn't care that she thought I had a resting bitch face—whatever the fuck that meant. What did it mean? Was that why she thought I was grumpy all the time? Was it from the way I looked at her? If she only knew that I had to be grumpy or else my beast would take over and ravish her, then she'd think differently of me.

Besides, what did it matter to me that she was on a date? She wouldn't be able to take too many of those for long. She would be pregnant with my pup before the end of the month, and I'd lock her away in my home to care for her.

Another low growl escaped my mouth, my vision blurring with red.

Yet my mind continued to wander back to one thought. *Who the fuck is she out with?*

And in the pits of my fury, someone banged on my front door.

CHAPTER
THIRTEEN

LUCIANO

ALL THE FURY dissipated from me, and I snapped my gaze toward the front room. Only a few people knew about my packhouse, and those people knew not to disturb me here unless something happened.

Yeosin flashed through my mind. I tightened my hands into fists, my claws slicing into my palms, and I walked to the front door. If it was Joseph, returning to tell me that Yeosin was refusing to come, I swore—

The bang became louder, and a low growl rumbled from underneath the door.

"Luciano!" a familiar voice shouted. "I know you're in there. Open the door!"

After unclenching my hands, I yanked the door open to see Alpha Theo standing outside in his beast form, blood dripping off his extended canines, eyes a blazing gold, and claws torn right into the doorframe, making it crumble.

At one point, he had been my sworn enemy. We fought against each other in bloody war after bloody war. But decades ago, the Dragon Clan took advantage of the war between the packs. They had ripped us apart one by one by one until there was nobody left except the alphas and a few packmates.

"Theo," I said. "What are you doing—"

He stormed into the house, his beast form slowly disappearing back into his human body. "Elizabeth is gone."

While we had never seen eye to eye, we had set aside our differences after we defeated the Dragon Clan in order to rebuild. We had carved out The Breeding Caves in Pine Grove to repopulate so our species wouldn't die. And from what I remember …

"Elizabeth?" I asked. "Isn't that the woman you invited to The Breeding Cave years ago?"

"She's gone," he said, voice shaking in rage. "She's gone!"

"What happened to her?"

"My home was ransacked … and I found this"—he pulled out a dragon scale—"in the mess they'd left. After we had tried for years, she'd finally become pregnant. She was carrying my pup."

"We'll help find her," I said, my mind drifting to Yeosin for a moment, hoping she was safe. If something happened to her, I didn't know what I would do. "And when we do, you should think about bringing her to live with the others."

He gritted his teeth and snapped his gaze away. "I shouldn't have to."

There was nothing wrong with living with the remainder of our pack so deep in Pine Grove that the Dragon Clan wouldn't be able to find them. I couldn't do it because I had a business to attend to, but Elizabeth could.

And maybe Yeosin too … especially if she had someone following her.

"We should kill the Dragon Clan," he said.

"We don't have the beasts for it," I said. "We barely survived last time."

"We might not have the beasts, but we have the money. We can pay for it."

"Pay who?"

"The Colossals."

"Fuck no," I growled. "They're nothing but trouble. Once we make an alliance with them, they might kill our enemies, but they'll steal our packs, our women, and the little children we have left."

When he didn't respond, I bit back a growl. He wasn't asking me. He was telling me.

"You already met with them without running it by me first?"

"We don't make decisions together."

"*We* have to look out for our own."

He paused. "They have a daughter they want you to meet."

"No."

"She's strong enough to be a warrior … or a luna."

"I'm not interested."

"You need to rebuild. We both do."

"Which is our reason for creating The Breeding Cave," I said, "to rebuild."

"The Breeding Cave is for just that—breeding. Not finding mates."

"We can't have mates anymore," I said.

"Well, we need to find someone strong, someone like us, someone with enough power to defeat the Dragon Clan right by our sides. Humans are only for pushing out more children to help expand our lineage. And if I were you, I would suggest having multiple of them."

"I'm already planning on having multiple pups with—"

"Multiple *humans* you bring to the cave. Better chance at getting one pregnant and better odds of your family surviving if you have a handful of women pushing out children every other year or so."

The thought made my stomach turn. How could he think such a thing?

"You're talking nonsense," I said. "What happened to having one mate?"

Fated mates had always been so important and innate to beasts like us. One person to obsess over, one person to live with, grow older with, to raise a family of strong warriors with. Maybe I was just too old for this shit anymore.

"Times have changed," Theo said. "We have to change with it."

I gritted my teeth and stayed quiet. I didn't have it in me to argue with him tonight. I had to meet with Yeosin in just a couple of minutes, and I needed to make sure that she was all right. I couldn't let his words get to me.

Still though, was that what this world had come to? Breeding with multiple partners?

"We'll speak more," I said, heading to the front door.

"I look forward to it, Luciano. I know we can take them down and get her back."

"We will," I said, though I hated the thought of working with those human-looking creatures who could shift into Colossal beings at a moment's notice. They were ugly monsters who lost control of themselves in that form.

Not only that, but they were selfish and believed everyone desired them.

Once he left, I headed toward The Breeding Cave.

If the Dragon Clan really had taken Elizabeth, then Yeosin might be next. Hell, they might have already been looking for her. I really needed Joseph to tell me who had been stalking her in that SUV earlier today.

Either way, I couldn't risk losing her.

I had searched for someone capable and fertile to birth my pups, and I wasn't planning on bringing anyone else to The Breeding Cave either. Yeosin needed to stay safe, and she could do that in my penthouse or with the others.

Her scent drifted through the woods from the cave. I nodded to Joseph, who was still parked, and then he drove off so we could be alone. He'd be back later, once I finished filling her up and claiming her tight little body.

When I reached the cave, Yeosin stood near the end with her back turned to me and her long black hair flowing down to below her mid-back. Moonlight glimmered against it as she brushed her fingers across the chains that I had tied her up with the last time she was here.

I walked toward her slowly, careful not to make a sound until my fingers grazed against the skin of her forearms, and all the worries of the Dragon Clan seemed to disappear for a moment. "Yeosin, I'm so glad you're safe and he—"

YEOSIN

I SHOVED HIM OFF ME. "Don't do that."

"Do what?"

"Touch me and pretend like everything is okay."

My body reacted way too much for that. He couldn't use his touch to comfort me. I had a couple of bones to pick with him, including him showing up at my workplace, not giving me aftercare or giving me that money in cash.

"Are you angry with me?" he asked.

"It's not like you care," I growled through my teeth.

Really, I wasn't angry with him. I was angry with myself for feeling this way about him, for allowing my body to react all gooey to him, for not putting my foot down to demand the money in cash like I'd thought I would receive it.

"Yeosin."

"Don't call me that!" I exclaimed. "My name is Alana."

No, it wasn't.

We both knew that.

I hated when people called me Alana, but when he said my real name, it did something bad to me. All my thoughts seemed to disappear into thin air because I was desperate for someone to respect and love me.

"You'd prefer I call you Alana?"

Just the sound of that nickname coming out of his mouth made me shudder in disgust. I furrowed my brows harder and pressed my lips together because I actually would hate it if he called me that.

"We need to talk," I said.

I had been thinking and overthinking everything since the Dragon Clan had followed me earlier and since I had seen Alvin in the city.

"You'd prefer I call you Alana?" he repeated.

"Why are you being a dick?"

"I'm not being a dick. I'm asking you a question because I know you hate that name."

"I put up with a grump at my job," I said. "I don't need it from you either."

While it wasn't completely a lie, it definitely was my excuse to get out of answering his question. I wanted him to call me Yeosin, but I didn't want to admit to it. Admitting to it would mean that I would hear it every day for as long as this went on.

"You can't show up at my workplace," I said. "I could've gotten fired on my first day."

He placed his hands on my upper arms and slowly drew them down. "I needed you."

"It couldn't wait? At least until I was out of the building?"

"No," he murmured deep into my ear.

I shivered underneath his touch and wished that I weren't in this situation with the Dragon Clan. My entire life would be so much easier. I would've never come to this cave, never felt these … *things* for this beast who wouldn't tell me anything.

Suddenly, a branch snapped just outside of the cave, and the beast pulled away from me. He sniffed the air, but didn't move toward the entrance of the cave or relax behind me. "Who was in that car earlier?"

"What car?"

"You walked out of your building with your boss and stared at an SUV with the license plate of JWGSH89 this afternoon. Who were they?" His claws began extending against my skin. "An ex?"

"No!" I exclaimed. "They were nobody."

"Who?"

"Nobody."

"Who?"

"Why do you care?!" I shouted, so caught up in all my emotions from earlier today and all the messages I'd been getting from the Dragon Clan. "You won't even show me your face. You don't trust me, so I can't trust you."

"You can trust me."

"Then tell me your name."

A low growl rolled out of his throat. "I can't tell you that."

"Tell me something!" I exclaimed. "Who are you? Why do you want me to have your child? What's with this cave? And why can't you show me who you really are? Do I know you, or are you just too ashamed?"

The words came out harsher than I'd expected. I was upset, but that wasn't an excuse.

"Sorry," I whispered, dropping my gaze. "I don't mean ashamed in a bad way. I just don't understand why I can't know anything." Tears welled up in my eyes. "You're expecting me to carry your child when I don't know anything about you."

After a long pause, he turned away from me and walked to the front of the cave. Moonlight bounced off his back, illuminating all the muscles that he had. I sucked in a breath and tore my gaze away because if I looked for any longer …

"I lead a pack of beasts," he started. "That's all you need to know."

"What kind of beasts?" I asked.

"Lycans."

"So, like … wolves?"

"No."

"Are you sure? Because I swore that I read a story where—"

"Wolves are weak," he growled, then suddenly, his voice dropped to above a whisper, so low that I could barely hear it. His shoulders rounded forward, and he quickly tilted his head to the side. "Maybe that *is* what we are now."

My eyes widened slightly, and I stepped toward him. The closer I approached him, the more I realized how scarred his back was, and parts of it almost looked … burned, as if he had been in a bad fire.

What had happened to him? Was his pack hurt? Destroyed?

"Is Molly in your pack?" I asked, deciding to shift the conversation.

"Yes."

"And Joseph too?"

"Yes."

I stepped closer to him, realizing how deep those scars were. Whatever had happened to him, it was bad. No wonder why he didn't want to talk about it. I could only imagine …

"How many people do you lead?"

"Only a couple hundred now."

"Were there more?"

He tightened his hands into fists, and I realized that I had overstepped this time. I hadn't come here to ask all these questions. My one goal tonight had been to demand that he give me the money in cash.

I can't be invested in his history. I can't have feelings for him.

"Never mind. That's not what I want to talk about," I said. "I need the money in cash."

"Molly already told you that it's not safe to walk around with that kind of—"

"I know the consequences, but I need it."

"Why?"

I pressed my lips together. "Please."

"Tell me why, Yeosin, and I'll give it to you."

I crossed my arms and glared at his shadow. "I'm not telling you."

I wasn't only embarrassed, but I also didn't want him to look at me any differently. He might be using me as a surrogate, and he might be a beast whose face I would never get to see, but I still … felt some type of way about him.

A type of way that I had never felt with Alvin.

"I'll ask you one more time," he said. "Why do you need it in cash? Is anyone threa—"

"No!" I exclaimed, turning away from him. "I like cash better. That's why."

It was bad enough that my parents were disappointed in me after Alvin had ripped me off, but I didn't want him to be disappointed in me too. I could handle this myself. I had been for the past few weeks now.

This wasn't his problem anyway. He seemed like he had a bunch of his own.

Besides, *I* would be fine …

At least, I hoped.

CHAPTER
FIFTEEN

YEOSIN

"YOU'RE GOING to have so many of my children," the beast whispered behind me, one hand on my upper hip from behind and his huge cock buried inside my pussy. "I won't need anyone else to give me pups."

I fluttered my eyes open to see darkness surrounding me, but we weren't in the cave. My body was relaxed against a comfy mattress that definitely wasn't mine back at my apartment. The beast pressed himself deep into me.

"What time is—"

"Shh, shh, shh," he murmured into my ear. "You can go back to bed, Yeosin."

"What's going on?" I asked, my pussy clamping down on his cock.

He hissed in pleasure. "I didn't mean to wake you."

Toes curling, I arched my back against him. "I don't mind."

Last night, I had been infuriated with him, but I was in too much of a groggy state to think right now. The pleasure rushing through my system made my head hazy, and him not giving me many answers last night seemed to float away.

He had answered one of my questions, but that was all I had gotten out of him.

Still, it was something. I was making some progress.

He pushed me onto my stomach, placed his thumbs on the small of my back, and wrapped his large hands around my hips from behind. His fingernails dug into my skin, which meant that he wasn't in his beast form this time.

No, he was human right now.

The blackout curtains were drawn, so even if I wanted to look back at him, I wouldn't be able to see his face. It didn't matter to me though. I had caught a glimpse of him and his scars last night.

"You're staying here now," he said, pushing into me.

"Why?" I asked in a breath.

I had no room to argue, no matter how much I wanted to, no matter how much he infuriated me by asking why I needed that money. I would live here with him now, which wasn't the worst thing in the world.

The Dragon Clan could've killed me by now.

"So I don't have to worry about you."

Worry about me? I tightened around him at the sound of his words.

Sure, I might only be the woman he wanted to have his kids, but deep down, I secretly hoped that he meant more than just that. I hoped he worried about what could happen to me because he … *liked* me.

Though that would never be.

Someone knocked on the door as he continued to pound into me, driving me higher and higher until I exploded around him.

"Excuse me, Alpha," Molly said from outside the door. "I have the breakfast and tea that you requested for Yeosin."

"You have to stop," I whispered. "Molly is at the door."

"No," he grunted into my ear. "Breeding is a natural thing."

"It's a private thing. She doesn't need to hear us having—"

"Come in, Molly."

"What?!" I exclaimed, fingers curling into the pillows. "She's just gonna come—"

Before I could finish my sentence, the door swung open. Light from the hallway flooded into the room and bounced against the wall behind the headboard. My eyes widened in horror as I watched her silhouette walk into the room.

Oh, I know that she didn't just walk in while he is fucking me!

With his arms posted on either side of my torso, he grunted and continued to pound into me. I stared down at the pillow, unable to believe that he hadn't even stopped. He hadn't even hesitated!

Molly walked all the way to the side table beside us and placed a tray of fruits down, along with some hot tea. I expected her to leave right then and there, but instead, she began pouring tea into the same teacup I'd used last time.

"This one is for you, Yeosin. Make sure you drink all of it."

"T-thank y-you," I squealed, then pressed my lips together so I wouldn't embarrass myself and moan in front of her. I squeezed my eyes closed and hoped she'd leave. "I-I'll be s-sure to drink all of i-it—oh my God."

After politely nodding, as if this wasn't weird as hell for her— or maybe the beastman did this kinda thing all the time—she walked back to the door and slipped into the hallway, and the sliver of light flooding into the room disappeared, leaving us in darkness.

"W-why d-did you—"

"Because breeding with you is more important."

"More important than someone watching us?!"

He stilled inside me and grunted, yet his arm curled around my hips, and his fingers found my clit. He rubbed it in small torturous circles, until I physically couldn't take it anymore and my body exploded underneath him.

I buried my face into the pillow and cried out in pleasure, wave after wave rushing through me. When he finally pulled his fingers away, he pushed himself off me and rolled to his side of the bed.

"You're lucky our old mating system isn't in place," he said, slipping off the mattress and heading away. "Or else I'd have to breed you in front of my entire pack during your heat and until your belly began rounding."

With my stomach still pressed against the mattress, I glanced over my shoulder just in time to see a brown head of hair disappear into the bathroom. I pressed my thighs together and closed my eyes, embarrassed but also a bit intrigued about his *mating* system.

Did they really fuck in front of each other? Was that why Molly was okay with it?

Once I gathered my thoughts—or at least came down from the high—I crawled over to my side of the bed and grabbed my teacup. The sweet scent of the hot tea drifted through my nostrils, stronger than last time.

Or maybe that was how it seemed because the other teacup hadn't had the same scent.

No, it smelled different somehow. Not as strong or as … potent.

Deciding that it was just my imagination playing tricks on me, I slipped out of bed naked and walked to the window while sipping on the tea. I pulled back the curtains and stared down at the city.

So, this is my life now?

Unable to coerce a beast to give me ten million dollars in cash.

Life could definitely be worse, but—who knows?—maybe it'll take a turn today at work.

I took another sip. Work.

My eyes widened as I peered at the digital clock on the nightstand.

Shit! I'm late for work.

"Oh no," I whispered, scrambling up in the bed and hurrying

to grab my clothes where he had laid them out last time. I stumbled around in the room, the darkness making it hard to see anything. "I'm gonna get in so much trouble!"

CHAPTER
SIXTEEN

LUCIANO

"ALPHA THEO PAID me a visit yesterday afternoon," I said to Brent, who stood in my office.

Just outside the window, I spotted Yeosin reading through some documents. I had made it to work just before she did—a half hour later than our typical start time—and I planned to question her about her tardiness later …

Just to make her squirm.

"Oh, yeah?" Brent asked, lounging in the cushioned chair across from me and tossing a tangerine in the air. When he caught it, he tore into it with a single claw. "What'd that asshole want anyway? Probably something—"

"He's made a pact with the Colossals."

Brent stopped peeling the tangerine and looked over at me through wide eyes. "He what?"

"I'd warned him against it, but he already made contact. One of his many surrogates was taken by the Dragon Clan, and I fear that Yeosin is next."

"Who's Yeosin?"

A low growl escaped my throat, and I hardened my gaze. "Alana."

Yeosin's American name tasted sour on my tongue. She had told me to call her that last night, but by the look on her face, I could tell that she was lying. Plus, every time I did say her name, her arousal became stronger.

"You're mating with Alana?"

"We're not mates."

A grin stretched across his face. "Sure you're not."

"We're not."

"Fine," he said, wiggling his eyebrows. "But you're still mating."

"Get out of my office," I growled. "I came to warn you about Theo and the Colossals, not talk about my love life."

"Love life?" Brent harped. "So, you're in love with her now?"

"No!"

"Mmhmm. Sure. We'll say that."

"Brent, I swear to the fucking Goddess, you'd better—"

Brent hopped up from his seat and walked to the door. "I gotta go anyway. Work calls."

"Send Yeosin in," I said to Brent.

He bowed his head with the biggest smirk ever, walked out of the office, and stopped at Yeosin's desk. After leaning against it, he flashed her an innocent smile and crossed his arms, speaking quietly to her. She leaned forward and kicked her legs underneath the desk.

Her smile quickly faded to fear, and she lifted her gaze to look at me through my office window, eyes huge. After standing and straightening out her skirt, she smiled at Brent—*I wanted to kill him for it*—and turned toward me.

"You wanted to see me?" Yeosin asked, peeking into my office with those huge brown eyes.

After I gestured for her to come in, she stood in front of the slightly ajar door and pressed her full lips together.

"If this is about yesterday afternoon, I didn't mean to run out like that. I—"

"Miss Cho"—I clicked my tongue—"you were late this morning."

Yeosin's eyes widened, and she stiffened in front of me. "I know. I'm sorry!" she said with a slight bow of her head. It was as if she didn't want to make eye contact with me anymore, like if she did, then I would know her dirty little secret. "It won't happen again!"

While shaking my head, I walked over to the door and locked it behind her. My back was turned toward her, hers to mine, and I couldn't hold back the smirk that crawled across my face. I was a terrible person for asking her a question like this.

But I loved watching her squirm for an excuse.

"Where were you?" I asked, turning toward her, her smaller body nearly trembling.

Suddenly, her cheeks blazed bright red, and she shuffled her feet. "I, um … I was …"

"You were …"

"I was … out!"

She pressed her thighs together, and I inhaled the scent of her arousal still lingering from this morning. I was sure I had made her come—not once, but twice—but her pussy was still wet for me. Smelling so sweet.

"With a guy?"

"No!" she exclaimed, dropping her voice. "He's not just any guy. I was with, um …"

I raised an eyebrow and tilted my head to the side slightly. "Hmm?"

"I was with my boyfriend."

"You have a boyfriend?" I asked, the nickname making me feel … things.

"Sorta," she said, her face scrunched. She wrapped her arms around herself, tearing her gaze away from me. "I forgot to set my alarm, and he snored all night, and—"

What? Snored?

"I don't—" I began, but stopped myself before it was too late. I cleared my throat and walked around toward my desk, leaning against the front of it and crossing my arms. I needed to change the conversation quickly before she caught on. "You weren't off gallivanting through my building yesterday afternoon?"

"Shit!" she murmured so quietly that a human wouldn't be able to hear it.

"What was that?" I asked, teasing her.

"D-did you see the security cameras?" she asked.

I lowered my gaze. "Something like that."

"S-sorry, I was lost. It's so n-new to me here."

"You weren't … getting yourself into trouble, now were you, Miss Cho?"

"No, sir," she said.

And I had to stop myself from correcting sir to Alpha.

"Because if you were, then you'd have to be punished."

She stared up at me, her nipples hardening underneath her shirt and her arousal becoming so strong that my beast was slowly claiming hold of me. "P-punished?!"

"Punished."

After shuffling her feet on the floor—rubbing her thighs together in the process—she tilted her head down and looked up at me through her lashes. "What kind of punishment?" she asked, her heart pounding so loudly that my beast could hear it.

Is she enjoying this?

I kicked myself off the desk and stalked closer to her. She sucked in a breath and craned her head up, furrowing her brows together. I grabbed hold of the beast inside me, desperate to stay in control. Yeosin couldn't see my eyes change color or the beastly qualities inside me.

I stared down into those big brown eyes. "The good kind."

"Oh, yeah?" she whispered, her arousal so strong that I knew I wouldn't be able to hold my beast back much longer.

But I couldn't stop pushing her. I wanted—needed—her here, on top of my desk, screaming out my name.

Right when I was about to respond, she sucked in a sharp breath and swallowed hard, her cheeks becoming even redder. "It, um, won't happen again! I promise, Mr. Bates. I'll be here on time tomorrow."

"And if you're not?"

She grabbed the door handle. "Then you can punish me any way that you'd like."

CHAPTER
SEVENTEEN

LUCIANO HAD DISAPPEARED into a meeting room, and I shot up to my feet. My stomach was growling, but I hadn't dared to take my lunch break yet because the thought of him punishing me kept me here.

My core was pulsing and warm, desperate to be filled by him.

I swallowed hard and pushed the thought to the back of my mind. I needed food.

So, once the coast was clear, I slipped into the elevator and pressed the Ground Floor button. I bounced on my toes, my heart racing at the thought of earlier, when Luciano had called me into his office.

All that talk of punishment had really gotten me going. My pussy had been pulsing all morning at the thought of that grumpy man bending me over his desk and having his way with me until he was satisfied.

But maybe I was reading this all wrong. The girls up front had said that Luciano had a thing for Ella, and we looked absolutely nothing alike. And he was my boss, so it wasn't like anything could actually happen between us.

It was my imagination making things up.

Besides, even if things *were* to happen and then the beast got me pregnant, how the hell would I explain that to him?

Oh, sorry, Mr. Bates, but I'm carrying another man's baby—but I'm just a surrogate, and the man is actually a monster. No, really, he's a monster, monster.

The elevator doors opened. I blew my bangs off my forehead and stepped out, looking from side to side so the beast couldn't surprise fuck me here again today. I couldn't let that happen again. Luciano was onto me.

After examining the foyer, I headed toward one of the exits. My stomach growled, and I desperately needed to shove something into my mouth. I had run out of the bedroom before I had time to eat this morning.

Once I decided to grab some ramen, I pulled my purse to my chest and smiled to myself.

Was Luciano really flirting with me? Maybe, but—

Suddenly, someone snapped their hand around my shoulder from behind, dragged me into an alleyway, then slammed me against the side of a brick building.

"Where were you last night?!" the man hissed into my ear.

I glanced to my right to see a black SUV with tinted windows at the corner.

The Dragon Clan.

"I-I'm sorry," I whispered. "I … I was out."

"We need our fucking money," he said, grabbing my arm as tightly as he could and shoving me out of the alleyway and toward the nearest ATM. "And you're going to fucking get it for us."

Heart pounding, I did as I had been told because I felt something hot poke me in my lower back, and I really didn't want to die today. I pushed my tears away and scrambled to get my card out of my wallet. When I did, I slipped it into the ATM.

What I didn't understand was why they hadn't taken my card.

They could steal it and use it every day to get as much money out of the ATM as they wanted. Why hadn't they … done that? Why did they have to harass me for it?

Was it a tormenting thing? Torture thing?

"We don't have all fucking day," the man growled. "Get it now."

The ATM spit my card out of the machine, and then hundred-dollar bills flooded out behind it. I grabbed them all in a shaky hand and counted them three times to make sure it was enough.

But it wasn't.

So, I pushed the card into it again and hoped that it'd let me withdraw more this time. The Dragon Clan wanted more money than they had last week, and I hadn't been convincing enough for the beast.

He didn't understand that he wasn't the only person with enemies. I had them too.

"Hurry up," the man growled, shoving something warm against my lower back.

I wasn't sure what it was, but it stung. Badly.

"I-I'm sorry," I whispered, keeping my head down so nobody would see me here with them. Not many people knew who the Dragon Clan was, but everyone in my family did, and they had stopped talking to me after Alvin betrayed them. "I-it's not letting me take out much at a time."

I could only imagine how much my family would talk if they saw me out here with them.

After typing in the most amount of money that it would let me take out, I waited for the machine to spit out my card and the cash like it had moments ago. But the loading circle on the screen continued to spin and spin and spin.

And all I wanted to do was cry harder.

"Come on," I whispered. "Please."

Why do I have terrible luck with technology every time I use it?!

A moment later, a message popped up on the screen.

Request denied. Daily withdrawal limit met.

Eyes wide with trembling tears, I hit all the buttons on the screen, hoping it would try again. The loading circle spun once more, and the same message popped up on the screen, followed by the machine spitting out my card.

"I'm sorry," I whispered, gathering the cash in hand. "This is all I have right now."

The man snatched the cash from me and counted it twice, and then he looked over his shoulder at the driver in the black SUV and shook his head. I gulped and made myself as small as possible.

"I can get more tomorrow," I whispered. "Please, don't hurt me."

"Alvin needs the money now."

My brows furrowed together. "Wh-what do you mean, Alvin needs it? I thought …"

"Alvin, our boss," he growled. "He said that you'd have the money."

"Your boss is Alvin?" I whispered. "I thought you were from the Dragon Clan?"

"We are."

"B-but …" I said, confused because Alvin wasn't part of the Dragon Clan.

I thought … I …

What is going on? Alvin is their boss?!

"Can I talk to him?" I asked. "Surely, this is some kind of mistake. I don't have money."

As far as I knew, they were after me because of Alvin. But maybe … maybe I had misunderstood them this entire time. I thought Alvin had gotten us into trouble. I didn't think that Alvin had told them to come after me.

The man slammed me into the ATM and snarled into my ear, the heat on my back getting even hotter. Tears pricked the corners of my eyes, and I bit my lip to hold back the sobs that I so desperately wanted to spill out of my mouth.

"Same time. Same place. Same amount of money. Tomorrow."

The man shoved me away and stormed back to the black SUV sitting at the corner of the street. After he slipped into the passenger seat, they drove away, leaving me at the ATM without any dignity left.

With tears welling in my eyes because my back was still burning, I walked back to work. The dried-up gum on the sidewalk seemed to fly by me, but I was too much in a daze to care or pay attention to anything right now.

My back felt like it was on fire, but I must've been ... imagining that.

Maybe they cut it with a knife, and the sting was blood seeping out of the wound. I sucked in a breath and tried to figure out how I would explain a bloody shirt to Luciano when I returned. I didn't have another pair of clothes to change into.

I grabbed the handle of the door and yanked it open, stepping into the warm building and hoping that it wasn't blood at all. After hissing to myself, I hit the elevator button, and the elevator doors popped open.

Two nice leather shoes stopped a foot away from me, and I stepped out of the way so they'd have room to get by and so I could get into the elevator, but they followed me. I peered up to see Luciano glaring down at me.

"Where have you been?"

I pushed away my tears and stood up taller. "Getting lunch!"

My stomach growled, and he narrowed his eyes, and then they softened.

"You're crying."

"N-no, I'm not!" I exclaimed. "I just had something super spicy, and I ..."

Luciano stepped closer to me and took my chin in his hand. "Lying will get you in trouble, Miss Cho. And you know what getting in trouble means, don't you?"

"Th-that I'll be punished."

He lifted my chin, so I stared into those dangerous eyes. "Do you want me to punish you?"

"I, um …" I sucked in a breath, and warmth gathered between my legs. "Yes."

CHAPTER
EIGHTEEN

YEOSIN

YES? *Yes?! Why did I say yes?!*

Luciano tilted his head down slightly, his eyes glowing under the dim elevator light in a way that I had never seen before, but maybe I had never really gotten the courage to look him in the eyes, especially at Pink Ivory.

"Yes?" he repeated. "You want me to punish you?"

I sucked in a breath, determined to take it all back and tell him no. "Yes."

Come on, Yeosin! We can't do this right after practically getting robbed!

But if it would stop Luciano from asking why I was crying and why there was blood all over my backside, then I had to go along with it. And even if I tried, I didn't think I would be able to refuse him. This feeling was worse than body betrayal syndrome that girls always got in those cheesy romance books.

I couldn't move. I couldn't say no.

A deep and feral need in me would only let me agree.

"Please," I whispered, pressing my thighs together. "I need you."

Luciano pulled me into the elevator and hit the Close Door button. When the doors shut, he had me pressed against the shiny metallic wall, his face buried into the crook of my neck and his hard cock against my stomach.

Slight pain shot up my back, but the adrenaline suppressed it. I arched my back to keep it from pressing too hard against the wall and tilted my head to the side to give him better access, a small moan escaping my mouth.

What am I doing? I have to stop!

"Don't you think this is … wrong?" I whispered.

"I think it's a perfectly acceptable punishment for lying," he murmured against the column of my neck, his slight stubble making me tingle in all the right places. He pushed a foot between mine and slid his knee between my aching thighs.

"I don't think it's enough."

Yeosin, what the fuck?!

"It's not enough of a punishment for you?" he murmured, dipping his hand underneath my skirt and rubbing my aching clit. "What if I push you all the way to the tip of coming all over my fingers and then just leave you there?"

I didn't want that. I wanted to come. I *needed* to come. So, I ignored him.

I furrowed my brows and whimpered. "Since the moment you walked into Pink Ivory, I've been thinking about you," I said, the confessions just tumbling out of my mouth at this point without me being able to stop them.

With his face buried in the crook of my neck, he moved his fingers faster against me. I spread my legs a couple of inches wider, desperate to forget about everything that had happened during my lunch break.

When the elevator doors began reopening, Luciano hit the Close Door button again so they snapped shut, then pressed the Top Floor button. I arched my back a bit harder so my wound wouldn't skim against the metallic wall and closed my eyes, the pressure unbearable.

And right when I was about to come, he stopped. "No coming."

"Please, let me come," I pleaded. "I need it. Badly."

While this felt so wrong because I had feelings for that beast, nothing could ever happen between us. He had made it clear that he was only looking for a surrogate and only cared that I was safe. Doing this once wouldn't hurt, right?

When he stopped moving his fingers, I bucked my hips against his hand, so desperate to get off. I really needed to relax after what had just happened out on the street, and coming would be the perfect stress relief.

"Don't stop," I cried when he pulled his hand away. "Please, don't stop."

"This is your punishment for lying to me."

"No," I murmured. "Please, no."

While he didn't put his hand back on my pussy, no matter how many times I pleaded, he didn't pull away from me either. He stood, pressed against me, his hands behind his back and his taut muscles flexing against his suit jacket.

I moved my pussy closer to his thigh and began grinding myself against it like a desperate little mess of a woman. I gripped on to the arm rail behind me and bucked my hips up and down on his suit pants, my skirt riding up my thighs until it was bunched at my hips.

"Desperate, fuckable," he murmured, "and breedable."

A wave of heat rushed through my core.

"Why did you lie to me?" he asked.

"I didn't," I cried, gripping on to his suit jacket. "I didn't lie, I promise."

Lie. Lie. Lie. Lie. Lie.

He clicked his tongue and shook his head, but didn't stop me from getting off on his thigh, ruining his nice suit pants with my juices, breaking all the rules of the corporate world that HR had told me that I had to follow.

"Breed me," I whispered because I thought it would break him like it had the beast.

I can't say that to my boss! Stop it!

"I want to be bred. Please, Mr. Bates. Breed me!"

Growls rumbled out from his throat, and I swore his eyes glowed even darker.

"Breed you? You want me to breed you?"

"I love the thought of someone getting me pregnant," I whispered, closing my eyes and thinking back to the beast's offer. "Of someone wanting me so much that they have to put a baby inside me."

The beast didn't want me that badly; he just wanted to continue his family name.

But if he did want me for that reason …

Fuck!

"You're not going to get pregnant, rubbing yourself off on my thigh," he said.

I ground my pussy against his hard cock in his pants. "Then shove it inside me."

His cock was throbbing against my cunt, creating the biggest imprint against his suit pants that I had ever seen. He was way too hard to pull away now. This was so forbidden, but I couldn't stop.

A low chuckle escaped his mouth. "I don't think HR would like that much."

When the words left his mouth, reality seemed to smack me hard in the face. I blew out a deep breath and stopped grinding against him, suddenly coming back down to reality and realizing that this was so wrong. I had to stop.

Before I knew it, he undid his zipper and pulled out his huge cock. "But it's not like I give a fuck about what HR thinks."

My nipples hardened, and I sucked in a sharp breath. "Mr. Bates, I—"

He stroked it against my pantyhose, his shiny black-and-silver watch glimmering underneath the light. My eyes widened. I swore I had seen that watch before, and it hadn't been on his wrist, but who …

"Beg for me to fuck your tight little hole again," he murmured.

"Again?" I whispered, brows furrowed. "What do you mean by ag—"

Luciano cursed under his breath, which sounded more like a growl, and slammed himself inside me, tearing right through my pantyhose. I pressed a hand over my mouth and cried out into it, coming almost instantly at the feel of his cock deep in my pussy.

Wrong. Wrong. Wrong. Wrong. Wrong.

This was so wrong.

CHAPTER
NINETEEN

YEOSIN

MY BOSS'S hands were all over my body, his face buried into the crook of my neck. I arched my back, the wound from the Dragon Clan stinging, and clutched on to his round shoulders.

Holy fuck! He feels so good though.

The pain almost didn't matter.

"You're so tight," he hissed, pumping into me slowly.

I curled my toes and bit down on my bottom lip to suppress my moans, trying to keep quiet. But it wasn't like that it mattered. The elevator doors could open at any time, exposing us to the entire office.

"Tell me how badly you want it."

"So badly," I cried out into his neck. "I want it so, so badly. I'll do anything for it."

"You have to promise me one thing, Yeosin," he growled.

"What? Anything!"

"You're not going to let a drop of my cum roll down your thighs when we get out of this elevator," he murmured, his nose buried in my black hair. "You're going to keep every last drop of me inside you."

I nodded. "I promise. I promise!"

When he curled his fingers against the upper part of my ass, pain shot through me from the gash—if that was really what it was. I tensed, but the pain quickly subsided from the pleasure. My mind was on overdrive right now, and I so desperately didn't want to feel a thing, except his cum in my pussy.

I shouldn't be doing this right now. *Luciano is my boss!*

But I wanted someone to love me, and I knew that this wasn't love ... but it was close enough to it, right? Someone desired me so much that they wanted to put a baby inside me. How couldn't that be confused as love?

With every floor we ascended, the elevator dinged, making my heart race. I tightened around him, letting him use my body for his pleasure. He bucked my hips back and forth on his huge cock, from base to tip until it almost slipped out.

"Fuck," he growled, the sound making me tingle all over.

"Please come inside me, Mr. Bates," I cried into his shoulder. "I need it so—"

Luciano gripped my hips and held them in place, pushing himself into me and shoving me further against the elevator wall. Pain pierced through my body, and I dug my nails into his back to displace all the pain.

Low growls left his mouth, and suddenly, his cock twitched inside me.

My eyes rolled back into my head from the thought of my grumpy boss being so into me that he just had to come inside me as a punishment for lying to him. The control he had lost because of me. The pleasure he had *because of me.*

When Luciano pulled out of me, I clenched my pussy so none of his cum would roll down my thighs, like I had promised him. Pain and guilt rushed through me, but I pushed it away before the elevator doors opened.

I swallowed hard and readjusted myself as the secretary came into view at the front desk. Luciano was out of the elevator before

I had time to think of an excuse and heading in the opposite direction of his office.

"Good elevator ride, huh?" she commented with a smirk.

My cheeks flamed, and I shuffled my feet. "You can say that …"

As soon as I made it into the office, I hurried to the restroom to check out the gash in my back because it was only getting hotter. Tears pricked the corners of my eyes from the pain after the pleasure completely wore off.

I really needed to figure out what the hell I was going to do!

When I pushed open the restroom door, expecting to not see anyone inside, Ella stood there with her arms crossed over her chest and her pointed gaze on me. It was as if she had been waiting for me to come here.

"What were you doing with Luci?"

"Luci?" I repeated, furrowing my brows and feigning innocence.

Nobody could find out what had happened! Except … everyone seemed to know already.

"Don't play stupid," she hissed. "Luciano Bates."

"What do you mean? We were just in the elevator …"

"Know your place." She shoved me. "It's not here. You don't belong."

I opened and closed my mouth a handful of times, then glanced back at the mirror. "I … I don't know what you're talking about."

"We can all smell it," she growled, nose wrinkling. "It's disgusting."

"Smell what?"

She looked me up and down, then drew her tongue across the front of her teeth, highlighting the pointed canines that she had. They weren't small like a human's, but much bigger, like those fake teeth I used to wear on Halloween as a vampire.

"Stay away from Luciano," she said, twirling around. "He's mine."

With wide eyes, I stared at the door as it swung closed. The secretaries really hadn't been kidding when they said that Ella had a thing for Luciano. Were they lovers? She sure acted that way. Maybe they had a past together.

When I finally overcame the complete confusion and shock from what had just happened, I locked the door so nobody else could come in and turned my back toward the mirror to peer at my shirt.

No blood.

At least none that I could see yet. But my back was burning still.

I swallowed hard and gently tugged up on the bottom of my shirt, revealing the huge red scar on my lower back. I squinted and moved closer to the mirror, eyes slowly widening in horror.

Is this … a burn mark?

A deep red outline with spots of yellow and a bubble already started forming in the center.

What had he used on me? A lighter? That would've burned my shirt though.

Someone wriggled the doorknob, and I pulled my shirt back down so that nobody else would see. How was I going to explain this to the beast when he saw it later? He would ask about it, saying that this was why I couldn't have the money. Because of *his enemies.*

Maybe I could hide it from him. It couldn't be that hard, right?

I could come up with an excuse that I was tired or that I was sore from this morning. I glanced down at my skirt and straightened myself out. Besides, I was feeling a bit guilty for what had happened with Luciano.

It wasn't like the beast and I were exclusive. He didn't even like me like that.

"Alana?" Brent shouted from outside the door.

After blowing out a breath, I pulled the door open and gave him my best smile. "Yes?"

"You all right?" he asked, hiking his thumb behind him. "Ella stormed out of the restroom in a huff. I thought I'd check on you."

"Yes," I whispered, lying straight through my teeth. "I'm fine."

I wasn't okay one bit. My back was somehow scarred. Ella had breathed down my throat for sharing a couple of minutes with our boss in the elevator. And worst of all, I needed to figure out how to get the money before the Dragon Clan burned me alive.

CHAPTER
TWENTY

LUCIANO

"CAN we start in the hot spring?" Yeosin asked, standing at the edge of the cave later that night, as if she were afraid to come in to see me. She shifted from foot to foot, hands clasped in front of her body. "Please."

I stalked toward her, noticing that her breasts seemed fuller than usual, her hips wider, and her eyes were almost glowing underneath the dim moonlight that flooded in from outside the cave. I had been inside her twice already today—not that she knew that—but my beast had been getting greedy.

Too greedy.

My fingers found her chin, and I gently drew the pads of my fingertips across her cheek. She stared up at me through soft brown eyes. I cupped her chin and lifted it a bit higher, trailing my fingers down her neck, the soft spot tingling against me.

Mark her, my beast growled inside me. *We need to mark her.*

"Please," she whispered. "I need it."

After releasing her chin, I forced myself to step to the side. "Go."

She bowed her head as a thank-you and scurried deeper into

the cave and down the walkway that led to the hot spring. When we reached the steaming body of water, she kicked off her shoes and peeled off her coat.

Instead of taking the rest of her clothes off, she faced me and nodded. "You go in first."

"I'm not going into the hot spring."

"Please," she said, the word faint and desperate.

What is going on with her tonight?

Once I realized she wasn't going to budge—maybe I had been too rough with her earlier and she needed to relax—I slipped into the hot spring and rolled my shoulders forward from the hot, relaxing water.

Yeosin chewed on the inside of her cheek for a couple of moments, then swallowed hard and peeled off her shirt.

Is she nervous about me seeing her naked? I have seen her body so many times now that it shouldn't matter.

She stepped into the water, moving farther and farther into it until it reached her waist. Then she paused, her face contorting into one of pain. She stepped farther into the water so her entire body was submerged and winced.

"What's wrong?" I asked, moving closer, the water rippling around us.

"Nothing."

"Come here."

After another moment's pause, she swam toward me, the water up to her shoulders. I moved behind her and placed my hands on her shoulders. She was more tense than usual, or maybe I was just shit at giving her proper aftercare. I had just run out of that elevator earlier, mostly in fear that I'd lose it right then and there in front of the secretaries.

If Yeosin was stressed out, it would make getting her pregnant harder.

My hands traveled further down her back. When my fingers pressed against her lower back, she winced. Immediately, I pulled my hand away from that spot and snaked it around her waist. Her body had never reacted that way before tonight.

"Did I hurt you?" I asked.

"No."

Her breasts were tender, and so was her lower back.

When I gently placed my hand on her backside again, her entire expression scrunched into one of pain. I picked her up in the water and brought her back toward the rocks that led down into the hot spring.

"No," she exclaimed. "I'm fine. I'm fine!"

"You're lying," I said. "I always know when you're lying."

"I'm fine," she said, wriggling in my arms.

I placed her belly-first on the rocks, lifting her hips out of the water, and I saw a huge bubble on her lower back from what looked to be like … a burn. I thought I had been too rough with her in the elevator, but I couldn't have done this.

"Who did this to you?" I growled.

"N-nobody!" she cried, clutching her back as if she knew exactly what I was talking about. She turned over, fell down into the spring, and stared up at me, but the light was shining from overhead so she couldn't see my face. But I could see the glow from my red eyes on her face. "It was nobody, I promise!"

"Who?" I snarled. "Who fucking did this to you?!"

"I was clumsy this morning," she whispered. "I-I spilled hot tea on myself."

"On your back?" I asked through gritted teeth. "You spilled hot tea on your back?"

"Yes," she said, nodding and staring up at me through innocent eyes that I almost believed. "I spilled tea on my back. That's what happened. That's why my back is burned … I swear it is."

"I'm going to ask you one more time, Yeosin," I whispered, trying hard to contain my emotions before they claimed my beast and took hold of me. "And if you lie to me, I'm going to fucking lose it."

"You're going to lose it either way," she said, scurrying back to the wall.

"Who hurt you?"

She gulped and shook her head. "I can't tell you. I don't want … I don't want you to look at me any differently," she finally whispered, tears welling up in her eyes. She dropped her head and wiped a tear away with her shoulder. "I'm embarrassed, and if you find out …"

"If I find out who did it to you, I'll kill them."

She sucked in a sharp breath and snapped her gaze up to mine. "No, you can't."

"Why not?"

"They're strong," she said. "My ex-boyfriend was really messed up with them. They don't care who you are or how much power you have; they'll hurt you. And I …" She wrapped her arms around herself. "I don't want them to hurt you."

Suddenly, my chest tightened, and I froze.

"I don't want them to hurt you."

What did she mean by that? Did she … *care* about me? Surely not. No, she couldn't. And I couldn't feel anything toward her. The only reason why I had gotten angry over this entire thing was because she was supposed to carry my pups.

Not because I liked her.

Really, I didn't.

Not at all.

As I swept my fingers over her jawline and she leaned into my touch, my fingers tingled.

Fuck.

"Who are they?" I asked one final time.

"They're part of this gang," she whispered. "A clan."

Fury overtook my beast, and I hurled my fist into the rock beside her. "The Dragon Clan?"

Her brown eyes widened. "How … how do you know about them?"

"Is that why you need the money in cash?" I asked.

She dropped her gaze. "Yes, but seriously, you don't have to do anything. I just need the money in cash, and then everything will be settled. I swear, you've already done so much for me by providing me the money, and I—"

"Is that why you left work today during lunch?" The words left my mouth before I could stop them.

"How did you know that I left? Are you following me? What did—"

"Don't try to get out of this, Yeosin," I growled. "How long has this been going on?"

She pressed her lips together and shook her head.

"How long?"

"Since the night before we met," she whispered, bursting out in tears. "They've been threatening me." She wrapped her arms around my torso and buried her face into my chest. "Hurting me … so badly. I … I don't know what to do. Please, help me."

CHAPTER
TWENTY-ONE

YEOSIN

THE BEAST'S eyes blazed in the darkness, leaving a trail of light in every direction he looked. I stared up at the monster who I had promised myself not to fall for, realizing that I had told him my secret.

Realizing that … that he probably didn't care.

We were only together so he could breed me. We were only together so I could give him children. We were only together because he had given me ten million dollars to have sex with him and because I was desperate for the cash.

Why would he care at all?

"Get out of the hot spring," he growled. "Joseph will bring you home."

"And where will you go?" I whispered, not wanting him to leave.

It was bad enough that I had just spilled everything to him, but I had also been feeling really bad since hooking up with Luciano in the elevator. And I hadn't even fulfilled my duties to the beast in the cave tonight.

All I had done was cry.

"I'm going to find which one of them did this to you and kill them," he snarled. "Out now."

My eyes widened, and a warm feeling washed over my entire body. I was in no place to feel all these feelings for a man who only wanted my womb, but ... but the way he had sounded so possessive ... made me feel *special*.

It was what I had been craving in the elevator with Luciano ...

"Yeosin," he growled. "Don't make me say it again."

I placed my palms on the rock and pushed myself out of the water until I sat on my knees. I turned back to face him, watching the water ripple around his taut frame as he walked to the edge and hopped out of the hot spring.

While I didn't know much about him, by the way his eyes were glowing so brightly that I could see him in the darkness ... he was about to do something stupid and get himself killed, leaving everyone who still relied on him.

"You don't have to go."

He stormed out of the room and down the chiseled hallway. "Yes, I do."

"They'll kill you," I said, hurrying after him.

"I don't care," he snarled, voice gruff.

I grabbed his elbow. "I do."

The beast froze with his back turned toward me. I walked around him to face him and finally caught a glimpse of his face underneath the shimmer of moonlight. But before I could see all of it, he turned his head.

"Don't go," I reasoned. "I take it back. I don't need help. I was just ... just scared."

I had asked him to help in a fit of terror and agony. It really wasn't my logical sense talking. I had been hurting since I got that mark on my back earlier, then in the elevator with Luciano ... I had ignored the pain then because I was full of adrenaline.

After wrapping my arms around myself, I shuffled my feet. "I don't want anything to happen to you. They're dangerous," I said again. "They don't care what they do, and I … I will gladly take the burns if that means you're safe."

"You're fucking crazy, Yeosin."

My eyes watered. "Why does that make me crazy?"

"You're crazy if you think I will do nothing after you've come to me in tears and in pain," he said through gritted teeth. "You're crazy that you would rather continue to risk your life rather than tell me. You're crazy for caring about me."

Lips quivering, I shook my head. "No, I'm not. You have people who you must care for. You have people who look up to you. You're important, and I …" Memories of Alvin and my parents rushed through my head. "I'm not important to anyone."

That was what this all really came down to, didn't it?

He took my chin in his hand. "Don't say that."

"It's true," I said, my voice cracking. "I'm not. And I'm okay with that."

"You're important to me."

"Only because you need me to give you pups."

While I wanted him to refuse that was the case, he did nothing but growl.

"I don't like asking for help," I said. "You don't need to do anything. I promise."

"How much money does the Dragon Clan need from you?"

"Several million," I whispered.

"I need an exact number."

"That's impossible." I chewed on the inside of my cheek. "Even if I pay it back, they'll want more because they know that I can get it for them. I'm always going to be indebted to them, no matter what I do. So … don't bother helping. I don't need your money."

The thought had never really sunk in until now.

It was as if they were purposefully trying to work me to the bone, to siphon as much money out of me as possible, to … to keep me distracted.

My mind wandered back to earlier in that alleyway when the

Dragon Clan had said that Alvin was their leader. And if Alvin was their leader, then he hadn't been in trouble with them. Unless … there were subclans within the Dragon Clan, or those people weren't part of the Dragon Clan at all …

None of this made sense to me. And, God, it'd be far too hard to explain to the beast.

I was in a freaking mess—a web—that I couldn't get myself out of.

"Joseph will take you back to the penthouse," the beast said.

"But—"

"And you're going to go."

"I really—"

Before I had time to argue, the beast walked to the exit of the cave and released a low howl. He paused there for a few moments, and then he howled again. I listened for the sound of tires against the dirt floor, but heard nothing.

"Where is he?" I whispered.

After letting out another howl, he cursed underneath his breath.

"Is something wrong?" I asked.

Instead of answering me, the beast held out his hand. "Come with me."

"Through the woods?" I whispered, staring out into the darkness around us. "It's dark."

"I'll protect you, *mate*," he said, voice … different than normal. He scooped up my hand and pulled me onto a trail. "From anything."

CHAPTER
TWENTY-TWO

LUCIANO

"YOU'RE BACK SO SOON," Molly said when I walked into the penthouse with Yeosin.

"Where is Joseph?" I asked, carrying a sleeping Yeosin to my bedroom.

Molly followed after me and shook her head. "I thought he was with you. The last I heard from him, he was dropping Ms. Yeosin off at the cave and trying to find information for you on that car."

"Shit," I growled under my breath.

After I tugged down the blankets so I could place Yeosin on the bed, Molly clasped her hands together and furrowed her brows. "Did you walk all the way back here with Ms. Yeosin?"

"Yes."

"You could've called me."

"No service in the cave," I said. "Get me a warm towel."

Without asking any questions, Molly retrieved a warm towel from my bathroom. I peeled off Yeosin's clothes, then gently turned her onto her stomach.

"Oh my Goddess," Molly said, wide eyes fixed on Yeosin's burn. "What happened?"

"The Dragon Clan happened."

"The-the Dragon Clan?" she repeated, gulping. "They're back?"

"They're back."

"Did you run into them? Did they find the cave? The packhouse?"

"No. Yeosin ran into them during her lunch break. *They're* the ones in that car, chasing her down, demanding her to give them as much money as she has. And you know they won't stop until they've worked her to death."

She opened and closed her mouth a handful of times, then bowed her head. "I'll let you heal her." She gave Yeosin one last longing look, then disappeared into the other room. "And I'll boil water for some tea. It will help with the pain when she begins to recover."

Once the door closed, I knelt beside Yeosin on the side of the bed. She snored softly, her mouth ajar. I gently placed my hand on her bare back and outlined her burn with my fingers, making sure not to put any pressure on her skin so she wouldn't wake up.

When I accidentally made contact with the wrinkled skin, a jolt rushed through me.

Flames suddenly burned all around me. Mom lay bloody in front of me, her body burning with blue flames—the hottest kind known to beasts. When I grasped her frail arms, they turned to ash in my hands. I grabbed for any part of her, to hold her one last time, but with every touch, more and more chalky ash covered my hands.

Packmates cried out from all directions, screaming in pain and terror. I lifted my gaze to the battlefield, knowing that if we continued ... there would be nobody else left in my pack, knowing that everyone was dying because I couldn't protect them.

. . .

I pulled my fingers away and jerked my head to the side to shake away the memory.

After all these years that we had been hiding in the shadows, after I had finally decided to settle down and start over, to rejuvenate my pack, the Dragon Clan were back to take it all away. But I refused to let them touch Yeosin again.

If they did … I'd rip off their heads.

I didn't care what they did to me. I didn't care how much they burned my body with fire. I drew my tongue across my lengthened teeth and growled. Yeosin was mine. Mine. Mine! I didn't care if she was pregnant with my pup yet or not. I would do anything to protect her.

Once I took a deep breath to re-center myself, I pressed my mouth to her burn to use my saliva to heal it. I wasn't sure how I could heal her last time—outside of pack doctors, only mates could heal each other, and I had been cursed without a mate for the rest of my life—but I hoped if there was still a Goddess who watched over the beasts, she'd give me strength.

I drew my tongue across her burn. Once. Twice. A third time.

And nothing.

I tried again. Still nothing.

After trying again and still not healing her in the slightest, I pulled back. "*Fuck.*"

Part of me had been holding out hope that I could heal her, that Yeosin might really be my mate. My beast had surely thought so earlier at the cave. But the feelings I had for her were just … they were just about me needing to continue my bloodline.

She shifted in the bed, a strand of her hair falling into her face.

Yeah, that's what it is. An innate need to continue my bloodline.

That didn't change the fact that I needed to protect her with my life.

Once I finally accepted defeat, I pulled the blankets up to Yeosin's shoulders, grabbed my phone, and walked out of the room to the kitchen, where Molly stood over the stove, nervously running her hands together.

I wasn't the only one in that war who wore burns. She did too.

"Find a way to heal her," I said to Molly.

"You weren't able to?" Molly asked, eyes wide.

I gritted my teeth. "No."

Her gaze dropped. "I thought for sure that you were mates …"

"I already told you that I can't have a mate," I said harshly.

She bowed her head. "I know, but you're happier with her. I just … I thought …"

"I'm not happier with her," I snarled. "I'm using her for pups, and that's it."

"Keep telling yourself th—"

Before she could finish her sentence, I snapped my hand around her throat and slammed her against the nearest wall, my beast taking full control. When I realized what I had done, I immediately pulled away.

"I'm sorry," I said to Molly. "That was my beast."

"No, no," she said, shaking her head. "I'm sorry. I shouldn't have spoken out of place."

"I need her to mean nothing more than that," I whispered, trying to convince myself.

This meant war with the Dragon Clan, and they already knew who Yeosin was. There was a huge chance that she wouldn't make it out of this alive. And if she didn't … I would have to find another mat—I mean, another woman to give me pups.

Yeosin had to mean nothing.

"I need to figure this out," I said.

After running a hand through my hair, I stormed out of the penthouse and headed straight for the elevator with my phone pressed to my ear. It rang and rang and rang. I balled my hands into tight fists, almost bending the phone.

"Come on, Joseph," I growled. "Answer."

When the call went to voicemail, I slammed my finger on the End Call button and dialed Brent instead. I didn't have time to wait around for Joseph to call me back. I didn't know where he was, but it wasn't like him to ignore my calls.

Nonetheless, we needed a plan.

I wouldn't let the Dragon Clan get away with this. As much as I didn't want to partner with Alpha Theo, it seemed like that was our only solution right now. At least, it was a temporary solution, a temporary army.

If it protected Yeosin, then I would have to move forward with it. I had no choice.

"Hello? Brent speaking."

"Meet me at the old packhouse," I said. "Twenty minutes."

"Luciano. Hey, what's—"

"Packhouse. Twenty minutes."

He paused on the line. "Why? I'm kinda in the middle—"

"Now!" I snarled through the phone. "This is war."

CHAPTER
TWENTY-THREE

LUCIANO

"WHERE THE FUCK ARE YOU, JOSEPH?" I growled into the phone as it rang for the third time.

Brent and I walked through the woods toward Alpha Theo's packhouse that had been partially burned to the ground during the last war. Some of it was still standing, and while he had taken a huge hit to his pack, none of his packmates lived there anymore.

They were with the others—the remaining few—several hundred miles away from here.

"Do you think the Dragon Clan caught him?" Brent asked.

"No," I said. I thought it was worse than that.

Joseph wouldn't allow himself to get caught, and if he did, then he wouldn't let them take him. His phone could've been off, but that wasn't like him. He had been due back at the cave an hour ago. If we weren't there, he would've confirmed with me.

"He's dead," I said, pursing my lips. "He has to be dead."

Brent sucked in a breath and shook his head. "No, he's not dead."

"He's dead."

There wasn't a doubt in my fucking mind that he was dead. I

didn't know where they would've killed him or dumped his body, but if they wanted to send a message, then they would lay his body out for me to find.

Alpha Theo stood at the edge of his property, waiting for us. "Thought you'd show up."

"We have to talk about the Dragon Clan," I said, shoving my phone into my pocket.

"You want in on this war now?" he asked, leading us to the packhouse. "Why?"

I flared my nostrils and glared at the back of his head, not wanting to tell him that they had hurt Yeosin. He obviously knew that they had hurt someone close to me if I wanted in on this war and if I wanted to team up with him and the Colossals.

"Before you answer that," Alpha Theo said, pushing open the door, "come in."

The scents of the Colossals drifted through my nostrils before I entered, and I tensed. They were here. Of course. But I hadn't expected to make this deal with them here. I wanted the upper hand with Theo.

Though ... I didn't have another choice.

So, I kept my mouth shut and walked into the packhouse, spotting two male warriors and two female warriors from the Colossals, one of the women harsh and the other so small and almost ... soft.

Alpha Theo placed a hand on my shoulder and squeezed. "Luciano, I'd like to introduce you to Ruby. She's a strong warrior in the Colossals and has been looking forward to meeting you. I think you two will really hit it off."

"It's nice to meet you," Ruby purred, her full lips pursed into a soft smile.

Who would've thought that a girl who looked as sweet as her could turn into a giant monster, fierce enough to take on a dragon herself? She resembled Yeosin a bit—long black hair, wide hips, an innocent smile.

But something felt ... off.

Brent glanced over at me, but I didn't dare look back at him. I couldn't give off that I didn't want help, that I didn't need help. We needed to defeat the Dragon Clan before they found my penthouse and killed Yeosin this time.

"Let's skip the formalities," I said, turning back to Alpha Theo. "I want in on the war."

"What changed your mind?" Alpha Theo asked.

I ran a hand over my face. "The Dragon Clan burned my surrogate."

Surrogate.

That was all she was to me, but the word tasted like shit in my mouth.

Brent looked at me. "Surrogate? Didn't seem like that when—"

Before he could say another word, I snapped my glare to him and made sure he knew to shut the fuck up before I had to do that to him myself. I balled my hands into fists, my claws slicing into the thin skin on my palms.

"Your surrogate?" Ruby repeated. "You're trying to have children?"

"Only to rebuild my pack."

She stepped toward me. "Mating with a human will only weaken you. You need someone strong, someone who can take on the Dragon Clan, someone who isn't threatened by creatures of the night." She paused and craned her head up at me. "Someone like me."

I kept my lips pressed together and flared my nostrils.

What she was saying wasn't false, and I needed help defeating the Dragon Clan once and for all. But I didn't want her. Though if the Dragon Clan found Yeosin and ended up killing her …

Never, my beast snarled inside me.

The voice startled me because he didn't talk much to me anymore. He only took control when I let him. Since the last war, I had blocked him out since I had been the only one of us to think logically. Thinking with my emotions had gotten the majority of my pack killed the first time.

If Yeosin died, we'd need someone else.

No.

The word came out harsh and final, without room for questions or argument.

"We will be part of this war with you," I said. "And we'll take down the Dragon Clan."

"You will have to make sacrifices," Ruby said. "Are you ready for that?"

"Almost my entire pack has been sacrificed. I'm willing to do what I need to do."

I was willing to do almost anything, except ... put Yeosin in harm's way. I would do anything to protect her for as long as I could. I doubted my beast would let me do much else anyway.

Ruby stared up at me through curious, large eyes, and I didn't pull my gaze away because I wanted her to know I was serious. She seemed to be the one calling all the shots because the other three hadn't spoken yet.

When she finally pulled away, I clenched my jaw and looked back at Brent, who had a visible grimace on his face. He didn't like this idea as much as I didn't like this idea. But this was our only hope.

Alpha Theo cleared his throat. "Then it's settled."

"Great. When do we start?" I said, moving this along.

The earlier we finished this, the less I had to associate at all with the Colossals and especially Ruby. I didn't like the way she looked at me. I didn't like the way she touched me. And I really didn't like the way she wanted to be mine.

That spot was reserved for one person and one person only. Yeosin Cho.

My employee. My partner. *My mate.*

CHAPTER
TWENTY-FOUR

YEOSIN

"STOP!" *I scream at the top of my lungs, but the smoke around me traps my voice.*

Flames burn my body—from the tips of my fingers to my shoulders and down to my toes. I roll around on the ground, back and forth and back and forth, like the teachers at school had taught me—because my parents never did.

Tears stream down my cheeks, but they quickly evaporate away from the fire.

"Stop it!" I shout, getting glimpses of dragons circling above and burning everything that I love to the ground.

Everything is so in and out, and I can't remember what happened directly before this.

All I know is that my entire body is on fire.

From across the forest, I spot the beast lying against the entrance of the cave, his entire body burned so badly that I can barely recognize him. But I can smell his distinctive scent, tormenting me because I can do nothing.

Absolutely nothing to stop this madness.

He confided in me about this happening before—I am sure of it.

And while I want to protect him, to make sure this never happened again, to give him a family lineage that he so desperately wants, I can't. I am nothing more than a helpless human, caught in this mess with creatures I never thought were real.

"Stop!"

Except the dragons continue to breathe fire down upon me.

The smoke around me becomes almost unbreathable. I cough and try to breathe as much as I can. I do what I need, what I think will help. But no matter what I try, I can't put the fire out.

Flames engulf the beast.

I need to help him.

Once I make it to the cave, I drag the beast's burning body down the small walkway to the hot spring. Will hot water cool him off enough? Will it stop the fire? I don't know, but I have to try.

I have to try. I have to try. I have to try.

I can't lose him.

Out of all the people burning in the forest with us, out of all the people important to me, he is the only person I recognize. He is the only person I care about, which is sad.

I don't know his name. I don't know who he is in real life.

All I know is that he makes me feel special, even if it is only because I will one day have his children. If that is all my life becomes, then I am fine with that. But I am not going to lose him like this.

The dragons—no, the Dragon Clan isn't going to win.

I refuse to let them win.

"Please," I whisper, dumping his body into the lake and jumping in after him.

Almost immediately, the water swallows the flames that emanate from both of our bodies. I pull his face out of the water and tug him to the rocks, using all my strength to lift him out of the water so he won't drown.

His body begins healing itself. Not all the way, but the immediate wounds.

I climb out of the water, watching his abilities make him whole again, and I curl my arms around myself and look down at my body. My skin is burned off almost completely—some to the muscle, some all the way down to the bone.

Tears well up in my eyes.

We are alive, but at what cost? Surely, the beast will find someone else. He can't have someone like me. How will it look for a beast like him to be with one like me? My insides are still on fire, somehow burning still.

After brushing my fingers across his face, which is slowly healing itself, I place a soft kiss on his lips and wish that things can be different. I wish that … I could've actually a relationship at some point. I wish that he actually loved me.

When my lips left his, I walk away from the hot spring and head toward the exit of the cave. While I will never get my happy ending, I can make sure he gets his with Ella, a strong woman who can give birth to his children.

I can surrender to the Dragon Clan.

I can end this.

"You wanted me?" I scream, arms up in the air to let them know that I am not a threat once I step out of the cave.

I have never once been a threat to them, though they treat me that way. I don't have any power. I don't have any magic. I am just a normal human who had fallen in love with a beast who doesn't love me back.

I drop to my knees and stare up at the dragons. "I surrender."

Instead of them stopping this madness, they breathe more fire down upon me until my body is engulf in flames. The smoke thickens around me, the direct line of fire blazing all over me.

"Please, stop this torture," I whisper. "I surrender."

But that isn't enough. It will never be enough.

My body is burning to a crisp, but my mind will not let me lose consciousness. I am forever in a state of pure torture. I don't know why they want to put me through this. They have tortured me enough.

Yet if it will save the beast and his pack, if it will give them some more time to escape and find somewhere new to start a family, to live a life, then I will happily endure this pain forever.

———

Suddenly, my eyes shot open, and I stared up at the ceiling in the beast's penthouse. Breathing heavily, I sat up in the bed and spotted Molly and Ella at the base of the bed, Molly with tea and Ella smirking.

"What's happened to her?" Molly asked, eyes wide. "Her body ..."

I opened and closed my mouth a handful of times, confusion spreading through me. Why was I back here? Last thing I remembered, I had been at the cave with the beast. And what was Ella, out of all people, doing here?

"What's she doing here?" I asked Molly.

"She's come to heal you."

"To heal me? But I—"

Before I could finish my sentence, Molly looked back at Ella. "What's going on?"

"I don't know," Ella said.

Molly grabbed Ella by the collar and slammed her up against the wall. "What did you do to her?! I brought you here to heal her. Why are there burns all over her body?! If you did this, he'll kill you!"

She held her hands up. "I didn't do anything. I haven't even touched her yet!"

Healing? Wounds? *Burns*? All over my body?

I slipped out of the bed and hurried to the mirror, eyes widening in horror when I saw myself. The burn from the Dragon Clan on my back wasn't the only one that I had anymore. There was one on my cheek, and another on my chest, and another around my forearm, and more ... so many more all over my body.

CHAPTER
TWENTY-FIVE

LUCIANO

"THANK the Goddess that you're home," Molly said, tugging open the door before I even had a chance to grab the knob later that night. She shifted from foot to foot, her head bowed and her gaze on the floor. "I … Yeosin … it's best if you see yourself."

"What happened?" I asked, breathing in a scent that definitely didn't belong here.

Ella.

Molly led me to my bedroom, where I had left Yeosin. Soft cries drifted out from underneath the door, the sound of my mate —*I mean, of Yeosin*—making my entire body fill with even more fury.

Something had happened. Something bad.

Before Molly could open the door, I snapped it open, my palm flat on the wood, and spotted Yeosin underneath the blankets. Her shoulders jerked back and forth. A glass of healing tea sat on the nightstand next to her.

"Don't look at me," Yeosin whispered, hiding underneath the blanket.

I balled my hands into fists by my sides to control my anger. What had happened here? I had left her alone for a couple of hours with Molly, and I came home to find Yeosin not wanting me to look at her. Someone had said something to her, *done* something to her.

"What's going on?" I asked Molly, who stood behind me.

"It's best if you see yourself," she said for the second time tonight.

"Remove the blankets, Yeosin," I ordered.

"No."

"I'm not in the mood," I growled.

"Neither am I."

When I couldn't deal with it any longer, I stormed to the bed and ripped off the blankets. Yeosin shrieked and covered herself with her arms ... her arms that were covered in burns. Why the fuck were they covered in burns?

Instead of looking at me, Yeosin kept her head down too. "Go away."

"What the fuck happened?" I snarled, turning toward Molly. "And why do I smell Ella?"

"She came over while Yeosin was sleeping," Molly said, bowing her head, her chin quivering. "I ... I left them alone for two minutes to make some healing tea for Yeosin, and I came back to see her burned. I'm sorry. She has healing abilities. She said she'd heal her."

"That fucking rat," I said between gritted teeth. "What did she do?"

Ella had healing abilities—or at least, she used to—but as far as I knew, she didn't have the ability to create these burns all over Yeosin's body, nor did she have the ability to mimic the burn on her back.

It didn't make sense.

Unless ... she hadn't come alone. Maybe someone from the Dragon Clan had come with her.

Molly bowed her head even more. "I'm sorry. This is my fault. You can punish me."

"Never let her into my penthouse again," I growled down at her, my claws digging into her throat and my beast completely taking over my body. *You will not put your luna in danger like that ever again. Do you understand?*

With wide eyes, Molly stared up at me and nodded. "Yes. Yes. I'm sorry."

"You willingly let another beast in here with the woman I'm mating with to make sure that this pack, that me, that you, that the legacy of everyone you've ever cared about survives," I snarled, struggling to regain control so Yeosin wouldn't see me like this. But my claws had cut through the skin on Molly's neck. "Don't fucking screw up this badly again."

Suddenly, small hands wrapped around my forearm. "Stop it. She didn't do anything."

"She put you in danger," I growled, my back turned toward her.

"It's not her fault." She released her harsh grip on my forearm and gently placed her hand on my back, rubbing it in soothing circles. "I promise that if she had done something, I would tell you. But she didn't."

Slowly, I released my grip on Molly. "Get out of here."

Molly shuffled into the other room and shut the door behind her. As soon as she was gone, Yeosin's fingers left my skin, leaving me cold. She walked toward the bathroom and stared into the mirror.

I stayed put next to the bedroom door.

"Are they bad?" she asked.

"Yes."

My voice came out curt and to the point, but I was trying my best to hold my anger back in front of her. If she was stressed, then it would be harder to get her pregnant, and I vowed to put babies in her belly before the Dragon Clan could kill me.

"How bad?"

I feared that if I touched her, then I would hurt her even more.

She needed rest—a lot of it. I could try to heal her myself because that bitch wasn't coming near her again—*I don't care if she did it or not*—but I didn't know how much I could heal. I could barely do anything with her previous burn.

After pulling down the blankets, I gestured for her to return to bed. "You need to sleep."

"No," she whispered, fear evident in her eyes. "I can't."

"You need it."

She shook her head again, eyes filling with tears. "Last time, I had a nightmare."

"Lie down and sleep, Yeosin," I growled. "I don't have time to argue with you."

Yeosin furrowed her brows. "Then go."

"Yeosin," I growled. "In bed now."

"No."

"I will throw you in bed if I have to."

She crossed her arms. "No."

My fucking Goddess, why wouldn't she listen to me tonight? It was a nightmare—that was all. As far as I knew, she had never suffered from them before. It was a onetime thing, and it wouldn't happen for a second time.

Because I didn't want to hurt her, I blew out a low breath and relaxed. "Please."

Yeosin stood there for a few moments, unfolding her arms. "I'm scared."

"There is no reason for you to be scared," I said softly. "I'm here to protect you."

"You just said that you're leaving."

"I'll stay until morning for you."

Her brown eyes widened, and she perked up. "You will?"

"Yes." I slipped into the bed. "Now come here."

Yeosin still hesitated, but then she shuffled over and climbed into bed with me, slipping underneath the blankets and curling up against my body. I sucked in a sharp breath because I wasn't used to this and stayed until her breath evened out.

I needed to find out where these burns had really come from. Soon.

Before it happened again.

CHAPTER
TWENTY-SIX

YEOSIN

THE NEXT MORNING, when Molly stepped into the bathroom, I yanked off my plush navy robe and dropped it onto the kitchen chair. The beast had forbidden me to leave today, but I needed to breathe. I hadn't left Molly's sight all night.

She shut the door, and I tiptoed to the front door and slipped out of it when I heard her start to pee. Don't ask me how I was able to hear something like that through that heavy door, but I was out of here.

Once I shut the door behind me, I ran to the elevator.

I don't have time to argue with you. I don't have time to argue with you.

It was bullshit. The beast did have time. He could make time. If he didn't have time to argue with me about not wanting to have any more nightmares, then what would happen when I carried his child? Would he have time for me then?

After balling my hands into tight fists, I hit the bottom button on the elevator. I didn't want to get Molly into any more trouble, but I wasn't going to sit in the house all day and wait for the beast to come back.

No. Screw that.

My mind was reeling at where he could've gone last night. He had come home with another woman's scent all over him. It was so strong, and I hadn't even really processed it until he left again last night.

Was he going back to see her? Who was she? My replacement?

Hot tears burned my eyes, and I crossed my arms all the way down to the bottom floor. I stepped out into the lobby and marched to the exit of the building. The doorman opened the door for me, and the freezing air chilled my skin.

I had work, and I wasn't going to let the beast stop me.

Luciano would be pissed if I was late *again*.

The walk down the street seemed longer than usual in the cold. While the burns still decorated my body from head to toe, I couldn't really feel the pain from them any longer. It had subsided substantially from last night.

So, I was all good to go to work.

I wasn't going to wait around for the beast not to come home tonight again.

My body might've been ugly to him now, but ... but ...

My thoughts seemed to freeze up as the thought of being so ugly to him circulated my mind. Between that and the smell of another woman on him, being ugly had to be it, right? Why would he—or anyone—want to be with someone like me? My body was ruined.

I was ruined.

Could I even grow a baby in my belly? I didn't know what had caused those burn marks last night, but they had seemed to happen in my nightmare. How was that even possible? What if it happened while I was pregnant and killed the child?

The beast would really hate me then.

After sucking in a breath, I headed straight for Pink Ivory. I needed to clear my mind, and maybe I could get on Luciano's good side if I brought him his black coffee—my apologies for being late.

Coffee beans drifted into my nose, and I remembered how much I hated this place.

"You're back, Alana?" Henry asked from behind the counter.

I offered him a small smile. "Just for drinks."

"I see how it is," he hummed in amusement, as if we were ever friends.

Once I decided to just be polite and forget about last night so my feelings wouldn't bleed over into work, I stepped up to the counter. "I'll take a green tea, no sugar or milk, and a hot black coffee."

"That all?"

"Yes."

"Eleven dollars, thirty-four cents."

Damn, they hiked up their prices, didn't they?

After swiping the beast's black card, I stepped to the side and scrolled through my emails from these past few days. I rocked back and forth on my heels, playing with the end of my sweater to tug it over my thumb, which was burned.

I didn't want anyone seeing the scars. Especially not Luciano.

I didn't want his pity or his questions. But if he got me alone like he had in the elevator the other day, then it might be hard to dodge the questions about my skin.

Why is it burned? The heck if I know!

"Alana!" a new worker called.

My phone buzzed, but I shoved it into my pocket and headed to the pickup area. I grabbed the coffee from her with a grip a bit too strong because the cap popped off and the piping hot coffee spilled all over my hand, burning it.

"*Shit!*" I sneered out of instinct.

Except it didn't hurt.

"Oh my gosh! I'm so sorry!" the barista exclaimed. "I have such a hard time with these caps." She grabbed a towel and placed it gently on my hand. "I'm so, so sorry. I didn't mean for you to get burned!"

"It's okay," I whispered, brows furrowed together at how ... much it didn't hurt.

"I'll make you a new one right away," she said, shuffling to grab a new coffee cup.

Once she turned away, I slid the towel off my hand to see the burn already bubbling. Maybe I was used to the pain, or maybe something was happening to me. But why ... why wasn't it hurting at all?

Was my body getting used to this? How? My skin was literally bubbling!

"Here you go," the barista said. "I'm so sorry again."

"It's okay," I whispered, concealing my hand from her. How would I hide this one?

I grabbed both my drinks and headed for the door, staring down at the bubble on my hand. It had hurt, initially. It had to have, right? But maybe the pain from last night had conditioned me to not hurt anymore?

No, that couldn't be it. That pain had just been in my nightmare.

Back against the door, I pushed it open. What was going on with—

"Yeosin," someone hummed from in front of me.

I snapped my gaze up and widened my eyes. "Alvin ..."

What the hell is he doing here?!

Alvin grabbed the cups from me. "Yeosin, we need to talk."

CHAPTER
TWENTY-SEVEN

YEOSIN

"I REALLY DON'T HAVE TIME," I whispered, keeping my feet glued to the pavement.

A harsh wind whipped my hair into my face, but I refused to move from this spot. My hands were full, so I couldn't push him away or else I'd spill these goddamn things on me *again*. But if he pulled, then I'd do what I had to do.

"Alana," he said, "I'm not playing."

"Look, I don't have any more money."

"What are you talking about?"

"The Dragon Clan," I clarified. "You're their leader, aren't you? Is that what this is about?"

While I didn't trust him, I needed to play stupid for a bit longer until I could get to work or to the penthouse. Anything to stall him, anything to get somewhere safe so he couldn't steal me away for whatever he was planning.

Alvin's soft expression was replaced with a small, twitching smirk. "They said that?"

"I don't understand why," I said. "You were indebted to them."

"Yeah, that's what it was," he said. "Listen, I can make all your problems disappear."

"You can get them to stop asking me for money?"

"Yes."

"What do I have to do?"

Alvin nodded to his car parked at the corner. "Come with me."

I chewed on the inside of my cheek and really wished I had listened to Molly and the beast this morning. I didn't have time to deal with him, nor did I have the energy. The Dragon Clan was after me, and they … they were really dragons, weren't they?

My body was covered in burns because of them.

"I have my hands full." I gestured to my coffee cups. "Can this wait?"

"No."

"What do you need to tell me?" I asked. "Can't you tell me here?"

"I don't need to tell you anything," he said.

"Then why do you need me?"

He snapped his hand around my upper arm and yanked me closer to him until he was basically breathing down my neck. "Get in the fucking car, Alana, and stop asking stupid questions like you always do."

My heart pounded so hard that I could hear it in my ears. "No."

Damn, I am so screwed!

A low chuckle escaped his throat, and he yanked me even closer. "I don't think you he—"

"I did hear you, and I said no."

"She was very clear," a familiar voice said behind me.

When I turned around, Gideon—one of the regulars that I'd had at Pink Ivory—stepped between me and Alvin. Gideon had always been nice to me and not grumpy, like Luciano, but there was something about him that told me he could snap a man's head clean off his shoulders and go about his day without remorse.

And thank God that he was here! His usual time too.

"Everything okay here, Alana?" he asked.

Alvin released my arm and took a couple of steps back. "We're good."

"I just need to get to work," I said, eyeing Alvin.

Once Alvin took another good look at Gideon, he stepped back again. "Ten thousand. I'll have one of my men swing by the apartment tonight. Leave it outside in a green envelope. No exceptions."

Green envelope?! This man is reaching with these requests.

"Where am I going to find a green envelope?" I asked. "Plus, I don't have the money."

"You work for Luciano Bates. You can get us money."

He knows Luciano? How?

Not something that I was going to ask him. I needed to get out of here now, and if I had a chance to escape, thanks to Gideon, then I was going to leave and sprint to the office since it was closer.

God, this is all my fault! The Dragon Clan was now after not only the beast, but Luciano and his company too. All because they wanted me for reasons that they wouldn't tell me. Bottom line: I needed to warn Luciano about the Dragon Clan. Now.

"Get the fuck out of here," Gideon said to Alvin.

Alvin narrowed his eyes at Gideon, but then—to my surprise—he walked back to his car, slipped into the passenger seat, and drove away with one of his men. My gaze didn't leave that SUV until it was out of my sight.

"Who was that?" Gideon asked.

"My ex."

"Ex, huh?"

I glanced up at him. "Yeah, sorry about that."

"It's no big deal. I'll walk you to work."

"You don't have to," I said, another wind chilling me. "Really."

"I'm not letting you out of my sight until you're safe, especially after that."

After a quick nod because I didn't want to fight with him—I didn't feel safe after that either—I headed down the road and toward the office. The beast was literally going to murder me once he found out that I had left the penthouse.

Hell, if he hadn't found out yet.

"You work for Luciano?" Gideon asked on our walk over.

"Yes. How do you know him?"

"Who doesn't know him?" He sipped on his pumpkin-flavored coffee. "The grumpy billionaire who'd rather hang out in a coffee shop than his own office just to watch you work." A low chuckle escaped his mouth. "I don't blame him though. When you have that kind of money, power, and influence, life can be lonely."

My mind was reeling with so many different thoughts—*Is he insinuating that Luciano ... stalked me when I worked at Pink Ivory? And what did he mean by "I don't blame him"?*—but we had reached my office building.

"Well, I should get going," I said, twisting around to face him. "Thanks for—"

But Gideon was already gone.

CHAPTER
TWENTY-EIGHT

LUCIANO

I HAD BEEN WAITING outside my office for Ella to arrive, barely keeping it together. What the fuck had happened last night? Why in Ella's right mind would she come to my penthouse and hurt Yeosin? I planned to find out everything from her.

The elevator dinged, and her repulsive scent drifted through my nose. She walked in, hair bouncing in a high ponytail and lips covered in red, and headed my way. I flared my nostrils and glared at her.

"My office. Now," I said when she was in earshot.

Ella curled a finger around a lock of her hair. "But, Luciano, I have a—"

I snatched her upper arm, sinking my claws into her flesh. "My fucking office. Now!"

As soon as I slammed my office door closed, I allowed my beast to take form. My nails lengthened into claws, and my teeth grew into canines that could kill her in a moment.

"What did you do to Yeosin?" I growled.

"I don't know what you mean."

My hand snapped around the front of her throat, and I pinned her against the wall, her feet dangling off the ground.

"I'm not going to play fucking games with you, *pup*. You were in my home last night, and Yeosin has burns all over her."

After blowing her bangs up with a *pffttt*, she growled back. "Your home? That penthouse isn't your home. It has never been your home. Your home—*our home*—is the woods, is the pack-house. I'm sick of living in the city."

"You think I want this?!" I snarled. "Over eighty percent of our pack is dead because we lived in those woods. Over ninety-five percent of our warriors are gone. We are rebuilding with the woman who lives in that penthouse—with my *mate*."

The words left my mouth before I could stop them, and while I was sure that the Goddess had removed my abilities to have a fated mate, my beast had recognized Yeosin as his twice verbally in the past twenty-four hours.

And honestly, I had known that it was always true. I had been drawn to her from the moment that I laid my gaze on her, but I had kept my distance for as long as I could, as long as my beast would let me.

Because nothing good could come out of being close to her. Not with the Dragon Clan.

"*I* should be your mate!" Ella exclaimed.

As soon as the words left her lips, I threw her to the other side of the room. Her body slammed into the bookcase, making the books on the second shelf from the top tumble out and land on the ground beside her.

"So you burn her?" I stalked toward her. "Who gave you the ability?! Are you working with the clan who killed your mate and your child?!" My gaze clouded with red, and I picked her up by her hair. "Are you working with the Dragon Clan?"

"No, no!" she exclaimed, eyes wide in fear. "I promise, I'm not!"

"Then why the fuck is Yeosin's body covered in burns?!"

For the first time, something idiotic didn't come out of this bitch's mouth. "I don't know. Molly called me over to heal her. She was asleep … and the burns began forming on her body before I even had a chance to touch her."

"Liar," I growled.

"I'm not lying," she cried, grasping at her hair. "Please, let me down."

After blowing a breath out of my nose, I tossed her down and walked back to my desk to calm the fuck down so none of the humans here would walk in and see my beast overtaking my body with his.

With one hand grasping her head, Ella crawled to my desk and pulled herself up onto a chair, a small whimper escaping her mouth. "I promise I'm not lying to you. I didn't touch her. But I hadn't come over to heal her. I had come over to see how it'd feel to be her." Her voice suddenly dropped. "I miss my mate, and I thought … since you couldn't have one …"

"I would never and will never mate with you," I snarled. "Get it out of your head."

Tears filled her eyes. "But I'm strong."

"You're strong, so you should be fighting the war that's coming. Not bearing my pups."

Not only that, but I don't like her. Neither does my beast.

Her expression changed from sadness to pride and then to surprise. "The war that's coming? Does that mean that you really are partnering with the Colossals? Brent told me this morning about your meeting with them."

"Yes." I flared my nostrils and looked away. "But I need more information about Yeosin's burns. When—how did they start? She was sleeping? You didn't see anyone else leaving the penthouse before you arrived, did you? No Dragon Clan member?"

Yeosin had said that she had a nightmare …

I cursed at myself because I had stupidly brushed it off like it was nothing, basically told her to get over it. If the burns had really formed while she was asleep …

What the fuck was I thinking, telling her that?!

"I don't know how they formed. I didn't have a chance to heal her. Molly kicked me out."

"Rightfully so," I snarled. "You just told me that you didn't come to heal her at all. The next time one of your packmates asks you to heal someone, *you fucking heal them.* Do you understand me?"

Ella dropped her gaze to the desk. "I understand."

"My mate *wouldn't* refuse to heal someone just because they didn't like them."

"That's not the reason why—"

"I don't give a fuck," I growled at her. "You're a healer. You heal, or you're useless to me."

"I know," she whispered. "I'm sorry."

An apology wasn't going to cut it, but I didn't have time to argue with her any more today. I needed to get paperwork done as soon as possible so I could get back to the penthouse and make sure that more burns hadn't formed on Yeosin's body.

What the fuck actually happened? I shouldn't have been an asshole to her last night, and I should've opened my mouth and asked her what happened like any normal fucking person would've. But my beast was caught up in revenge.

A whiff of pumpkin drifted through my nose, and someone knocked on the door.

Who is—

"Mr. Bates," Yeosin said from outside the door, peeking inside the room. "Are you free?"

What the fuck is she doing here?! She's supposed to be at the penthouse!

"What are you doing here?" I growled once the door opened enough for me to see her entire body.

Carrying two coffees from Pink Ivory, Yeosin shuffled into the room, briefly glancing at Ella—who didn't spare her a look—and then the books that had fallen and headed straight for my desk. She set a hot coffee in front of me and smiled softly.

"Sorry that I'm late. I wanted to pick you up a coffee before work and—"

"I asked you a question," I hissed at her. "You're in—"

Before I could finish my sentence, I bit down on my tongue and balled my hand into a tight fist, my claws cutting through the skin on my palm. Any more anger, and my beast would begin to emerge again.

He was already riled up at the sight of her.

I cut my glare to Ella. "Out. Now."

Instead of putting up a hissy fit like she usually did, she scurried past Yeosin without a snide remark or even another look.

Yeosin furrowed her brows together for a moment, then looked back at me. "Is Ella in trouble?"

"Yes."

"Because of ... me?"

"*You* shouldn't be here," I growled, changing the subject.

I grabbed her wrist and yanked up her sweater to reveal another burn. This one was still hot. Where were all these coming from?!

"M-Mr. B-Bates," Yeosin whispered, her pupils dilating. "Your eyes ..."

"Who did this to you?" I growled. "This wasn't here last night."

She widened her eyes. "What?"

I stalked toward her. "This. Wasn't. Here. Last. Night."

She opened and closed her mouth a handful of times, and I realized that I had slipped.

"Y-you're the billionaire," she whispered, "who wants to breed me?"

CHAPTER
TWENTY-NINE

LUCIANO

"WHAT THE FUCK HAPPENED TO YOU?" I growled.

Yeosin stared up at me with curious eyes, stuck on the fact that I was the beast. "Wow …"

"Yeosin," I snarled, snatching her chin, "answer me."

Still caught in her trance, she parted her full lips. "I saw Alvin at Pink Ivory."

"You what?!" I roared. "You saw the Dragon Clan?!"

"It's okay. One of my regulars walked me here." She moved closer and tucked some hair behind my ear, her eyes searching my face, probably for any sign of my beast. "I can't believe it. Is it true?"

"I told you to stay home," I growled. "You love being punished, don't you?"

"Yes," she breathed out the way she always did at The Breeding Cave.

Her pumpkin scent, mixed with the sweet smell of her cunt, drifted through my nose, and I tried to stay in control. But my wolf had been aching to be released since she had stepped into my office. Except … she'd had strict orders to stay home.

"Are you really the beast?" she whispered, moving closer to me and staring up.

I gritted my teeth. Yeosin knew how to get on every last one of my nerves.

"I'm bringing you home," I growled, snatching her wrist.

"I've been cooped up there all night."

"You're lucky that I don't lock you in there for the rest of your life."

Yeosin shrugged. "Maybe you shoul—"

"Be fucking careful about finishing that sentence."

If I brought her home, then she'd sneak out again unless I either tied her up or … didn't let her leave my sight. I dropped my grip on her, opened my closet door where I kept items—in case something happened at work—and grabbed a couple of chains from the second shelf.

"Mr. Bates …" Yeosin's eyes widened when she saw them, and she stepped back. "You're not serious."

"Call me Luciano," I ordered.

"Luciano," she whispered, "what are you doing with that?"

I tugged her arms behind her back and wrapped the chain around them.

"Luciano!" she cried softly. "What are you doing?!"

"Making sure you don't go anywhere."

Once I sat her in the middle of my desk, I placed my hand over her top and ripped it off at the seams, and then I did the same with her bottoms. Her nipples were taut, and her pussy was dripping over the wood. Then I returned my gaze to my computer to the right of her. She inhaled sharply and tried to squirm out of the binds, but she wasn't going anywhere.

"You want to sneak out and put yourself in danger. Then here's your punishment."

"Being naked in the middle of your office?!"

"Yes, so I can keep my eyes on you."

"But don't you have to work?"

"You should be worried about getting *your* work done."

"How can I get my work done like this?!" she exclaimed.

I drew my tongue across my canine teeth. "Figure it out."

Yeosin flared her nostrils and struggled against the chains once more. "Why are you always grumpy?"

"Because *you* are set on getting yourself killed."

"Wouldn't that be better for you so you could find someone else to have your babies?" she asked like a fucking madwoman. "Why would you want me like this? My body is covered in burns. I've turned ugly."

"Don't fucking say that shit." Before another word could leave her mouth, I ripped off my tie and stuffed it into her mouth. "I'll grant you the right to speak again when you can find something nice to say about yourself."

"Luciano," she said, voice muffled, "it's true."

"Try to say it again," I growled, "and see what happens, Yeosin."

If she thought this was a punishment, she didn't fucking know what punishment was. But if another self-deprecating word left her mouth, I'd make sure she knew every punishment known to man until she loved herself.

Yeosin sat like a doll on my desk, whimpering to herself, staring at me, and drooling all over my papers. Her nipples were hard as ice, and I'd bet that they were aching. But I had to stay in control.

This was her punishment for leaving the penthouse. She shouldn't get rewarded.

But the chains restraining her made her a perfect … fuckable … breedable …

Breed, my beast growled to me. *Breed now.*

"Are you ready to be good for me?" I found myself asking, pulling the tie out of her mouth.

"Please, release me," she whispered.

Instead of granting her request, I stood and stuffed some paperwork into my bag to bring home. I couldn't control myself here with her. She struggled against the chains, trying to release herself from them, only for them to get tighter.

"We're going home," I said.

"Luciano, I can't go out like this!" she exclaimed.

"You're right," I murmured. "I need to fill you with my cum first."

Her eyes widened, but her little pussy clenched. "No, you need to release me!"

"Look at this body," I murmured, pushing two fingers into her pussy, my beast taking over. "You've been waiting for me to fuck you all day, haven't you? You have to learn to be a good girl and follow orders, and I won't have to be so harsh on you."

"Luciano," she whispered, "we can't do it here!"

I snatched her hips, pulled down my zipper, and lined myself up with her entrance. Her pussy tightened around my head, and then I slammed all of me inside her, grunting and groaning from how tight she was.

"Mr. Bates!" Ella called from outside the room.

"Whatever it is, leave it at the door. I'm busy."

"It's really important."

Goddess, I fucking hated her. "Leave. It. Outside. The. Door."

After a moment of silence, her scent disappeared. I gripped Yeosin's hips and pulled her closer to me, growls escaping my throat at the thought of filling her with my cum, getting her pregnant, *marking* her.

She bit down on her lower lip and whimpered.

Brent knocked. "Hey, I think you'll want to—"

"What?!" I growled, buried deep inside Yeosin.

Brent swung the door open like it was nothing and walked into the room. Yeosin scrambled—not that she could move much —and then completely froze when he looked at her, her cheeks reddening.

"What do you want?" I growled at him, not pulling out of my mate.

Our mate needs our cum. Every drop.

Yeosin's hair fell into her face, and she turned back to me. I pressed deeper inside her until my balls were pushed against her entrance. Brent wasn't going to ruin this for me. With a slight thrust of my hips—one that Brent wouldn't be able to see, but one that she could definitely feel—she came undone around me. Her pussy pulsed around my dick.

"Fuck," I grunted against her, slamming myself deeper inside her.

In the middle of my office.

In front of Brent.

I didn't care. She was mine.

My cum filled her pussy, and I released a low groan.

"You know …" Brent said, his shoes shuffling against the floor. "It can wait."

Then he slammed the door, leaving me alone to breed my mate.

CHAPTER
THIRTY

YEOSIN

"WHY ISN'T MOLLY HERE?" I asked.

After our little sexcapade in his office, Luciano brought me right back to the penthouse. And I couldn't help but notice that it was empty. No sign of Molly anywhere, which was extremely unusual. She was always here. By always, I meant *always*. She didn't even go out to get groceries.

"Molly isn't watching you any longer. This is the second time in less than twenty-four hours that I asked her to keep watch on you and something happened," Luciano said. "She's not fit at the moment."

My lip quivered. "B-but it's not her fault."

"You're right," he said. "It's not Molly's fault that you can't follow orders."

"Sorry," I whispered. "Can she come back?"

I didn't want to admit this to him, but she was my only friend. It was sad, really. But Alvin had completely upended my life, secluded me, and when I wasn't having it anymore, he decided to break up with me and demand money from his clan.

Then, of course, my stupid self had had to betray Molly and run away this morning.

"Did you punish her?" I whispered, chest aching.

"Do you want me to?"

"No!" I exclaimed, tears pricking my eyes. "Please, don't. She doesn't deserve it."

While his punishments to me had been nothing short of pleasurable, I had a feeling that Luciano had more than just a bit of a temper with everyone else. Since he had been a regular at Pink Ivory, he had scared the living daylights out of me.

I could only imagine what those hands were capable of …

Heat coursed through my body. *Get yourself together, Yeosin! Torture is NOT sexy.*

But if it was Luciano doing the torture to someone—like Alvin —for me …

I shook my head to get the thought out of my mind. *No, no, no, no, no, no! Stop it!*

"Brent will watch you while I attend my meeting," he said.

"What's your meeting about?"

"Killing every last member of the Dragon Clan."

I opened and closed my mouth a handful of times. "B-but I thought you said you tried …"

"We did," Luciano said. "Decades ago, and we lost."

"So, how are you going to defeat them this time around?"

Luciano stared at me for the longest time, his gaze shifted back and forth between his grumpy one and his beast's possessive one. Luciano was doing this for both of us, but mainly because I had asked him to help me.

But I didn't want him hurt or putting himself into danger.

Someone knocked on the door.

"That must be Brent," Luciano said, ignoring my question.

Before heading to the door to answer it, he captured my jaw in his strong grasp. I expected him to say something harsh, something grumpy that only Mr. Grumpy would say.

Instead, his voice was soft, pleading almost. "Please, don't be difficult for him. Don't leave. Don't sneak out. You're in danger."

"I know," I whispered. "I won't sneak out."

"You said that last time."

"Well, I mean it this time," I said.

After my run-in with Alvin at Pink Ivory, I knew that I had massively fucked up. This wasn't a game. Luciano really was trying to protect me, but I didn't think he could do it. He had promised he would, but how could he protect me from the flames in my dreams?

His beast's gaze flickered through his eyes. He pulled me closer to him and kissed me on the mouth. Not a heated type of kiss, but a soft one that made me feel like he wanted me more than for me to have his children.

Though I knew that was the only reason he cared.

I will never be more than that to him, but that's okay. At least I have him now.

The knock came again. Luciano pulled away and headed to the foyer. When Luciano opened the door, a doorman stood in the hallway with a square package.

"Delivery for Mr. Bates."

Luciano sniffed, as if he could smell something … unpleasant. He stepped into the doorman's line of view of me, dropped his gaze down to the box, then lifted it back to the doorman.

"Who is it from?" he asked, not taking the package. "I'm not expecting anything."

The doorman's gaze shifted to me. "From Alvin."

Moments passed, and then Luciano reached for the package. But instead of taking it, he wrapped his hand around the doorman's throat and slammed him up against the wall so hard that the wall dented and the drywall fell in chips at his feet.

A wave of fire burst out from the doorman's throat. The flames, aimed at Luciano's face, spread around and licked my skin. But before they could burn him badly, Luciano ripped out his throat, and the dragon fell to the floor. Dead.

When Luciano turned toward me, a burn stretched from the bottom right side of his face up to the left side of his forehead. "Grab your stuff and don't fucking argue with me. You're leaving tonight, and we're never coming back here again."

I moved closer to him. "Are you okay?"

"Yeosin," he growled. His burn mark suddenly began healing itself as his beast emerged from deep within his body. Eyes burning brightly, he drew his tongue across his canines. "Grab. Your. Stuff."

"What's going on here?" Brent asked from the doorway with a jar of pickles.

"You'll take Yeosin to the cave," Luciano said as if the man he had just killed wasn't lying in a puddle of blood. He rolled up his sleeves and picked up the package. "This building has been compromised."

"Any sign of Joseph?" Brent said. "I've been asking around, and nobody has seen him."

"Joseph is gone?" I asked, eyes wide and worry building up inside my belly.

Is he gone because of me too? Did I come into Luciano's life and hurt everyone?

"Yes," Luciano said, lengthening one of his nails into a sharp, bloody talon and cutting through the tape of the package. It ripped open with ease, the blood from the doorman dripping off his fingers and into the package.

My nosy ass looked over his shoulder into the square package, and a piercing scream escaped my lips. I shuffled backward until my back bumped against Brent's chest, my heart thumping in my ears.

It wasn't just anything in that package.

No, it was Joseph's head.

CHAPTER
THIRTY-ONE

LUCIANO

"JOSEPH!" Yeosin cried, dropping to her knees in the puddle of dragon blood.

Steam emanated from her knees, the only part of her body in direct contact with the blood, and I quickly pulled her to her feet, examining two new burns on her legs.

What the—was she allergic to dragons?

No, that couldn't be it. She had said her ex-boyfriend was the leader of the clan.

If she were allergic, then she wouldn't have been able to survive with him. Never mind how she could get burns in her sleep, if Ella really had told me the truth earlier at the office. Who the fuck knew anymore? None of this made sense.

But I had to figure it out. It was the only way to keep her safe.

Brent furrowed his brows. "Why is she burn—"

"I don't know," I said.

Yeosin's knees wobbled, and I placed her on the couch. She doubled over and threw her head into her hands, her body trembling. "How could they do this to Joseph?! He was the nicest person I'd ever met. W-w-why?"

As much as I wanted to, I didn't have time to answer questions, nor did I have the answers. The war between the beasts and dragons had started so long ago. They had taken so many of my friends, family, and pack for reasons that I would never know.

"If you run into any trouble at the cave, contact me immediately," I commanded.

Brent nodded. "I'll protect her."

I snatched him by the collar and yanked him closer. "If I find out that you've touched her, I will do to you what I did to him," I said, gesturing down to the dragon at my feet with his throat torn out of his body.

He held up his arms. "I won't. I won't! Who do you think I am?"

"A wild animal."

A smirk crossed his face, but when I tightened my grip on his collar, he immediately dropped it.

"I swear I won't. You can trust me to keep her safe. I know she's important to you. I got an entire show of it this afternoon."

After giving him a once-over, I released him and grabbed some clothes for Yeosin, stuffing them into my backpack and handing it to Brent. Then I held the door open for them. Yeosin stood and glanced down at Joseph's head, tears streaming down her face.

"Wh-why did they do that to him?" she sobbed. "Is it because of me?"

"No," I said.

"I-it is!" She sniffled. "Can't you revive him?"

"No."

"Jeez, you could be nicer," Brent said, ushering her out into the hallway and lowering his voice. "This is the first dead body she's seen."

"There's not a body," I said.

Brent rolled his eyes. "I know you don't have any, but you could fake some compassion."

I glared. "You can't have compassion in war. The Dragon Clan has now tried to kill her twice—that I know of. I don't fucking know why they waited until now if her ex is their leader. But find something to occupy her with."

Once he offered a nod, I placed my hands on Yeosin's shoulders and steered her to the elevator. Brent followed after, and we rode it down to the garage. Brent slipped into the driver's side of an SUV, and I placed Yeosin in the passenger seat.

"Wh-why do you have to go?" she stuttered, curling her fingers around my jacket. "Please, don't go."

"I have a meeting."

Tears shone in her eyes. "Luciano, please."

I cupped her face in my hands. "This is to keep you safe."

After she wiped her cheeks with the back of her hands, I shut the door and watched them drive off. Brent would be smart enough to leave the SUV at the base of the mountain, cover her scent among the woods, and walk up to the cave. I had to put my trust in him.

But my beast … my beast didn't trust anyone after what the dragons had done to us.

Once they were out of my sight, I pressed my lips together, shoved my hands into my pockets, and walked down the chilly streets toward my meeting with Alpha Theo and the Colossals several blocks away. I needed to clear my head, and sitting in a car wouldn't do that.

The sun had set an hour ago, and the streets were dark with shadows.

What is going on with Yeosin? Legs burning from dragon blood? Burns in her sleep?

I had never seen this in my entire life, not even during the last war with the Dragon Clan, and I hadn't heard it in any stories passed down through my family. I'd have to stop by the pack-house tonight and find any history books we had left.

At the crosswalk, I stopped and glanced to my right into an alleyway, immediately feeling like someone was watching me. Someone leaned against the brick building, but I couldn't see their face with the shadow. Hell, it almost didn't even look like they were there.

"You're not strong enough to protect Yeosin," he said. "You'll never be."

"Who are you?" I asked, nails lengthening into claws.

"Yeosin knows who I am."

"Well, I don't," I snarled. "Tell me before I kill you too."

"Killing me would be a mistake."

"Then answer my question."

A long pause.

"I'm an ally."

When he turned his head, the moonlight illuminated the right side of his body. And before he vanished into thin air, I caught sight of the burns that covered his skin from head to toe, burns deeper than Yeosin's, burns that should've killed any beast.

I turned around to find where he had gone off to, only to see him behind me.

This time closer.

"You should stay away from the Colossals," he said. "They're good at mind games."

"I am the last person who wants to work with them," I growled, not liking how much he knew about Yeosin, me, and our arrangement with the Colossals. "We don't have any other choice to keep Yeosin safe."

"You have Yeosin," he said.

I narrowed my eyes at the figure. "How the fuck do you know so much about her?"

"Because she's my fated mate."

And then he was gone again. This time for good.

CHAPTER
THIRTY-TWO

YEOSIN

I PUSHED a tear off my cheek and squeezed my eyes closed, seeing Joseph's head in my memory. It had sat in that box like a present that I was meant to find. After biting back a sob, I continued forward behind Brent through the forest to the cave.

While I hadn't known Joseph for long, he had brought me to the cave that first night, calmed my nerves, and seemed so genuinely trustworthy. I swallowed hard and wiped my cheeks with the back of my hands.

Seeing him dead had screwed me up.

Joseph was gone because of me, because he had brought me to the cave, because … the Dragon Clan was after me.

And they weren't going to stop until I was either dead or belonged to them.

"We're here," Brent said, pausing at the cave entrance. "Go clean off in the hot spring."

Brent had covered me in thick mud before we walked through the forest. He said it was to cover my scent because we had to take extra caution after the Dragon Clan murdered Joseph. Yes, murdered him.

He didn't just die. They had beheaded him.

Fire burned inside me at the thought of Alvin doing that to him. I could only imagine what his body had looked like—*if* he still had a body left and *if* they hadn't burned it to a crisp. I gritted my teeth. They would pay.

I headed through the cave toward the hot spring with Brent keeping a distance behind me. When I reached the water, I peeled off my clothes and sank into the water to clean off the mud, anger reeling inside me.

This isn't fair! How could they have done this to him?

"So … you come here with Luciano?" Brent asked, back turned toward me.

My muscles relaxed slightly in the warm water. I curled my shoulders forward and blew out a low breath, closing my eyes. "Yes."

Brent—who usually was very *not* awkward—rocked back on his heels and looked anywhere except at me. I shook my head and wondered why this was happening.

The scars, the fire, Alvin?! Most importantly, killing Joseph!

When I reopened my eyes, Brent still had his back turned and hadn't even inched toward the hot spring to clean himself off. He had smothered me and himself in mud earlier, and I didn't want to spend the rest of the night with his stinky butt.

"Are you going to clean yourself?" I asked. "There are soaps over there."

Tensing, Brent glanced over his shoulder at me. "Good. I can't see anything."

"What's that mean?" I asked, brow arched.

Instead of answering me, Brent walked into the shallow end of the hot spring and slipped right into the water, completely clothed. He wouldn't get clean like that.

"You're going to clean yourself in your clothes?"

"Listen"—Brent held his hands up—"I'm not trying to die."

"Why would you die?"

"Are you kidding me, Yeosin?" Brent asked, splashing the

water onto his shoulders. "If Luciano found out that I was naked in the same hot spring with you, he would rip my throat out and feed it to me."

While I might've wanted Alvin dead, Luciano really wouldn't do that to Brent, would he?

"Where did Luciano go?" I asked, nerves pricking at my stomach.

"A meeting."

"With who?"

"Warriors who will help us defeat the dragons."

My mouth dried. "Nobody can defeat the Dragon Clan."

Brent stayed quiet, and I took that to mean that he believed my words too. Once he finished, he jumped out of the water with his clothes soaked.

"There should be an extra change of clothes back here somewhere," Brent said, heading deeper into the cave through a walkway that I hadn't seen before, his voice becoming more distant by the moment.

Once I finished cleaning off, I waited by the rocks inside the water. Brent returned with two towels and clothes so big that they looked like they fit Luciano. He set them down by the edge of the rocks and walked toward the main area of the cave.

"I will change and find some firewood just outside the cave. It's getting cold." Brent tugged off his wet shirt and looked back at me. "Don't wander off anywhere, or Luciano will deliver my head to you like Joseph's."

My mouth dried, and I nodded. "Okay."

After he left, I climbed out of the hot spring and sat on the rock. My burns glistened underneath the thin layer of water that coated my body. I gazed down at them, my lips curling downward into a frown.

They were red and bubbly and ugly and disgusting.

No wonder why Luciano wants to fuck me, then leave.

No. No, I didn't really think that, did I?

Stomach twisting into knots, I patted myself dry with the towel and slipped into the oversize clothes to hide the scars that decorated my body. What was going on with me, and how could I stop it?

Did the Dragon Clan really have this much power over my body? Over me?

I wanted to see *them* burn. I wanted to see *them* covered in scars.

With my hands balled into fists, I gritted my teeth, a million thoughts racing through my head about how I would do it if I had the chance, if I had the upper hand. But those were just daydreams of a time that would never happen.

Every scar and every burn made me weaker.

Though I couldn't explain it, I could feel my body becoming closer and closer to death. The burns didn't hurt as badly anymore like they used to, but … I could feel it burning on the inside. I could feel … life slowing down.

Before I could achieve any of my dreams …

Do I even have any dreams anymore?

"I'll be back!" Brent called from down the walkway.

After smoothing out Luciano's shirt, I headed toward Brent's voice.

While I didn't have many of my own clothes–or much of my own life–anymore, not after Alvin completely took my life from me, I did have a dream, a goal—give Luciano a child before the Dragon Clan killed me.

When I returned to the main area, where Luciano had bred me that first night, it was empty, yet Brent's scent lingered in the air. I walked to the front of the cave and sat against a rock to wait for him to return.

My gaze traveled around the dark forest, and the hairs on my arm suddenly stood up.

I looked up at a tree in the distance and froze, spotting two glowing blue eyes from high up above. They were so far apart from each other that they almost looked like stars shining around the tree branches.

But then the creature, which must've stood twenty feet in the air, moved toward me.

YEOSIN

"WHAT THE FUCK IS THAT?!" I whispered to myself.

When the monster stepped into the moonlight, I nearly peed myself. At her full height, she stood at least twenty-five feet in the air. All she had to do was step on me, and I would be nothing but splat on the ground. One flick with her finger, and she'd send me spiraling into the wall with lethal force.

A branch snapped to my left. I looked over, expecting to see Brent, but saw a beast almost the size of Luciano charging my way. My eyes widened, and I shuffled backward into the cave because Brent had told me not to leave.

But where the fuck is he?!

The monster stopped at the entrance of the cave in his beast form and stood to his full length, towering over me. I had been coming to this cave for what felt like weeks now, and I had never once seen this one here before.

"Please, don't kill me," I whispered, backing up and holding my arms in front of my face.

He growled, the sound echoing through the cave. Luciano had told me that not many people knew about these caves and that the only people who really came here were … other beasts like him who had lost their packs.

Light from the moon flooded into the cave, bouncing off his muscles. He stalked closer to me and snatched up my wrist. I yanked it away and stumbled back into a rock, falling over it and landing on my ass, legs up in the air.

Shit! Where the hell is Brent?!

"Please, stop," I whispered.

He had that same hungry look in his eyes that Luciano always had when he trapped me in this cave with him to fill me, to *breed* me. Was that what this guy was doing here too? Did he plan on breeding me? Luciano … wouldn't let that happen.

But Luciano wasn't here.

Stomach twisting into knots, I shook my head as he grabbed my ankle and pulled me back up onto the rock, moving between my thighs. The full moon … it must've made beasts like him angry or horny … or both.

"Please," I whispered, tears pricking the corners of my eyes.

The twenty-five-foot monster outside the cave suddenly reached in and grabbed him between her thumb and forefinger, which were both at least six inches wide. She dragged him out of the cave and flicked him across the trees.

My heart pounded so hard that I could hear it in my ears. I scanned the forest at lightning speed in an attempt to find where Brent had gone off to. He was supposed to have supersonic hearing, wasn't he?!

Where the fuck is Brent?! How long does it take to retrieve firewood?

As she took another step toward me, her bones snapped inside her body, and she shrank from a twenty-five-foot monster into a five-foot-something human woman with raggedy blonde hair and an expressionless face.

"Fertile women shouldn't be here alone. Other beasts will take humans like you who aren't marked, especially during a full moon like tonight," she hummed. "Who was the stupid beast that left you alone?"

"Brent!" I shouted, backing up into the cave and not taking my gaze off her. "Brent!"

"You can yell for him all you want," she said. "He can't hear you."

"Who … *what* are you?" I whispered, backing up to keep space between us.

Instead of answering me, she crossed her arms and looked me up and down. "You're the woman who forced Luciano to make the pact," she noted, a low chuckle escaping her mouth. "*Interesting.* A fragile human who can't fight to protect herself."

"What pact?" I asked, brows furrowed. "I didn't force him to do anything."

"The only way he beats the Dragon Clan is without you," she said, tilting her head and looking down upon me. "You will do nothing except hold him back from achieving his dream of avenging his pack and his family."

"Who are you?" I asked again because she was …

She was just trying to get in my head.

"Stay away from him," she growled.

Fire bubbled up inside my stomach, and I narrowed my eyes at her. "Who are you?"

She hadn't answered my questions and had only come here to hurt me with her words. That had to be it. I needed to keep her away and ask Luciano about her later. If she knew him, he had to know her.

And where was Brent? Firewood shouldn't take this long to gather!

Her expression remained completely emotionless. "You're weak."

"No, I'm not," I said.

Though … I knew that I was weak. Really weak.

"And useless."

"I'm not useless," I said, straightening myself out. "I'm fertile." The words left my mouth before I could stop them.

It wasn't a secret that Luciano was trying to get me pregnant so he could continue on his legacy. I was more than that. But not to him. That was the only thing that I was useful for ... giving him kids.

"Besides, the scars you hide underneath your clothes are horrendous."

I tugged my sleeve down over my thumb to hide the burns and pressed my lips together.

"Stay away from Luciano," she warned again. "He belongs to Ruby."

Ruby? Who is Ruby? Was Luciano promised to her? Maybe made by the pact?

Jealousy burned inside me, and I balled my hands into fists behind my back. She had just saved my life. It would be rude manners to make demands of her now. But something deep inside me wanted to do more than that.

I wanted to rip that name from her mouth, torture her until she told me who Ruby was and why Luciano was promised to her, *kill* her. When the last thought raced through my mind, my eyes widened. *Kill? Me?*

This had to be ... someone else talking, getting into my head.

"You should leave," I said, glancing toward the trees where Brent had disappeared.

Luciano wouldn't like that this mysterious woman was at the cave with me. Or maybe he wouldn't care. Despite him telling me that I was only for him to breed, he talked to me and treated me like I was the only person he craved. Except he was flaky.

He was gone now, like he had disappeared last night.

Had he gone to visit Ruby both times and given me the excuse of meetings?

The woman moved closer to me, her eyes glowing blue once more, the way they had in the trees when she was a giant creature. "If you stay with Luciano, it will be the death of you. He has more enemies than just the Dragon Clan."

CHAPTER
THIRTY-FOUR

YEOSIN

"BRENT!" I shouted once the monster had disappeared into the woods. "Where are you?!"

Adrenaline rushed through me, and I placed a hand over my racing heart in a measly attempt to calm it. Why—*how* was this happening? Was this a dream? Was I having another one of those nightmares?

Someone grumbled outside the cave, and I grabbed a rock to my right, ready to hurl it at the next monster that walked in here. I wasn't taking any more chances. I didn't care if they weren't an enemy or—

"Yeosin," Brent murmured.

My eyes widened, and I clutched the rock to my chest and peeked around the cave wall outside to see Brent lying against it, slowly opening his eyes. He had a bundle of branches gathered on his lap.

"Brent," I said, grabbing his biceps and tugging him to his feet. "What happened?"

After placing a hand against his head, he walked with me back into the cave and set the firewood next to the entrance. When he pulled his hand back, thick blood coated it. "Something must've hit me in the head."

"Something or someone?" I asked. "There was something outside."

"Like a monster?"

"Something like that. At least, she could turn into a monster," I whispered, wrapping my arms around myself because a few weeks ago, I would've never believed that anything like this was real. "At least twenty feet high."

Maybe I was hallucinating.

"And a beast like Luciano. He tried to come in here and … and …"

My mouth dried at the thought of what that beast had wanted to do to me. He wanted to do to me what Luciano had done that first night under the full moon, but at least Luciano had some restraint.

That beast … had been wild, unrestrained, and terrifying.

"What'd he do?" Brent asked.

Tears welled in my eyes, and I found myself wrapping my arms around Brent's waist and burying my face into his chest. While it wasn't the same as Luciano, my heart was pounding so hard that I thought I'd have a heart attack.

Brent wrapped his arms around my shoulders and pulled me closer, gently stroking my hair. He didn't say anything for a long time, and honestly, I was grateful that he didn't because I didn't think I'd be able to say anything without letting out a sob.

My entire mind was rattled. First Joseph, now this. What was going on?

"Where is the beast now?" Brent finally asked when I pulled away.

"The monster flicked him away." Literally like he had been a gnat.

"Fuck. Luciano isn't going to like this," Brent growled. "Did she say anything to you?"

"She told me to stay away from him," I said. "Among other things."

Those other things being that he belonged to Ruby and that Luciano would never truly love me for my scars. Luciano had told me that it wasn't true, but he had only started this little thing with me so I could birth his children.

Why would he keep me around after that?

"If she's going to threaten you, why save you?" he muttered to himself. "To save face?"

I wrapped my arms around myself and rocked back on my heels. "Who's Ruby?"

Brent snapped his gaze up to mine. "Ruby?"

"Yes, Ruby. Who is she?"

"You don't have to worry about her," Brent said. "She's nobody important."

I hesitated to ask the next question, but forced myself. "Is she important to Luciano?"

"No."

"Then why did she—"

Before I could finish my sentence, branches snapped and leaves cracked in a rushed succession outside the cave, as if someone was running at us. Brent pushed me behind him, his nails lengthening into claws, preparing for a battle.

For heaven's sake, why can't we have a quiet night?!

My heart slammed inside my chest, and I inhaled a familiar scent.

Suddenly, Luciano appeared at the cave's entrance. Disheveled.

"Out," he growled to Brent, his canines glistening underneath the moonlight. Except his gaze was on me. "Now."

"Luciano, I think you should hear about what happ—" Brent started.

Luciano snapped his hand around Brent's neck, lifted him into the air, and squeezed, his blazing gaze still not leaving mine.

Warmth gathered between my legs, and a wave of pleasure rushed through me.

Ruby or not, Luciano did something feral to me, especially under this moon.

Another ferocious growl left his mouth. "Out. Now."

Once he released Brent, Brent scrambled out of the cave.

"Luciano," I whispered.

"Who is he?" he growled.

My eyes widened. "Who is who?"

"You know who I'm talking about."

"If you're talking about the beast who came to the cave earlier, I don't—"

"Another beast was here with you?" he roared.

This didn't look or sound like a man who was promised to someone else.

I opened and closed my mouth a handful of times, unsure of *who* he was talking about. Alvin maybe? Didn't he already know that he was my ex-boyfriend that led the Dragon Clan and wanted to make my life a living hell?

"*Your fated mate,*" he snarled.

"I don't know what you're talking about."

He stepped closer to me, his eyes blazing. And if I said that it wasn't the sexiest fucking thing that I had ever witnessed, I'd be lying.

"You're mine," he growled, stalking closer. "Mine." Another step. "All mine."

I stumbled back, loving the way he moved closer to me, the way he trapped me between him and the cave's rocky wall, the way my body was on fire and a deep innate need inside me was begging for him to breed me.

When he stepped closer, my fingers curled around his muscular shoulders. I stared up into the beast's eyes, which weren't on mine like they usually were. Now he was staring at the crook of my neck.

Like he wanted to eat me.

"Breed me," I whispered, pressing my thighs together. "Please, breed me."

Though I wasn't sure he heard me, as his eyes only grew hungrier. He grasped my chin in one hand and tilted it away from him, then buried his face into my neck, drawing his large teeth down the column of my throat.

"Nobody is going to take you away from me, and I'm going to make sure of it, *mate.*"

And then he sank his canines into my neck.

YEOSIN

AS LUCIANO PLUNGED his canines deeper and deeper inside me, pleasure exploded through my body. I dug my nails into his shoulders, my head lolling away from him to give him better access, a moan escaping my lips.

Oh my God.

I drew my hand from his shoulder to the back of his head and pulled him even closer to me, never wanting him to move. My limbs tingled with ecstasy, my knees nearly buckling. I curled my toes as blood rolled down my chest.

What is this? Some kink?

Hell, I wasn't sure, but it felt so good.

He wrapped his arms around my waist and lifted me right into the air. I wrapped my legs around his waist and my arms around his neck to hold myself up. His cock was hard inside his pants, and he was grinding it against my pussy.

"Put a baby inside me," I said in a breathy whisper. "Please, put a baby inside me."

"My mate wants a baby inside her," he murmured, licking the wound. When it was closed, he drew his nose up the column of my throat and sucked my earlobe between his bloody teeth. "Anything for you."

Once he reached between us, he ripped off my pants with his claws and tugged his huge, hard, and veiny cock out of his pants. The head dribbled with pre-cum. I clenched at the sight of it and whimpered when he started rubbing it against my entrance.

"Please," I cried. "I can't take it any—"

Luciano slammed inside me. I threw my head back and cried out in pleasure.

He thrust into me slowly at first, making sure that every bit of him slid all the way inside me. And then he pulled out agonizingly slow. With my legs wrapped around him, I tried to pull him closer, but he kept the thrusts steady.

"I need you," I moaned. "Please, Luciano."

With his hands around my waist, he thrust into me faster and faster and faster. My legs trembled around his body, and I gripped on to him with everything that I had. His balls were slapping against my cunt, driving me higher and higher.

"Don't stop," I said. "Don't stop. Don't stop. Don't stop!"

He pumped into me, his mouth all over the mark he had left on my neck. I clenched my pussy for him, desperate for him to lose it and dump his load inside me. I needed to get pregnant.

It wasn't a want anymore.

My body was burning up for his cum.

A layer of sweat covered my body, but I had quite literally done none of the hard work. The carnal need craved more and more of him, craved him to be deeper and deeper inside my pussy.

"Fill me up," I begged. "I want to have our baby."

A guttural growl escaped his throat, and suddenly, his quick thrusts stopped, and he grunted deep in my ear. Warm cum filled my pussy, and I moaned in pleasure. While we had done this so many times before, this time felt different.

This time felt like he had actually put a baby inside me.

Or maybe it was the heat getting to me.

Once he dumped every drop into me, he slammed deeper to push in his cum. And when he finished, he slipped out of me and placed me down. My knees wobbled, and I dropped to my knees, breathing heavily.

"I'm not done with you," Luciano growled, his hard cock swinging between his muscular thighs. "I'm going to fill you with everything I have tonight, and then you'll drink your fertility tea."

"My ... my ... fertility tea?"

Was that what I had been drinking? Molly had been giving me pregnancy tea?

"Fuck," I whispered, my cunt clenching at the thought of Luciano doing the absolute most to get me pregnant without telling me. If I had been on birth control, then I swore he would've ripped it right out of me.

Luciano tugged me closer to him, then knelt and sank his cock deep into my pussy again. His hands came around my waist, and he pulled me to him with every thrust. I arched my back and cried out in pleasure.

He sucked one of my nipples into his mouth and bit down gently. "Mine. All mine."

God, this can't be real!

Even after all these weeks that I had known the beast and months of knowing Luciano, I still couldn't believe that grumpy billionaire was inside me, calling me his and breeding me with everything that he had.

But he was, and something was telling me that I was carrying the billionaire beast's baby.

CHAPTER
THIRTY-SIX

LUCIANO

"MINE," I growled, stuffing my fingers into Yeosin so none of my cum would leak out of her. My dick throbbed against my thigh, and I wanted to fuck her over and over again, but she was nearly bleeding already. "You're mine."

My mark on Yeosin's neck glistened underneath the moonlight that flooded into the cave.

Goddess, I can't believe she is mine.

After years of torment, after years of a vicious curse that promised I'd live a life alone, we had finally found our mate. We had finally marked her. We had finally completed a bond between us.

A bond that the monster who had stopped me in the city couldn't break.

Who was that fucker from earlier, claiming Yeosin was his anyway?

It was bad enough that I had to deal with the Dragon Clan. Now him? I gritted my teeth and held Yeosin a bit tighter. No way was I going to let anyone waltz into Yeosin's life now that she wore my mark.

"Who is he?" I growled. "Who is the monster who claimed you as his?"

"I don't know," she whispered, curling her fingers around my shoulders. Her head lolled back, and a breathy moan left her mouth. "I don't know who it was, but do it again. Please, bite me again, Luciano."

The scent of her arousal became stronger, and I growled against the mark on her neck.

"Please," she said, sinking a hand into my hair and pulling my face closer to her neck.

After pulling my fingers out of her, I lifted her into the air and walked with her to the hot spring in the next sector of the cave. We had tea back there for her to drink so my cum would catch. But I was pretty sure it already had.

When we entered the room, I pressed my mouth against her mark and kissed it. She trembled in my arms, another orgasm ripping through her body. She would become a beast soon, just like me.

It would make her stronger, but she needed rest in order to get there.

Her moans drove my beast wild, and I found my canines lengthening once more. I drew them against her mark, my dick hardening between my legs.

Control. I needed to control myself before I fucked her again.

Once she came down from her orgasm, I forced myself to put the canines away, and I walked into the hot spring, laying her on a rock. She lay there, the water making her black hair wet and cling to her body.

The burns on her body reddened in the water, but she sighed so I assumed that it felt good for her. I needed to find a cure so Yeosin didn't discover any more burns on her body. While I didn't look at her any differently, she looked at herself differently. She thought of herself as ugly because her body was covered with them.

Fifteen minutes later, Yeosin crawled out of the hot spring and into my lap.

"Will you stay with me?" she whispered, clutching on to me, even in her sleepy state.

"I won't leave the cave," I said, placing her down on a rock. I tugged up on a blanket to cover her naked body. "But it's getting cold. I need to find some firewood for us so you don't freeze to death."

"No," she mumbled, dozing off. "When Brent went out there …"

Instead of finishing her sentence, Yeosin drifted to sleep. I grabbed another blanket and placed it over her smaller body. The mate bond had snapped into place quickly, and I could feel everything that she was feeling. She was cold and filled with pain that I couldn't understand.

Once her breathing evened out, I tugged on some pants and walked out to the main entrance of the cave, where I had been inside her more times than I could count now. I sniffed around, faintly smelling Brent's scent lingering in the air.

"Brent?" I called, heading to the entrance.

Brent leaned against a tree, his arms crossed and a bundle of firewood at his feet. Next to the wood was Alpha Alf, one of the alphas who owned a cave farther down the mountain. He and his pack had fallen victim to the Dragon Clan years ago too.

Now, he was barely holding on to his life.

"What happened to him?" I asked from the cave.

After slamming his foot into Alf's side to turn him over, Brent picked up the bundle of firewood. While I expected to see burns all over Alf's body, he wasn't covered in any burns at all. No, but his body was contorted in ways that it shouldn't be.

Brent couldn't have done that.

"What happened?" I said, my beast becoming possessive as we caught Yeosin's scent.

"Alpha Alf tried to attack Yeosin when you were gone," Brent said. "I tracked down the scent through the woods and found him. He was about three miles south from here, lying in a puddle of his blood."

"What do you mean, he tried to attack Yeosin?"

"It's the full moon, and he's an alpha without a mate," Brent said, refusing to make eye contact with me. Pain crossed his face, almost as if he was disappointed in himself. "What do you think I mean?"

Did he try to … to rape her? To claim her? To make her his?

"Where the fuck were you?" I snarled, sight clouding with red.

"I went right outside to get firewood," Brent said. "I wasn't more than five feet away from the cave. Somehow, I passed out. The Colossals had something to do with it. It had to be them … you know about their powers. Messing with monsters' minds."

"I knew it was a bad idea to work with them," I growled underneath my breath.

But how? How could we defeat the Dragon Clan without them? We had tried so many times before, only to be utterly destroyed and almost annihilated. I couldn't put Yeosin in that kind of danger, going at them myself.

"Thank Goddess they can't do it to humans," Brent murmured, "or else the dragons wouldn't be the strongest monsters in the forest anymore. The world would be ruled by Colossals."

My gaze dropped to Alpha Alf, and I growled. "Chain him up and bring him into the cave once you're finished. I don't care if he was overcome with anything during the full moon. He will pay for what he tried to do to Yeosin."

And I'd make Yeosin watch the man who had tried to torture her get tortured himself.

CHAPTER
THIRTY-SEVEN

YEOSIN

MY ARMS ARE BOUND *behind my back to a metal pole planted in the ground. Fire, ash, and smoke surround me in the barren field that once was part of the forest. I desperately try to escape the binds.*

"Show yourself!" I scream at the top of my lungs.

The shadows of dragons drift overhead in the thick gray smoke. My eyes burn from the ash, yet I glare up at them anyway. If they want to kill me, they should do it already. They should kill me!

What is with all this torture? Why won't they stop? I didn't do anything to them.

Luciano, Brent, Molly, and everyone that I have come to know and love aren't around. I can only imagine that they are dead already, that the Dragon Clan has obliterated them and forced me to watch.

At the far edge of the field, from what I can see at least, a giant comes into view. She looks similar to the monster I saw earlier at the cave with piercing eyes, but this is someone new.

She shifts into a human, standing a measly five feet tall, and walks through the field toward me, her hair blowing almost perfectly under-neath the harsh and warm dragon breath from above, her body one that any man will die to have in his bed.

Is this her? Is this … Ruby?

While I am not sure of anything anymore, especially why I am tied up to the metal pole that burns my arms from the heat, I know one thing that is innately true. These giants aren't good people.

No, they aren't here to help me escape.

Neither of them killed me, but they have tortured me, one way or another.

But it seems like nobody wants me dead. Not the giants or the Dragon Clan. However, they do want me weak. They want me weak enough so that I can't move. Weak enough so that I can't think. Weak enough so that I can't defeat them.

"You won't get away with this," I say through clenched teeth as she approaches.

The smoke clears up, and I notice Luciano behind her, his beast's penetrating gaze fixed on me. Except this gaze isn't the inviting one that I saw so many times, nor is it the possessive one.

He looks at me like he hates me.

Without saying a word, Ruby stops several feet away from me and turns toward Luciano. She places her hands on his face and pulls him into a kiss. Pain swells inside me as tears prick the corners of my eyes. I want to scream at her to stop, but when I open my mouth, nothing comes out.

I try escaping the bind that the Dragon Clan placed around me.

Useless.

What hurts the most isn't that she kissed my mate, but Luciano has placed his hands on her waist and is now kissing her back, deepening it in front of me, staring at me as she leans into him, pressing her body against his, claiming him.

Of course, Ruby is so much prettier than me. She looks younger and fitter and stronger than I can ever be. Why wouldn't he choose her? Luciano needs a strong woman who can carry his baby.

Not someone like me.

Not someone who burns in my sleep from my dreams. Not someone who attracts the psychos from the Dragon Clan. Not someone who Luciano has to protect from war and sacrifice himself.

"Stop it," I cry.

She is getting inside my head. This isn't real. It can't be.

But when Luciano deepens the kiss with Ruby, my mark burns on my neck. Hotter than the fire the Dragon Clan has burned me with more than once now. Hotter than what I imagine hell feels like.

A shriek leaves my mouth this time, and my burns from previous nights reignite. I kick my legs and flail my arms around the binds in an attempt to escape, but instead of them loosening, the rope begins burning off from the heat my body is emanating.

I can't handle this anymore. I need to escape.

Yet every time I take a breath, I inhale smoke and heat. Yet every time I try opening my eyes, they burn from the sight of Luciano with another woman, with my mate kissing someone else.

He is mine. He is supposed to be mine!

After licking Luciano's kiss off her lips, Ruby saunters over to my blazing body. Her bones break, one after another after another as steam radiates from her body. She transforms into her Colossal beast and places a hand around my torso.

She lifts me into the air and tightens her hold around my stomach.

Suddenly, pressure erupts through my round belly, and my eyes widen. I glance down at Luciano, who stares up at me with a smirk on his lips. If she doesn't stop, then she is going to … she is going to kill our baby.

"Stop!" I scream, but nothing comes out of my mouth. "Stop, please!"

Luciano waited so long for this. Luciano chose me. Not her.

"He doesn't want you," she says with a smile, her eyes almost as wide as my stomach. She lifts me so I am level with her face. "I will have his child. I will give him a family. You will be nothing to him."

With that, she squeezes me in her fist. My ribs shatter in her hold, blood beginning to gush out of my mouth. I spit it up, my sight becoming hazy. My insides feel like they are being turned inside out.

Death will be easier than this pain, than this torture.

I let my eyes flutter closed. It is never-ending.

"Stay with me," a soft voice says from a distance.

Everything is so loud yet so quiet at the same time. Yet I see a flame in the woods behind Ruby and past Luciano. Someone is coming for me. Someone is here for me. Someone is trying to pull me out of this nightmare that is life.

CHAPTER
THIRTY-EIGHT

LUCIANO

AFTER BUILDING A FIRE FOR YEOSIN, the crook of my neck began blazing. I placed my hand over it and seethed. Suddenly, the pain spread from my neck to the rest of my body like a wildfire, overtaking every inch of me.

Mate, my beast howled inside my mind. *Mate is in trouble.*

My gaze traveled from the fire to the cave's pathway, which led to the hot spring. I chucked a log of wood at Brent and ran through the pathway, following Yeosin's scent to the hot spring, immediately spotting her seizing on the rock where I had left her.

And her body … her body was on fire!

Flames burned from her scars. I scooped her body into my arms and leaped right into the hot spring. The water sizzled around us as her body continued to seize in my arms. I cradled her head and dunked her underneath the water to put out the fire on her face.

"Yeosin," I murmured, pulling her into my arms and holding her trembling body. My fingers curled into her sides as she continued to sleep, the flames out but her body still steaming. "Wake up. Wake up. Wake up. Wake up."

No response.

I leaped out of the hot spring because maybe the warmth of the water was making it worse, and I brought her to the other room. After stumbling right past the fire, I exited the cave and let the cold air hit her skin.

"What the fuck happened?" Brent asked, hurrying over.

"Her scars were on fire."

"What?!"

"Get me a towel from the back room and some lotion."

Brent disappeared deeper into the cave. Suddenly, the seizing stopped, and her burns didn't feel quite as hot. Her eyes fluttered open, and she peered up at me through tears, seeing my face.

"Luciano," she whimpered.

"I'm here," I whispered. "It's okay."

Yeosin's quiet tears turned into hiccups, and she began trembling in my arms again. She gripped on to me tightly, her nails digging into my shoulders. "I don't want you to leave me," she cried. "Please don't leave me."

"I'm not going to leave you."

"Y-yes, you w-will!" she sobbed. "Because Ruby is better."

"Ruby?" I asked. "How do you know who Ruby is?"

"Why didn't you tell me about her?" she asked, wiping her eyes.

"She's not important to me." I rocked her. "What was your nightmare about?"

"The dragons had burned down the entire forest. I was tied up to a metal pole in the center of the chaos, and ... and Ruby was there as a monster. And ..." She paused and let out another sob. "And you were with her."

"We were working together, but not for long ..."

"No, you were there as a couple," she whispered. "You kissed her. You *loved* her."

"I don't want to kiss her, and I really don't love her," I said.

Yeosin stayed quiet, but then slipped out of my arms and put distance between us, her tears gone and her arms crossed. "I'm sorry. I shouldn't have cried. I … you … I think you should be with her," she whispered.

"What?" I exclaimed.

What the fuck was going on with her? Moments ago, she had told me not to leave her. Now she wanted me to be with Ruby? What the fuck had happened in her nightmare that caused her to think this?

"You should be with her," she repeated. "She's strong. I hold you back."

"No, you don't."

"Look at my body," she whispered. "These scars will continue to burn."

"We will find a cure."

"What happens when they burn so badly that I miscarry? Or can't get pregnant at all?" She shook her head and stepped away from me, her gaze on the ground. "It's not like you mated with me because you love me. You mated with me to have children."

Not true.

"Do you love me?" she whispered.

Yes.

"Yeosin," I said, staying in control, "it's not that simple."

Again, she stayed quiet.

"Was that all that happened in your nightmare?" I asked after I realized that was all she'd say unless I asked her.

"There was this voice …"

"A voice?"

"Someone who said—never mind."

"What'd the voice say?"

"That they were coming to save me."

I gritted my teeth. In her nightmare, I had been the villain. Not the savior. So, it had to be someone else's voice. Someone else who had promised my mate that they'd save her. And I'd bet it was whoever the fuck that monster had been in the shadows this afternoon.

"Was it a female's or male's voice?" I asked.

Yeosin stayed silent.

"Yeosin, female or male?"

"Luciano …" she whispered. "I …"

"Who was it?"

"It was a female," she said.

But I didn't believe her.

I moved closer to her until we were inches apart. She was lying, but I wasn't going to push it. I doubted that she even knew who it was.

"What was your first nightmare about?" I asked, drawing my fingers over her scars. "The nightmare that gave you these scars. What happened in that one? Did you see the dragons then? The Colossals?"

Tears pricked the corners of her eyes. "I saw the dragons."

"What did they do?"

"We were at this cave," she said. "And they burned everything in sight, including you."

Why had the nightmare changed from killing me … to me hurting Yeosin? Both included dragons burning the world to the ground, except this one included the Colossals. What had happened?

"They didn't try killing you in either of the dreams?" I asked.

"No. They don't want to kill me."

"How do you know?"

"I just know," she whispered. "They want to torture me, to make me weak. They want total submission. Submission that I will never give them."

THIRTY-NINE

YEOSIN

THE FIRE CRACKLED in front of me. I pulled the blanket further around my shoulders and curled up next to it. While I wasn't in that nightmare any longer, my body still burned, especially my mark. I didn't know what to think, what to do.

"Do you think it's the Colossals?" Brent whispered to Luciano.

Luciano and Brent stood at the edge of the cave, speaking quietly to each other, but I could hear them crystal clear. I gently brushed my fingers against the bite marks that Luciano had given me earlier.

My body had gone through so many transformations over the course of the last few weeks, but this was definitely the biggest one. If I focused hard enough, I could hear the forest noises from miles away.

"The nightmares?" Luciano growled, canines lengthened. "No."

The Colossals must've been what that giant monster was earlier, who had paid me a visit in the cave, the one who had saved me from that monster who, if I was putting this together correctly, must've been Alf. Luciano and Brent had been talking about Alpha Alf too.

"Who are the Colossals?" I asked.

Whoever the hell they were … I didn't know if they were enemies or allies. That woman earlier had saved me, yes, but … I couldn't shake the feeling that she had secretly wanted me dead. And for Ruby to show up in my dream as an enemy?

"Nobody," Luciano snarled, snapping his gaze to me. "You should be resting."

"No," I said, standing. "I want to know what's happening. They're torturing me."

"It's too dangerous for you," Luciano said.

I crossed my arms. "No, it's not."

"Rest," he snarled. "Or I will send you to the mountain where I sent Molly."

After marching over to him, I poked him hard in the chest. Sure, he was always possessive and controlling, but ever since he had bitten me, it seemed to be knocked up a few notches. I didn't know if I thought it was the hottest thing or if it pissed me the fuck off more.

"I thought you said that she wasn't fit to watch me," I said.

"She isn't the only person living in the mountains. There— actually, you know what?" The moonlight bounced off Luciano's sculpted face. "That's the perfect fucking place for you. The dragons will never find you."

"Then you won't see me either," I said.

He clenched his chiseled jaw. "I won't."

"Is that what you want?"

"Of course not," he growled. "I want you *alive*."

We glared at each other for a few more minutes, and my gaze drifted to his lips.

Control yourself, Yeosin! I am supposed to hate him right now. I should not want to fuck him, especially in front of Brent.

"Should I leave?" Brent asked, hiking his thumb back. "Are you going to hate fuck again?" He waved his arms in the air.

"Because that is not something I would like to see for a second time today."

"No," Luciano and I both said at the same time.

But his gaze dropped to my lips, and that gleam returned to his eyes.

"You sure?" Brent said, stepping back. "Because—"

"The Colossals can't mind-control a human," Luciano said, pulling his gaze away.

"You marked her, and *then* they showed up in her nightmare," Brent said.

"How does that explain the burns on her body from her first nightmare?"

"All I'm saying is, it's suspicious," he said. "And she might've gotten burns in her first nightmare, but Molly and Ella didn't say anything about her body igniting on fire. If it had, your sheets would've been burned."

I tugged the blanket tighter and turned around to put distance between us because what the fuck was going on with me? Luciano didn't need me to be a horny mess right now, and he really didn't need to wake up nightly to my nightmares. Honestly, I wasn't sure why he didn't just dump me off for Ruby.

Because he loves me.

The thought crossed my mind, but I pushed it away. He couldn't. He had said he didn't.

After sitting back down next to the fire, I stared into it and saw my nightmare in the flames. The fire licked my toes, and I inched them closer to stay warm. The pain in my dreams had always been worse than the pain of fire in real life—at least as of lately.

It was a sick illusion. My mind was playing tricks on me, or maybe I was becoming numb to the pain in real life. The fire didn't hurt me the way that it did in my dreams.

"Get your toes away from the fire," Luciano growled. "Are you fucking crazy?"

But I didn't move them away.

Within the flames, I saw that barren field. I saw the ash. I saw the burned bodies of beasts, just like Luciano. I could smell the horror, the blood, the rotting bodies. Within the flames, I could see the future.

"They won't get away with this," I whispered, tears burning my eyes. "I refuse."

If I hated Alvin before, I really loathed him now. I wanted to see every single one of them in his stupid little clan dead. Burned to ashes themselves. Body parts littering the forest. All while torturing him with my two hands.

"So, what do you want me to do with Alpha Alf?" Brent asked, peering outside the cave.

"Let me do it," I said, standing up.

All I felt was pain, and I wanted him to feel it too. I wanted him to feel the fear run through his veins like I had felt when he rushed into the cave and tried to fuck me. I wanted him to fear for his life, to beg me not to touch him.

"Yeosin, you need to rest," Luciano growled.

"No." I walked over to Luciano and Brent, peering out into the forest. "Bring him to me. I want him to feel the pain, the fear that I did. I want to kill him myself."

CHAPTER
FORTY

YEOSIN

WE STOOD in front of Alpha Alf—Luciano in front of me, shielding him from looking at me. I gritted my teeth and glared up at his huge, muscular back. Why couldn't he let me do anything that I asked for?!

"Move," I growled at Luciano, shoving him out of the way with force.

To my surprise, Luciano actually stumbled back a bit, as if I'd pushed him off-balance. I ignored it and stepped in front of Alpha Alf to get my revenge. Granted, he was a bit fucked up already, but I didn't care.

"Yeosin," Luciano snarled from behind me. "Let me do it myself."

My heel came down on Alf's jaw, and the cracking sound echoed through the cave. Blood trickled out from the corner of his mouth. I kicked him again in the same spot, and again, and again, and then again to release all my anger.

When his face wasn't even recognizable anymore, the fury still bubbled inside me.

"Yeosin—"

"I'm not finished," I growled, walking past Luciano and out of the cave. After finding a hefty rock in the forest, one with enough jagged edges that it could stab Alf, I walked over to his body. "I already told you that I'm going to kill you."

On one side, the rock was sharp, and the other was blunt. I smashed the rock's blunt side into Alf's groin. Once, then twice, then a third time. Every time it hit his cock, he grunted and groaned and began sputtering incoherent words.

"I hate you," I said, hurling the rock at him. "I hate you. I hate you. I hate you."

Adrenaline rushed through me.

"I hate you!" I screamed at the top of my lungs, my voice echoing through the forest.

I kicked him as hard as I could in his chest, imagining that it was Alvin who was receiving all my torture. That bastard deserved it for what he had put me through, then and now. He deserved something worse than death, something more ... sinister, more gruesome.

His dick cut up into a hundred million little pieces, birds pecking at his open wounds, watching his body decay day after day after day and being able to do nothing about it. I wanted to bathe in his tears and blood.

This was what he deserved.

I wanted to torture Alvin more than I thought possible. I wanted him to suffer, to beg to die.

Once I dropped the rock onto Alf's balls, I turned away from him and looked up at Luciano, who had an unreadable expression on his face. Behind him, Brent's mouth was dropped wide open, and he was looking between me and Alf.

"Have your way with him," I said to Luciano. "I'm finished."

When I stepped away, Luciano wrapped his hand around Alf's bloody neck and hurled him into the closest tree. I watched on through the pain. Alf's deformed body snapped at the spine so loudly that I didn't think he could stand if he tried.

A wail left his mouth, and pleasure ran through my body.

God, it felt so good to be the one in control. To be the punisher. The torturer.

Luciano picked him up again and squeezed his throat so tightly that it popped. Alf's head lolled forward, and blood gushed out from between his lips. The blood pooled underneath him, and I swore I could see flames flickering off it.

"Eat shit, you fucker," my man growled.

With brute strength, Luciano grabbed his lower jaw in one hand and his upper jaw in his other, fingers in Alf's mouth, and quite literally tore his head into two pieces. The last thing I heard leave his mouth was a piercing wail, and then his body fell limp.

Luciano dropped Alf's head, and it rolled to my feet. I kicked it away, bloodying my toe, and watched it hit the nearest tree. I had never once thought this would end up happening, but I also hadn't thought that I'd see Joseph's head as a present, that the Dragon Clan would be after me, that monsters were real.

But I knew better now.

Monsters were real. And there was a monster in all of us.

"Bury him," Luciano ordered Brent.

I had seen Luciano give orders before in the boardroom, but something about this …

God, control yourself, Yeosin. How can you be horny and angry at the same time?!

Luciano scooped up my hand. "Come. Let's wash the blood off you."

Before Luciano, whenever something major had happened like this and I became this angry, I'd return to my bedroom to be alone, to process my thoughts, but today, I found myself following after him and enjoying his company.

He hadn't stopped me from lashing out. He hadn't scolded me. He'd protected me.

Once we made it to the hot spring, I stripped off my clothes and slipped into the warm water. The heat felt good against my burns, and I closed my eyes as the blood seemed to melt off me. Luciano stepped in and swam over to me.

While he had been more jealous and possessive of me since he'd marked me, he was also more … loving. Maybe *caring* was a better word because he had already said that he didn't love me. Though he could care for me.

We didn't say anything as he washed the blood off my body, using the soaps that Molly had brought down here a while ago. How long had it been since I had met him? How long had we been together?

At this point, I wasn't too sure.

A few moments later, when my body was submerged into the water, I listened to footsteps approaching, and Brent's scent drifted through my nose. He appeared at the entrance to the hot spring.

"He's taken care of," Brent said to Luciano, then smirked at me. "Welcome to the pack, Luna."

YEOSIN

WATER BUBBLED AROUND ME. Luciano grabbed my hand and led me out of the hot spring, blanketing me with a towel and drying off my body. Once he was finished, I wrapped it around myself and followed him back to the main cave area, the stone cold under my feet.

My stomach twisted into knots. It was almost bedtime.

And I would do anything not to experience those flames again.

In the front, Brent must've laid out some pillows and blankets for us. Luciano sat down on them, the fire still flickering a few feet away. The warmth from the flames was the only good thing about them on this cold night.

"Come here," Luciano growled.

"I want to sleep in a real bed," I whispered.

Though truthfully, I didn't want to sleep at all tonight. It was just an excuse because I knew that Luciano didn't have a bed here. Anything to stay awake for a bit longer so I didn't have to experience that nightmare again would be optimal.

"We don't have a bed here." After reaching for me, he took my hand, his facial features relaxing for the first time tonight. Somehow, I had never noticed how handsome he was without looking all angry. "You won't have another nightmare."

I tugged my hand away and wrapped my arms around myself. "Yes, I will."

"I promise you won't," he said. "Not when you're sleeping with me."

Tears welled in my eyes, but I pushed them away and hesitantly sat beside Luciano. I didn't want to visit the flames again. I didn't want to be tortured again. I didn't want to see Luciano with another woman again.

Because I loved him.

Yes, it was foolish. Yes, he didn't love me back. Yes, I had only met him about a month ago. But, God, I loved him. I hadn't felt this way about Alvin during all the years that I had been with him.

"I won't let anyone hurt you," he whispered, tugging me closer. "Please."

I curled into his chest. "Monsters hurt me when you're not around."

Every single time he wasn't with me, some monster found its way to me. It was almost as if I attracted them, almost as if they knew where I was, had orders to hurt me. I wouldn't put it past Alvin to have told them to.

Especially Alpha Alf earlier.

They could blame the full moon all they wanted, but how people had begun acting around me when they never did so before … something had changed in the past few weeks since I'd met the beast within Luciano.

Luciano curled his arms around my smaller body and rested his head against mine. "They won't hurt you when I'm here beside you. They'd have to burn me alive before they could get to you."

Truly, I wanted to believe him. But I didn't. I couldn't.

Alvin might've won the war a long, long time ago, but Luciano didn't know anything about Alvin. He didn't see Alvin the way I did. He didn't witness what Alvin was capable of, the manipulation and torture.

"One day, when this is all over and the Dragon Clan ceases to be, we'll get out of that city. We'll rebuild the packhouse. We'll have the nicest bed to sleep on. And you'll never have to worry about a thing."

I turned onto my back and gazed up at the ceiling of the dark cave. Some moonlight flooded in through the cracks and crevices, gleaming against the rock. My hand found Luciano's, and I intertwined my fingers with his.

It was nice to dream, wasn't it?

Only he didn't know that I'd probably be dead before then.

Luciano lifted my arm into the air so he could see my scars, but didn't let go. With his free hand, he drew his fingers against them. When he turned our intertwined hands over so he could see my fingers, I could see the faint scars on his hand.

They were just like mine—burns from the Dragon Clan—but his had healed, almost to where they weren't visible. Though I could still see them.

"Tell me about it," I whispered, listening to his even breathing, feeling the heat of his breaths, touching his skin that was rougher than mine. "About your past, about your pack, about life before the Dragon Clan."

"Life before the Dragon Clan," he said. "It was so long ago that I almost don't remember it."

I playfully rolled my eyes. "You're not that old."

A low chuckle left his mouth as he continued to mindlessly play with my fingers.

"We were comfortable. Too comfortable. And I ... I was a terrible leader. I should've been more on edge, more untrusting of people. I should've protected them more when they attacked."

I released his hand and rolled over onto my stomach. "I said, life *before* the Dragon Clan, not during the war."

"What do you want to know about?" he asked.

"Your family."

Sadness shone in his eyes, which was quickly replaced with hardness.

He wasn't going to tell me. He was trying to block it all away.

But he didn't know that I knew that look all too well. I'd mastered that look. I had forgotten things about my childhood, before the Dragon Clan, that I couldn't remember anymore. I had these long stretches of time that I had no recollection of. At all.

Thoughts and memories that I would never recover, and if I did... I wasn't sure I *wanted* to remember them.

I gently cupped his face and kissed him on the mouth. He stiffened at first, then suddenly melted into the kiss, seizing my waist and tugging me closer to him.

When I finally pulled away, I rested my forehead on his. "Tell me about your family."

"I had two younger brothers," he whispered. "We did everything together. We made promises to travel the forest one day and see the world, to visit every type of species that we could find."

I brushed some hair out of his face. "What were their names?"

"Elijah and Gideon."

While I wanted to ask what had happened to them, I already knew that the Dragon Clan had killed them. And I didn't want him to become even sadder or shut down like he had before ... I wanted him to be happy.

I never saw this grumpy man happy.

"What is your favorite memory with them?"

"Three weeks before the Dragon Clan destroyed everything, I brought them to the lake. Elijah had just turned eighteen, and he told us that he had met someone who felt like his mate. We couldn't know for sure; we had all been cursed not to have a mate."

His lips curled into a smile. "I didn't know how it felt at the time, and I had pushed the thought of it out of my head ... but it just came back to me. He must've felt the way that I do with you —the warmth, the need, the desire to be a better man."

My stomach did one of those flippy things, and I pressed my lips to his.

"I may know how he feels, but he will never know how I feel now that I have you," he whispered, drawing his hand over my stomach. "He will never know what it's like to finally have a family of his own. One that needs to be protected like this."

After crawling up into his lap, I gently grasped his chin. "Do you believe in an afterlife?"

"Yes," he said, eyes glowing as he wrapped his hands around my waist.

"Then show Elijah and Gideon what it's like. I know they're watching."

"How?" he asked. "I've tried for so long."

"I don't know how, but we need Alvin's head."

He tugged back on my hair and placed a wet kiss on my neck. "If you want Alvin's head, I will bring you Alvin's head."

YEOSIN

"LUCIANO," I whispered, trailing behind his quickened pace and seizing his elbow.

Brent was a few paces back in the woods, on the lookout for anything or *anyone* following us.

I chewed on the inside of my cheek. "I don't know if this is a good idea."

"You either come with me or I bring you to the mountain."

My stomach twisted into knots, and I clamped my mouth closed. I didn't want to go to the mountain with the others. I didn't know them, and something deep inside me was yearning for Luciano, now more than ever.

"Do you trust them?" I asked.

Apparently, we were heading to meet with the Colossals because Luciano planned to break their pact. We had talked about it all morning—or more like he and Brent had talked about it while I tried to chime in.

Luciano grunted, "No, I never did."

It had to just be my imagination playing tricks on me, making it seem like the Colossals were a threat because that girl wanted my man. Luciano had made a deal with them only because he thought he needed them to win the war.

Now he was planning on breaking that agreement because of these stupid dreams.

After all, that Colossal had saved me ... after letting Alpha Alf approach me.

I glanced over my shoulder, noticing that the trees were becoming further away from each other and large footprints were imprinted into the thick mud underneath our feet. I swallowed hard and found Brent grimacing at them.

When he made eye contact with me, I turned away from him. "You and Brent should talk this out more. If you think that they are the only way that you—that *we*—can win the war, then we should turn back now and keep the pact."

"We already agreed," Luciano said. "We don't need them."

"Don't you think we should have a plan before making any rash decisions?"

He clenched his jaw. "This isn't a rash decision. The Colossals threatened you more than once in your dreams, and they knocked Brent out in the woods so they could get you alone in the cave. I don't trust them."

Almost instinctively, I placed a hand on my stomach. I didn't have a bump yet, but I knew there was a baby growing inside me. I didn't know what the right choice was anymore. Honestly, I never did. But I had to think more than just about myself now.

I made a vow to have his baby before I died, and I wasn't going to break that.

Suddenly, bile rose in my throat, and I dropped Luciano's elbow and stopped in the forest. Luciano paused and glanced back at me. I stumbled back a bit, finding the nearest tree to support myself, my head swaying.

After hurling up the breakfast we had made at the cave, I wiped my lips. *Hell, this is going to be a long pregnancy.* Would this happen every morning and into the early afternoons? Were beast babies the same as human babies with the pregnancy term and symptoms?

Mom had always avoided conversation about her pregnancy whenever I asked, so I wasn't sure if the women in my family had a rough time or not. Already, after experiencing the first day, it definitely wasn't going to be all sunshine, like I'd imagined.

"Are you okay?" Luciano asked.

"Yes," I said, letting go of the tree to continue walking.

But as I moved ahead, the dizziness clouded my vision again. The trees wobbled in front of me, and I squeezed my eyes shut so the sudden sensation of hurling would pass quickly again. I really didn't want to burn the back of my throat for the second time today.

"Yeosin," Luciano said.

When I looked his way, all I saw was a blurry outline of his body. Behind him, deep in the forest, was a spark, a flame, moving toward us. As the object approached, the fire seemed to disappear, and a monster stood behind Luciano.

Though he wasn't a threat like the Colossal had seemed yesterday.

Standing at the same height as Luciano, the monster had large wings and eyes as golden as the sun. Luciano and Brent hadn't noticed him yet.

"*Turn back now, Yeosin,*" the monster said, his voice so familiar.

"Yeosin," Brent shouted.

The monster moved closer. "*You're in danger with the beasts.*"

"No, I'm not," I said. "I'm in more danger alone."

"Yeosin," Luciano said, placing his hands on my shoulders and snapping me back to reality for a split second.

Then the dizziness came back, and the man with wings returned behind Luciano.

"*Luciano doesn't know your true power,*" he said. "*He can't protect you from what's to come.*"

"What's to come?" I asked. "My nightmares?"

"*Some of them, yes.*"

"Fire will rain down upon us," I whispered, my chest tightening and nerves nipping at my stomach. I stared ahead at him, his outline becoming more visible, the longer he stayed in place. I knew this man from somewhere. "Do you work with the Dragon Clan?"

"No."

"Then who are you?"

"*I can't tell you,*" he said. "*Not now. You're not ready.*"

I pulled myself out of Luciano's hold and stepped closer to the monster. "I am ready."

"*No, Yeosin. You're not ready until every part of you burns alive.*"

When he started to walk away, his body still turned in my direction, I followed after him. Luciano grabbed my wrist to hold me back, and I stopped because I realized that I was running after a delusion.

This might not even be real.

"What can you tell me?" I asked.

"*I can tell you that I'm your kind,*" he said. Then his body turned into flames, and he disappeared into them.

CHAPTER
FORTY-THREE

LUCIANO

"WHAT WAS THAT? WHO WAS THERE?" I asked, looking behind myself with Yeosin in my grasp. She had been talking to someone, but neither Brent nor I could see them. "Yeosin, say something to me."

She shook her head. "Nothing. It wasn't anyone."

"Yeosin," I snarled, "tell me."

After snapping her gaze back to mine, she stared up at me through those innocent brown eyes. "I promise it wasn't anyone. I think … I think I just had another one of those hallucinations."

I growled under my breath. I would get it out of her today after we finally broke this pact. It had to be the Colossals playing tricks with her mind again, and I wouldn't stand for this anymore. We were done. Fucking done with this shit.

"Come with me," I snapped, grabbing her hand and tugging her along toward our meeting point with Alpha Theo and the Colossals. We had scheduled a meeting for today, so I knew they'd be here.

And I was going to fucking kill one of them if I found out it was true.

We walked for about twenty more minutes in silence, until we reached the small stream. After crossing it, I listened to Alpha Theo chatting with the Colossals about a quarter mile south. I steered Yeosin in that direction.

When we approached, the chatting stopped.

"Luciano," Alpha Theo said. "You're here early."

"We're done," I growled at him, dropping Yeosin's hand. "The pact is over."

"What the fuck are you talking about? We just had—"

"It's fucking over!" I snarled, cutting my gaze to the group of Colossals. "I'm not dealing with any of this shit anymore. I'm not going to be played and have Yeosin put in danger because of you."

"Yeosin?"

"The human I brought to The Breeding Cave."

Alpha Theo looked over my shoulder at Yeosin, who stood small behind me, her arms wrapped around her belly, as if she were trying to protect it. She eyed Ruby, the woman she had seen in her nightmares.

"Is she pregnant?" Theo asked.

Flaring my nostrils, I stared at Alpha Theo because it wasn't any of his business.

"She is, isn't she?" He rolled his eyes. "Just what we fucking need right now."

I shoved him back, canines extending. "This is what we set The Breeding Cave up for. To reproduce so those fuckers wouldn't burn us out of existence. Don't get fucking pissed off because you've been trying for years and not gotten anyone pregnant."

He pushed me and seethed. "I did get someone pregnant, and they took her!"

"Did you?" I asked, stepping closer to get into his face. "Or was she really your mate and you lost her because you couldn't protect her? Because *you* had your eye on another woman when she was supposed to be your only priority?"

Theo fucking pissed me off beyond belief. All this talk about this human woman that he had found to reproduce with. She was perfect for him, and yet he had been with the Colossals probably for a while now.

"We've already planned on saving her," Theo said. "We *need* to save my mate."

"You're willing to sacrifice mine to save yours who you never loved until it was too late?"

"Love? Don't talk about her like you fucking know what it feels like to love someone."

Man, I want to punch him in the jaw so badly right now.

I balled my hands into fists by my sides. "I do."

"That's fucking bullshit," he growled, putting his hands on me again. "Don't fucking li—"

Before he could finish his sentence, a dragon swooped overhead and breathed fire down on the forest around us, trapping our group of beasts and Colossals within a ring of scorching fire. Just like Yeosin's nightmares, the Dragon Clan had found us.

CHAPTER
FORTY-FOUR

YEOSIN

ONE MOMENT, Luciano had been fighting with Alpha Theo. The next moment, we were trapped within a ring of fire, being smothered by the smoke. I was pushed around and separated from Luciano as the group of warriors tried to find where the dragon had disappeared off to.

The sound of large wings flapping through the air echoed around the forest, and suddenly, there wasn't just one dragon, but three of them, breathing fire down upon the forest around us.

My heart pounded inside my chest so loudly that I could hear it in my ears. I scanned the forest for a place to escape, but couldn't find any openings that weren't thick with fire. Flames licked my shins, and I scrambled back on my ass to get away from them as quickly as I could.

The heat …

God, it is getting so hot so quickly.

Beads of sweat rolled down my forehead. Warriors shifted into Colossals. Where was Luciano? I couldn't see or hear him above the cackling of fire, through the giant bodies, the blood, the chaos.

I gasped for fresh air, inhaling nothing but smoke.

I need to get out of here now.

One of the dragons locked eyes on me from above and suddenly swooped down, flying right toward me. Ruby, who had barely looked in my direction since we had made it here, shifted into her huge form, knocked him out of the air with one hand, and picked me up with the other.

A piercing scream left my mouth, and I flailed my legs in the air.

What is happening? How do I get out of here? I need to protect my baby.

Once she squashed the dragon underneath her foot, she placed me on the other side of the fire. I landed with a thud and stumbled back to regain my footing. After peering at me for another moment, she turned back to the attack.

Chaos ensued around me, and I backed away from the fire while scanning the woods for any sign of Luciano. I hoped that someone had gotten him out of there because I had lost sight of him, and I *couldn't* lose him.

As I looked around, my gaze landed on a figure in the woods —one that was on fire, but wasn't fazed by it, one like the monster that I had seen earlier. When his eyes found mine, flames suddenly engulfed my body.

They didn't hurt, but my skin melted.

"Yeosin!" Luciano scooped me up in his beast form and pulled me to his body, the flames almost evaporating on contact. He pressed me against his chest to shield me and ducked under a canopy of trees. "We're getting you out of here now before they find you."

But the Dragon Clan had already found me. They were here, weren't they?

As we retreated through the woods, I stared over Luciano's shoulder at the battle unfolding behind us. Colossals swapped at the dragons swooping through the air, breathing fire down upon the trees.

My eyes burned from the smoke, and I shifted in Luciano's arms.

We couldn't leave them there. Ruby had actually protected me from a dragon. While we thought they were the enemy, an enemy wouldn't help us. An enemy would let me burn and laugh as it happened.

"We have to go back," I said, clawing at his back. "Please."

He continued running. "No."

"Yes."

"No!" he growled, silencing me. "We're meeting Brent at the cave, and then I'm going back."

"I'm coming with you!" I shouted. "You're not going alone. I'm not going to lose you."

"As long as a baby is in your belly, you'll always have a piece of me, Yeosin."

All my brattiness disappeared, and I remembered the promise that I'd made to myself. I would have the baby for Luciano before I died, which meant that I couldn't die yet. I couldn't run into the fire. I had no powers. I was helpless.

But the monster from the forest earlier was right.

Against the Dragon Clan, the beasts were weak without the Colossals. The beasts couldn't save me. They were very strong, but they couldn't reach the skies. They couldn't fly. They couldn't protect me.

Maybe only I could protect myself.

CHAPTER
FORTY-FIVE

YEOSIN

TEN MINUTES LATER, Luciano approached familiar territory with me still in his arms. We had gotten way too far away, and I couldn't remember which way the battle was anymore, so I couldn't go back to help if I tried.

"Fuck!" someone hissed from about a quarter mile ahead, near the cave.

Luciano set me down, and I followed the rambling of curses. Brett stood with a pair of jeans hanging low on his hips, a pained expression on his face. A sizzling burn stretched from his right shoulder, across his chest and ribs, then down his abdomen to his jeans.

My eyes widened, and I grabbed his hand and tugged him into the cave. Would the hot spring help soothe his burns? I wasn't sure, but I knew that Luciano had some medication back there. I believed Molly had brought it at one point.

Some jealous hothead growled behind me, but I shot him a glare and continued walking with Brett toward the back of the cave. How could Luciano be jealous right now out of all times? I was directing Brett to get healed, for fuck's sake!

Once we made it into the back room, I dropped Brett's hand and rummaged through the goods in the corner. There had to be something, somewhere, right? There were scented soaps, lotion, shampoo …

In the middle of my search, I heard chatter coming from the other area of the cave. I glanced over my shoulder to see a group of Colossals walk into the room, including Ruby. Luciano stepped in front of me and growled at them.

I stopped what I was doing and turned around to see Brett eyeing them down too.

"Get the fuck out of here," Luciano snarled, claws and teeth lengthening. "Now!"

The Colossals were burned so badly. So, so badly …

My mind wandered back to the battle. What scared me the most was that the dragon who had tried to capture me … he looked so familiar. His facial structure was one that I had seen before, but I swore that I had never laid my eyes upon a dragon in real life.

Maybe he was one of Alvin's goons.

"Stop it," I shouted at Luciano, standing in front of the Colossals. "They protected me."

"Get out of my way, Yeosin," he growled at me.

I glared up at him and crossed my arms. "No."

His lip twitched. "Yeosin."

"Luciano, they haven't been the cause of the fire in my nightmares," I said.

"You don't know that."

"Yes, I do."

"Then who?" Luciano growled. "Who burned you?"

I opened and closed my mouth a handful of times, my heart racing. Should I tell Luciano about the monster? He hadn't seemed like he would harm me, but when his gaze landed on me in the middle of the battle, my body had burst into flames. It wasn't the Colossals.

"The monster that I saw in the forest on our way to the meeting," I admitted. "It was him."

"And how do you know that wasn't one of their sick illusions?"

The Colossal who had appeared outside the cave the other night stepped forward. "I will admit that I put Brent to sleep just outside the cave so I could speak with Yeosin and warn her away. But I have not touched her in her sleep."

"You don't like her, so I don't fucking believe you," Luciano snarled. "How do you know it wasn't them?"

I shrugged because I knew he wouldn't believe me. "It's just a feeling."

"Who is the monster?" he asked.

"He's … he has wings, and his body can erupt in flames."

"A monster with wings who can erupt in flames?" Ruby said. "Sounds like a dragon."

My throat dried. He did sound like a dragon, didn't he? But he wasn't dangerous.

At least, I didn't think he was.

"It is obvious that the Dragon Clan doesn't want to kill Yeosin," another Colossal said. "If they did, they would've used fire to kill her back in the forest. She was out in the open, easily targetable. One of the dragons tried to snatch her away."

"They want to torture her," Luciano said. "They've burned her before."

"Why? Why burn her, but not kill her?"

"Alvin is my ex-boyfriend, but he always seemed so uninterested in me." I shook my head, not able to understand it myself. "I'm not sure what he wants with me, though he loves control and power over people."

"And this other monster, this other dragon, wants to burn you alive?"

I squeezed my eyes closed, my head beginning to dully ache. "I don't know."

Every single day that passed, more questions popped up.

Why did Alvin want me back after breaking up with me? Who was this other dragon? What did *he* want with me? And why had this all suddenly started to happen after Luciano gave me a proposition?

CHAPTER
FORTY-SIX

YEOSIN

FIRE BURNS *the forest that surrounds me. Completely alone, I stand in the center of it, the flames licking every part of my body. Luciano isn't here, nor are any of the Colossals, which means that … this is all a dream, a nightmare.*

And if that monster is really causing these burns, then he has to be close.

Though my body is burning, I stay calm and scan the area.

Empty. Empty. Empty. A shadow …

My eyes widen, and I follow the shadow with my gaze as it moves around the trees it burns. Then my legs move faster than my mind can come up with a plan. All I can think about is finding that bastard and killing him so this anguish will stop.

So, I run through the flames as my skin melts under the heat. I pump my legs faster and faster to catch up with his quickening figure. This can't happen. I can't let him get away from me.

When he sees me picking up speed, he extends his wings and flies into the air above me. I pick up a rock and hurl it at him.

"Get back down here and face me!" I scream. "Don't be a fucking bastard!"

No response.

I pick up another rock, this one quite larger, and use all my strength to throw it at him. It hits him in the left wing, and he flies backward a bit.

"You're becoming stronger and smarter, Yeosin," he says. "Good."

"Stop this fire!" I scream. "Stop burning me alive."

"No."

"Why not?!"

He floats down toward me. "If things stay the same, then your baby will die."

Rage bubbles through my stomach, and I grit my teeth, shoving him back. "Don't you say anything about my baby." Adrenaline rushes through my system, and I find myself pushing again and again, one arm cradling my belly in protection. "Don't touch my baby."

"I would never hurt it," he says. "I'm telling you the truth."

"No," I shout. "You're lying to me. You're hurting *me!"*

"I'm helping you."

"You're fucking psychotic!"

"Yeosin."

"Stop this!"

"Yeosin."

"Get away from me!"

"Yeosin!"

Shouting from above me shook me awake. Luciano gazed down at me, his hands on my shoulders and huge gashes in his bare chest. My eyes widened as his blood dripped down onto me, and I struggled to sit up.

"Luciano," I whispered, reaching up to his wounds. "What happened to y—" Before I could finish my sentence, I noticed that my fingers were bloody, but what scared me the most was that they weren't fingers anymore.

No, they were huge claws. Sharper than Luciano's.

"Calm down, Yeosin," Luciano whispered, releasing his grip on me. "It's okay. It was just a nightmare."

I stared in horror at his chest, tears welling in my eyes. "Did I do that?"

Luciano didn't answer me.

"Luciano," I whispered again, sitting up and cradling his face. "Did I do that to you?"

"It will heal," he said. "Did you see the monster in your nightmare?"

Tears stung my eyes and ran down my cheeks. "I-I hurt you … I'm s-sorry. I didn't—"

"It's okay, Yeosin. It's okay. I'm fine." He sat back slightly, giving me a chance to see the wounds I had caused him again. "See? They're healing already. They'll be healed by morning. But tell me, your nightmare?"

"Where'd you go?" I asked. "I only have nightmares when you're gone."

Luciano grimaced. "I had to piss. I'm sorry."

After blowing out a low breath, I placed a hand against my stomach and felt the faintest of heartbeats inside it, which meant that … my baby was still okay for now. But if that monster found me again, if that monster *touched* me again …

We would have a problem.

"I saw him again. That dragon …" I whispered. "He's causing these burns. He's hurting me."

CHAPTER
FORTY-SEVEN

LUCIANO

"WHY ARE WE HERE?" Yeosin asked, her arm wrapped around mine as we ascended my office building in the elevator.

When the door opened on the top floor, I stepped out and started toward my room in the back.

"I need to grab a few things, and then we're out of here. We're out of the city. We're out of the forest. Well, at least you are."

"What do you mean, I am?"

Instead of answering her, I pursed my lips to not get angry. I knew she wouldn't like what I was going to propose, but I didn't care. This was all to protect her.

"What do you mean, Luciano?" she asked, tugging me back.

I clenched my jaw. "You're going to the mountainside."

Yeosin crossed her arms and glared. "Do you think that's going to solve it?"

"It's going to keep you away from harm, so I don't have to worry about you during battle."

"And what if the dragons find me at the mountain? You won't be there."

"They won't find you."

"Yes, they will," she hissed, then dropped her gaze. "They always find me."

Knowing that I would get nowhere arguing with her, I continued toward my office and turned on the lights. She followed after me, staying quiet.

"What do you have to get here anyway?"

"Nothing. Nothing important."

"It obviously is important if you're bringing me here after what just happened."

I hurried to my desk. There were a few important, essential papers that I needed to take. My laptop too. But that wasn't why I had come; I could've gotten those any day. Could've had someone send them to me if I needed them that badly.

No, I was here for one thing and one thing only.

When I opened the bottom drawer of my desk, I saw the shiny gem that had been passed down through generations glowing at the bottom. Yeosin looked over my shoulder and stared down at it, the glow bouncing off her big brown eyes, making them look magical.

Things were getting bad. And I didn't know how to solve them. All this time, we had been hiding away, running away from those wild dragons. I just wanted to live a simple, quiet life. But after seeing them today, I knew I had to do something.

No more sitting around. No more trying to protect her in a cave. We couldn't. Soon, they would find us, if they hadn't already discovered where we were staying. There was only one place that I knew should be safe. And I really, really, really didn't want to leave her alone. I knew that I couldn't, that I shouldn't.

But the mountainside was far, far, far away. Would the dragons venture that far, or could they?

"Don't answer me then," she said, glaring at me. "I'm still not going to that stupid mountain. Not without you."

"Yes, you are."

"You don't understand," she growled, her nails lengthening into claws. "The Dragon Clan always, always, always finds me.

You can try to hide me for one hundred thousand years, and still somehow, they will find me. I could die and come back to life, and they would know that it's me. You don't understand, Luciano. You can't understand."

"I do understand, and I'm not going to let it happen."

"You don't get a choice. They will find me. They will torture me. They will kill me if that's what they want to do." She dropped her gaze and shook her head. "I still ... I still can't wrap my mind around what they want with me. But they want something."

"There are warriors there who will protect you."

"Those warriors aren't you."

While it was never my intention to fall in love with her, I found myself softening at her words. She had done something to me that I couldn't quite understand, but as her mate, it was still my job to protect her.

"Luciano," she whispered. She placed a hand over her belly. "We have a child now. I don't want you getting hurt, never mind losing your life. After what I saw today ... I know there's no way you can kill them. There's no way I could kill them. The only people who could help us are the Colossals."

I gritted my teeth. I didn't want to work with them. I hated them. I swore that they were the cause of this. They never had anything good in mind.

"Please, Luciano, listen to me. If you're going to make me go to the mountain, then you're coming with me."

"You don't understand," I growled. "This is my pack. They killed my family. I promised to avenge them, and all I've been doing is running and hiding. No more. I'm not gonna do any of that shit anymore."

"But—" she started.

"No," I cut her off, shaking my head. "You said it. We have a family, and I'm not going to let them take away my family again. Not the one that I made."

Instead of responding to me like I thought she would, she grabbed my hand and pulled me closer to her. My body was rigid, tense. But her hand, it felt so good. She intertwined our fingers for a moment and blew out a little breath, her eyes fluttering closed. Then she placed my hand right over her stomach, and I could feel the second heartbeat inside of her.

The baby ... the baby was growing quickly. Or maybe ... maybe she had gotten pregnant far before I thought she was. Maybe she had gotten pregnant that first night after I met her. Could she have? I had sworn up and down that I couldn't have a mate. But we clicked so effortlessly.

Had she really gotten pregnant that first night together?

Never mind that ... she was right.

I couldn't defeat the dragons. But I wasn't going to stop.

I scooped up the gem and stuffed it into my pocket. It burned on touch, and it was a scar that would never fully disappear. Whatever this gem was, it was important. My mother had given it to me, but had never fully explained what it meant. But it was fire —that much I knew.

And if it was fire, maybe it had something to do with the dragons. And if it had something to do with the dragons, maybe it could defeat them.

I didn't know, honestly. The only person my mother had told was Gideon. He had been obsessed with that gem hanging around her neck. Now I would never know. I would never fucking know what it meant.

But I would do anything—any-fucking-thing—to figure it out. Maybe this gem, this fire, could defeat the dragons once and for all.

CHAPTER
FORTY-EIGHT

YEOSIN

"WHAT'S THAT?" I asked, spotting Luciano putting something into his pocket. It was an orange gem, something that I knew I'd seen before. But I wasn't sure where. Maybe from my childhood.

Mom … she had something similar. Or maybe I was getting things confused.

Because I didn't remember the last time I'd seen her wear it. Actually, I didn't think it was my mom at all who had been wearing those. The memory was so old, faded. But it was a woman. I knew it was a woman who'd had earrings like that. I swore …

"It's nothing," Luciano said.

I didn't know what took hold of me, but I reached for it in his pocket. I grabbed the gem. And then my hand started burning. It started burning and burning and burning, hotter than any dragon fire I had ever felt before.

But I didn't pull my hand away. I couldn't pull my hand away. It was like it was attached.

It was like my body wanted to burn. Like it *had* to burn.

I hissed underneath my breath, and Luciano suddenly grabbed the gem from me and stuffed it back into his pocket.

"What are you doing?" he growled at me. "I said it was nothing." Then he dropped his gaze to my hand, which was burned, and he clicked his tongue. "Why must you always burn? I don't understand it. You burn from dragons. You burn in your nightmares. And this gem? This gem has made you burn now too."

"Are you mad at me?" I knew that if I made him mad, he might really bring me to the mountainside and drop me off there and never return. I couldn't let that happen. "Please don't be mad at me."

After a long, low breath, he shrugged his shoulders forward and grabbed me by the waist. He rested his forehead against mine and gently closed his eyes. "I'm not mad at you. I'm stressed out. I fear that they'll take you away from me. That this fire, whatever the hell it is, will take you away from me. I fear that it will kill you and our baby."

"What are you saying?" I asked, my stomach twisting and turning and filling with butterflies from not his words, but how he had said them. Soft, vulnerable, desperate to keep me safe, not only because of the baby, but because he felt something deeper for me.

"What do you mean, what am I saying? I'm saying that I can't lose you."

"Because of our baby?"

"Not because of our baby," he snapped. "Because I love you."

My eyes widened as the words rolled out of his mouth. And then suddenly, he mirrored my expression, his lips parting. I thought he meant to say something more, to take it all back, but he didn't. I stared at him, and my lips curled into a small smile. I didn't know what to say. Did he really mean this ... had the baby ...

"I love you too," I whispered.

At the moment, I didn't care if he was lying. I didn't care if it was all for the baby. I loved him. I really, truly loved him.

He stared at me as if he didn't believe it, then shook his head. After a couple of silent moments, he grasped my face and pulled me in closer, placing a kiss right on my lips. It was hungry, filled with desire.

"I love you ..." This time, his words were stronger. "I love you," he murmured and mumbled against my lips over and over and over again. "I've never loved someone as much as I love you. I can't explain it."

Warmth spread through my body, and I slipped my fingers through his hair, tugging.

I didn't know if this was usual for his kind—the innate desire. But I was sure it was. The beasts had spoken about mates before, right? Yes, yes, they had to have. I swore I'd heard them talk about it when we were with the Colossals.

Was that what this was? He loved me? Or was this just a thing? What were mates? Were they to be together forever?

Before I knew it, Luciano's hands were all over my body, more than they had ever been.

In the beginning, it had just been lust when he brought me to that cave. I'd thought he was the handsomest man ever all those times that he walked into the coffee shop.

And now ... this was something so much more, and it felt ... better? It felt so much more intense, like nothing I'd ever experienced before.

Luciano placed me on his desk and slipped between my thighs, his mouth moving down the column of my neck. "Goddess, I love you."

"If you love me, promise you won't ever leave me. Promise you won't take me to the mountainside without going yourself. Promise you will never die from the dragons, even if I do."

"I'm not gonna leave you. I'm going to love you until the very end."

CHAPTER
FORTY-NINE

YEOSIN

ONE MOMENT, Luciano had told me that he would never leave me, and the next, his hands were finding their way up my thighs. I sat back on his desk, one that I doubted he would ever see again after today, and spread my legs.

I grabbed at his tie and pulled him closer to me. "Please, give it to me. I need it."

Somehow, even though I was already pregnant, I craved him even more than I had before. Maybe it was because he had finally admitted that he loved me, so I knew that this … it wasn't just physical anymore.

No, Luciano loved me.

Luciano wrapped his fingers around the waistband of my pants and panties and tugged them down to my ankles, ripping them right off me to give himself complete access to my body. He dipped his head and buried his face against my tits, covered by my shirt.

"Yeosin, I love you," he murmured, sucking on my nipple through my shirt. "I *need* you."

After wrapping my hands up in his hair, I let my head loll

back and moaned softly, my toes curling from the pleasure of Luciano—the billionaire and the beast—telling me that he loved me. *Me.* Some random chick who had been in an abusive relationship with a dragon a few weeks ago. A girl who never thought she'd be anything more than someone's girlfriend.

Now I was the beast's mate. The love of his life.

"You're mine. You've *always* been mine."

I tugged him even closer, wrapping my legs around the back of his knees and forcing him to move near me. He nestled himself between my thighs, his hard cock grinding against my bare pussy. I reached for it, but instead of letting me have him, he dropped to his knees.

With one of my legs on his left shoulder, he held the other one apart and placed his hot, wet mouth on my cunt. I whimpered, my pussy quivering just from the touch. I laced my fingers into his thick dark hair and tugged.

"Oh my God," I whispered. "Oh my God!"

"I know. I know. I know," he murmured against my pussy. "Tell me. Tell me."

"You feel so good!" I cried, legs beginning to tremble.

He moved his tongue in circles around my clit, back and forth and back and forth.

"If you don't stop, I'm going to—"

"Come for me, baby. Tell me how good it feels."

Holding my breath to build myself up quicker, I threw my head back further and gripped his hair as hard as I could. The pleasure ... God, the pleasure was too much! It was too much. I was going to ...

"Fuck!" I moaned, my eyes rolling back into my head as the ecstasy pumped through my body. My legs trembled wildly, and I expected Luciano to stop and fuck me already, but he fastened his mouth on my clit and sucked on it. "Fuck. Fuck. Fuck. Fuck!"

When he refused to pull away, more and more pleasure flooded my body, making it tingle all over. I dropped my hands to the edge of the desk and sank my claws into the wood, bending it in my grip.

"I want your claws in my back as I fuck you, *mate*," he murmured, kissing up my stomach, between my breasts, then against the column of my neck, nestling his cock right up against my aching pussy.

I placed my hands on his back and sank my nails into his skin as he pushed himself into me. As I moaned, he slipped his tongue into my mouth, eating up all the sound. I curled my toes and cried out, his huge cock filling me up.

"More. More. More. More. More. More!" I mumbled into his mouth. "Please, more!" The pressure built higher inside me, and I bit down on his lower lip, sucking it into my mouth. "God, it feels so good!"

Luciano wrapped his arms underneath my arms, grabbing my shoulders from behind, and began pounding into me. I cried out into his mouth and clawed at his back, my body on fire from the pleasure.

"Fuck, you feel so good," he murmured into my mouth. "So, so, so good."

"You're mine," I mumbled, exploding around him. "All mine."

Luciano spilled out inside me. "Yours."

LUCIANO

"I REALLY HAVE a craving for tea. Can we stop to get some at Pink Ivory before we leave?" Yeosin asked, bouncing on her toes in the middle of the elevator. Her hair was a mess from our fuck session on my desk. "At our favorite place. The one we met at."

"No," I said sharply, not wanting her to complain. "We need to get out of here now."

"Please," she whined. "The baby wants some."

"The baby does not want tea. You do."

"Please, Luciano. That's all I'm asking for before we leave. We don't know when we're gonna be back in the city—*if* we ever will be back in the city. And … you never know when it's gonna be your last day."

"Stop," I growled. "Don't fucking talk like that. Never again. Do you understand me?"

"But …"

"No, I asked if you understood me. Don't talk like you're going to die tomorrow."

"Okay," she whispered in the softest voice I'd ever heard from her. "But can we please just get some? Then I won't ask for another favor like this. I know what we have to do. I know we have to leave and never come back. Just this one thing is all I'm asking for."

I gritted my teeth and blew out a low breath. I didn't want to go. I knew it wasn't going to be safe. But she was right. We probably wouldn't be back—or not for a long time if we ever did return. And this was the place where we had met. It was a place where I had fallen madly in love with her, even if I didn't want to admit it. It was where I knew deep down that she was my mate.

"Fine, but you have to be quick. We grab tea, and then we're out of there. We're not drinking it there. We're not going on a date there. We're out of the city before eight o'clock tonight. We're not taking any chances."

"Okay," she agreed, nodding. "I understand."

Once we left the office building, I took her hand in mine, and we walked down the road to the coffee shop where I had met her. It was getting dark, and I was scanning every street, every alley-way, everywhere for anyone who might try to hurt us.

I didn't trust them fuckers.

I still wasn't sure what I wanted to do with her. Honestly, Yeosin should've been sent to the mountain because I knew that she wasn't safe here. But she had a good point. If I didn't go with her, they would find her. Somehow, someway, they were always able to find her.

My mind was a mess. And it didn't help that she was preg-nant; it was making my beast so much more riled up. I couldn't leave her anywhere alone. Anywhere that she went, I had to go with her. It was the only way to protect her.

I was the only person who I trusted to keep her safe.

Sure, Brent could've kept her safe, too, but I had thought the same about Molly. I had thought the same about Joseph. I had thought that my brothers were able to protect themselves and our family when I went off to war.

But what was funny about war was that you never knew who you could trust. And I wasn't even talking about who might betray me; I was talking about their strengths. Their will. Their abilities. People could train forever and still not be prepared.

I hadn't been.

Not that time around at least.

"Yeosin," someone called from above.

I tugged Yeosin behind me and stared up at a beast suddenly floating down into a dark alleyway, tucking his wings behind him. Not this fuckhead again.

"Yeosin, you can trust me," he said.

Yeosin placed a hand over her belly, tensing up behind me. "Trust you?"

"Don't talk to him," I scolded. "Stay quiet."

"Yeosin, please," he murmured, still shielded by the dark that I couldn't see his face.

I needed to get Yeosin out of here now, before he hurt her.

"I can't even trust you when I'm sleeping," she said. "You burn me."

"It's for your own good," he said.

A feral growl escaped my throat, and I swiped my claws at him, lunging into the darkness. He swiftly used his wings to pump away, deeper into the dark alleyway. Fury was rushing through my body. I hated this fucker. How could anyone trust him? He couldn't even show his face.

"Who are you?" she asked. "If you tell me, if you show us, then maybe we can trust you. But we can't trust somebody who doesn't trust us."

"We're not going to trust you, no matter what," I snarled at him.

I didn't care who he was. All I cared about was keeping her safe. Keeping our baby safe. If I lost them, there would be no fucking point in living. None. Everybody in my family was dead already. If I lost her, I'd rather just end my life right then and there.

"I know a place where you will be safe. Luciano, you could come too."

"No, get out of here now."

"I promise, I swear it's safe."

"Get the fuck out of here," I growled, finally making contact and shoving him backward. "Before I kill you."

If what she had said was true, then he had been the one hurting her. He had been the one setting her on fire, into flames. Causing all of her pain. And if he didn't stop soon, he could kill our baby.

But, if he had wanted to kill her, he could've done it already. He could've taken her plenty of times when she was alone. He could've killed me when I wasn't expecting it. I couldn't understand his motives. What was he doing here? Was he really trying to help? Or did he want to kill her for good? And if so, why?

"I swear I'm not here to hurt you."

"You've set me on fire more than once. What makes you think that I will ever trust you?"

"Stay behind me," I growled at my mate as she moved forward.

"No," she growled back, standing right at my side.

Her hands were balled into small little fists, and I could see the beast in her eyes. Ever since I had marked her, she had become more and more beast-like, but there was something to her that was different. Something that I couldn't put my finger on.

"Why are you here? Why do you keep doing this? Why do you keep following me and burning me?"

"You don't understand."

"Then explain it to me."

"It's not that simple."

"Then I'm not coming with you. You need to stay away from me and my family."

I was fed up, and now he was pissing me off. We didn't need this right now. I needed to get her to safety, somewhere. And I wasn't planning on following him, no matter how many empty promises he made.

The truth was that I didn't trust him. And I never would.

Yeosin didn't trust him, and she was very trusting of people. Almost too trusting.

When he stepped forward again, I grabbed him by the collar and hurled him to the ground, into the light. The dim light shone down upon his face, and for the first time, I saw him. I saw the beast. I saw the man who claimed my mate was his.

I saw my brother who I'd thought was dead.

CHAPTER
FIFTY-ONE

YEOSIN

"GIDEON?" I asked, eyes wide. "What are you doing here?"

Gideon …

The man who had been a regular at Pink Ivory, who had saved me from Alvin, was this dragon who had been following me around? I mean, he had seemed pretty protective of me all those times I served him coffee.

But why is he here? What does he want with me? Is he really a dragon?

Luciano looked back at me, half angry, half confused. "You know him?"

"Yes, he was one of my regulars at Pink Ivory. How do you know him?"

"He's my fucking brother who I thought was dead."

"What do you mean, your brother?" I asked, jaw slackening.

Gideon and Luciano are related? No, there isn't any way. Luciano is a beast, and Gideon is a … a dragon, right? How are they related when they are two separate types of beasts living in the woods?

"What are you doing? Where did you go?" Luciano turned back to Gideon and shook his head, as if he still couldn't believe it. Maybe this was a trick by the monster with wings or the Colossals. They could control someone's mind, right? "And what the fuck are you?"

Gideon exhaled harshly through his nose. "I can't explain. It's too hard. It will take too much time. But I need the orb in your pocket. It'll be easier to explain that way. We can talk on our way back to the—"

"No," Luciano growled, tensing. "Absolutely fucking not. Answer my questions first."

Gideon looked toward the street. "We're not safe here. Follow me."

"Fuck no," Luciano said, grabbing my hand and pulling me back toward the road. Buses flew by, on their way to pick up passengers during rush hour. "We're not going anywhere with you. You're a dead man, talking to me."

"I'm not dead. I never died. You have to let me explain."

Luciano took another step toward the street, into the light. "Explain then. Here. Now."

After he turned toward me, Gideon's features softened. "Come on, Yeosin. You can trust me. I protected you from Alvin at the café a few weeks back. Don't you remember?" He reached out his hand, and I noticed that it was covered in burns. "Please."

I stared down at it for a few moments, my heart pounding so loudly that I could hear it in my ears. Something inside me tugged me to him, and I didn't know why. But I couldn't trust it. No, I trusted Luciano.

Didn't I?

"We're going," Luciano growled, yanking me toward him. "Now."

Deciding that he was right, that I couldn't trust Gideon, no matter how nice he was to me … I grimaced in his direction and followed Luciano out onto the sidewalk. My mind raced with thoughts, with … memories almost.

Memories with Gideon before Pink Ivory. Memories of that scarred hand. Memories of …

Something else …

"Is Gideon a dragon?" I whispered to Luciano, glancing over my shoulder at Gideon, who hadn't moved from the alleyway, yet his gaze was on me the entire time as we departed. "He has wings and can manipulate fire."

"I don't know what the fuck he is," Luciano said. "That's not the brother that I knew."

"Why does he want the orb in your pocket? What does it do?"

Luciano tensed. "I don't know what it does. My mother never told me. She only told him."

"Then maybe we should hear him out," I suggested.

Before I could get another word out of my mouth, Luciano twirled around to face me. His canines lengthened past his teeth, and his eyes were darker than I had ever seen them. "Do you have feelings for him?"

"What?" I asked, eyes wide. "What do you mean?"

"Do you have feelings for him? Do you like him? Have you ever liked him?"

"No, of course not."

A low growl left Luciano's mouth. "Don't lie to me."

"I'm not lying."

Luciano snapped his hand around the front of my throat and pinned me to the side of a building. He buried his face into the crook of my neck, pressing his canines against the mark he had left there. My body trembled from the mere touch.

"You're mine," he growled into my ear. "*Only* mine."

I curled my fingers against his chest. "I know," I said in a breathy whisper.

"You don't belong to him, no matter what he tells you."

"I'm yours, Luciano," I whispered, but when I closed my eyes, I faintly remembered Gideon—the man that I swore I only knew from the coffee shop and the beast who followed me around— telling me that I was his … his mate.

CHAPTER
FIFTY-TWO

LUCIANO

I TIGHTENED my grip on the steering wheel and glanced in the rearview mirror, spotting a flash of fire in the distance between the trees. *That fucker is following us.*

Gideon had tried his hardest to hide himself from me, but I knew he was there.

Rage rattled inside my rib cage. I gritted my teeth, my canines slicing through a couple of thin layers of skin on my lip. Yeosin had one hand on her growing belly and her eyes on the road, surrounded by forest, in front of us.

"Are we going to the mountain?" she asked.

"No."

"To the cave?"

"No."

She twisted her head toward me, brows furrowed together. "Where then?"

Truth was that I had been driving around these back roads in the forest to try and lose Gideon. I eyed the number of miles until the gas tank was empty on my dashboard and growled under my breath. If I didn't lose him soon, we'd run out of gas.

"We're going to run out of gas soon," Yeosin noted, following my gaze.

"We are."

"Do we have another container somewhere? I doubt there's a gas station this deep."

"No."

"Then what are we—"

"Yeosin," I growled, harsher than I should've, "you're not helping."

Usually, I was okay under pressure, but since finding Yeosin and admitting that she was my mate who was carrying my child, everything had become much more stressful. I needed to protect her, but all I could worry about was losing her.

Yeosin's eyes filled with tears, and then she turned her body away from me and faced the window. I blew out a sigh through my nose and glanced over at her, my beast whimpering at the thought of upsetting our mate.

With my free hand, I placed my hand on her thigh, squeezed, and turned her back toward me. "Gideon is following us, and I'm trying to lose him, but I can't think straight. Don't be mad at me. I'm sorry."

"It's okay," she whispered. "I'm stressed out too."

"Why?"

She shifted uncomfortably in her seat and peered in the rearview mirror, shrugging.

She was intentionally keeping something from me because she thought I couldn't handle it, which pissed me off. But honestly, I had been keeping something from her since we had met Gideon in the alleyway.

Long ago, when I had been cursed to never have a mate again, there was one exception to the curse. I would only be granted a mate who would be shared among the strongest creatures in the forest. Those creatures were named, and a bird of fire was one of them.

All this time, I had thought that it was a fire dragon. That it was Alvin.

Though it was Gideon. It had to be Gideon.

I sank my fingers against Yeosin's thigh and squeezed. No way was I going to share her, not when she had my baby inside her. I had waited for far too long. I couldn't have anyone take her away from me.

No fucking way.

The dashboard began blinking with the Low Gas message, and I cursed to myself. I had maybe twenty more miles of gas left. The last thing I wanted was to be stranded in the middle of the forest with a pregnant mate.

So, I pulled off the road and began forging my own path, heading straight toward my old packhouse. If this really was Gideon following after us, he had to know where we were going. And if it wasn't, then I had the upper hand.

I could kill him if I needed to, and I could prove to Yeosin that he was not to be trusted.

Because years ago, I had buried Gideon with my very two hands underneath our childhood swing set. Either this was a fake Gideon, or he had risen from the dead, or my brother had died and been reborn into the bird of fire who was fated to have my mate.

CHAPTER
FIFTY-THREE

YEOSIN

I CHEWED on the inside of my cheek as Luciano parked his fancy, sleek car in front of a half-burned-down house.

"This is my old packhouse," he said, jaw twitching. He peered in the rearview mirror. "The dragons burned it during the war. I don't come here much anymore, but it is the only place that I can bring you right now, especially with this fucker following us."

The structure, though ravaged by flames, still had a certain type of … familiarity to it. In its former glory, it must've been a homely place, where young beasts ran around with their friends; elders sat around a fire, talking about life; and leaders like Luciano made war plans.

Once Luciano stepped out of the car, he grabbed my hand, his warmth around mine.

"Yeosin," he murmured, his voice a soft growl that sent shivers down my spine, "this used to be our home. One day, I will rebuild it for you and our family. I don't care how long it takes. I promise you that our life won't always be like this."

I squeezed his hand and stepped into the house. What had it looked like before the dragons ruined it? The walls were now crumbled, blackened by fire. The roof had caved in several places, leaving only ash.

Still, somehow, I knew that it had once been beautiful.

"I can't believe they did this," I whispered, clenching my fists.

I knew that they had. I knew they were capable. And part of me knew they would happily cause this destruction.

But how could anyone want destruction and death like this? What had caused the dragons to hate the beasts this much? Why had the war begun again? And why weren't the dragons satisfied that they had killed almost every one of them?

While I might've been born human, I was becoming more beast every day, and these ruins were a part of our history. The dragons had stolen something precious from us, and I couldn't stand the thought of them going unpunished.

"I won't let them get away with this," I growled, canines lengthening.

We walked through the ruins, Luciano pointing out where the dining hall used to be, the grand staircase that had once led to the upper floors, and the courtyard where pack members would gather for celebrations.

I tried to picture it all, imagining the laughter and the sense of community that had once thrived here. But it was hard, especially when Luciano was looking over his shoulder, waiting for Gideon to walk in because he was definitely here with us now.

"It must've been beautiful," I said.

"It will be again," Luciano said, tugging me behind him in the kitchen that led out into the backyard. He turned toward the door we had entered, his body tensing. "If you're going to follow us, you might as well show yourself, Gideon."

Gideon emerged from the other room, his gaze cast on the ground. Usually, he wasn't so submissive, so saddened. I had only seen the nice but stern part of Gideon a handful of times at the coffee shop.

But he looked … almost sad here.

"I was just about to bring Yeosin to your grave," Luciano said. "Care to join us?"

"No, I am here to ensure Yeosin's safety," Gideon said, straightening himself out. "She's not safe here."

Conflicting emotions surged inside me, but I buried them all away and stayed put behind Luciano. He didn't trust Gideon for a reason, and I trusted Luciano. I wanted answers just as badly as my mate, but I had made a promise to myself that I would have Luciano's baby.

Our baby.

"I'm fine," I finally said once the tension became enough.

"Is that so?" Gideon peered at Luciano. "She carries our future after all."

"Our future?" Luciano growled. "Yeosin is my mate, Gideon. Don't overstep."

Gideon's expression remained calm, but there was a glint of mischief in his eyes. "I've tried to be nice. I've tried to protect her. Most importantly, I've tried to keep quiet about the curse, but Yeosin deserves to hear the truth for her own protection."

I furrowed my brow. "What are you talking about? What don't I know?"

"Shut your fucking mouth before I tear it off," Luciano snarled.

Gideon stepped forward. "Do you want to know why you feel this connection with both—"

Before Gideon could finish his sentence, a deafening roar echoed through the ruins. The sky darkened as massive, winged creatures descended upon us. The dragons were here. They had found us, and we were alone.

YEOSIN

FLAMES LICKED at my skin as I huddled behind a crumbling wall, clutching my belly. Out of all the fucking times that the dragons could attack, why did it have to be now?! The scent of charred wood filled the air, the smoke nearly choking me.

I held a hand over my mouth and nose in a measly attempt to block it from entering my body. My mind was racing, but my anger burned hotter than any dragon fire. Luciano had already shifted into his beast form, standing a few feet from me and throwing a fallen beam away from me. His canines were lengthened, and parts of his fur were burning.

Wings sprouted from Gideon's back, and he took flight to chase down the dragon spurting fire from his mouth. They raced through the air, flying in circles so quickly that even down here, I could feel the wind from their speed.

Gideon's shriek pierced through the darkness, as the dragon had taken a chunk of meat off his abdomen. My eyes widened, and I kept myself hidden behind the wall, not knowing what to do.

I didn't want to stay hidden. I wanted to fight.

But I knew it wasn't smart. I knew they were here for me. Maybe for my baby.

"Come with me!" Luciano shouted.

After peering around the wall, I caught Luciano holding back his hand for me. My heart pounded in terror as a dragon who had been hiding suddenly swooped in through the broken roof, spreading fire all inside the kitchen.

"Luciano!" I screamed, my voice raw. "Watch out!"

Luciano dragged his claws against the dragon's underbelly, opening it up. Blood and guts rained down upon us, and the dragon lost balance and dived headfirst into the living room beside me. I screamed and backed up into the wall.

Before the dragon could regain control, Luciano leaped at him, his howl sending shivers down my spine. He ripped the beast to literal meat pieces, throwing them back in the living room until nothing was left, except bare wings and a carcass.

As Luciano finished him off, another dragon swooped low and snatched me with its talons. I dived out of the way, the sharp claws cutting into my ribs, and shrieked out in pain, grasping the open wounds.

I couldn't let them take me. I ... I wouldn't. I'd promised myself I'd have Luciano's child.

Gideon swooped down toward the packhouse, blocking the dragon he had been fighting from breathing fire down onto Luciano. His wings ignited into flames, yet he didn't seem to be in pain.

"Get out of here!" he shouted at me. "Both of you."

Luciano snatched my hand and pulled me through the rooms toward an exit on the opposite side of the house. Fire crackled and popped above us, and the roof caved in, falling inches from me. We hurried out the door and into the woods.

"We need to get you to safety," he said.

I grabbed his hand tightly. "I'm not going anywhere without you."

"Yeosin," he snarled, tugging me through the woods, "it isn't an option."

"I won't run from them, not while you're fighting to keep me alive."

"I'm fighting to keep you alive because you're my mate," he said. "It's what I was made to do. To protect you. To protect our family and the baby inside your belly. I'm not allowing you to argue with me this time."

We began moving so fast that the forest became a blur of shadows and flames as Luciano and I darted between the trees, the roar of dragons echoing right behind us. They were on our tails, almost quite literally.

My breath came in ragged gasps, my heart pounding so loudly that I could hear it in my ears. Luciano tightened his grasp on my hand, but my legs couldn't move that much faster.

"Keep moving, Yeosin! We need to find shelter."

Move faster, Yeosin. If not for your life, then for your baby's!

Suddenly, a deafening roar filled the air, and a massive shadow loomed above us. I peered up in time to watch a dragon swoop down with its talons outstretched. Before I could react, Luciano pushed me aside, taking the brunt of the attack, sprawling to the ground.

The dragon landed right on his back, his talons sunk deep in his muscle.

"Luciano!" I cried, reaching out helplessly.

"Run, Yeosin!" he shouted. "Don't let them take you!"

I wanted to run to protect our family, but my legs and my heart ... couldn't make me. I struggled to my feet, but I had twisted my ankle on the fall down. Alvin descended, his massive wings beating the air around me and his talons circling around my belly.

He lifted me off the ground. I kicked. I screamed. I tried to escape.

Yet the world tilted around me, and I found myself staring

down at my mate. At the father of my unborn baby. At the man I loved.

"Luciano!" I shouted with all my might, reaching out for him as if he could change all of this, as if he could ... make all my problems go away. He had always done it for me before. "Luciano!"

Alvin pulled me higher into the air, then suddenly, the treetops became a blur of dark green and fire underneath me as we flew quickly.

Alvin nestled me closer to his body. "I have you now, Yeosin. You're all mine."

FIFTY-FIVE

YEOSIN

DAMN IT, *my eyes burn.*

I stirred on something rough against my bare skin and wiped my eyes furiously with my fists. When the pain subsided, I slowly blinked my eyes open and sat up the best I could on a nest of twigs, stones, and gold.

Where am I?

I squinted through the dim light that flooded into the room through cracks in the cavern walls. My entire body ached, especially my ribs, but I did my best to support myself and pulled my knees to my chest, the sound of metal scraping against the ground making me jerk.

When I glanced down at my ankles, thick metal shackles were snapped around them. Slowly, memories began rushing through my mind, and I sucked in a sharp breath. The dragon, Alvin … he had captured me.

After dropping my gaze, I swallowed hard and realized that I hadn't just been captured by Alvin, but that I was sitting in … I was sitting in a nest, one that reeked of long, endless nights filled with pleasure.

Except … nothing about Alvin had ever been pleasurable.

Wiry twigs and rough stone lay underneath me, hiding the scattered bones and torn woman's underwear. I inhaled the scent of smoke drifting in from the other room and realized that … I needed to get out of here. Now.

I stood on wobbly legs, the chains clinking with each movement.

How do I get out?

After stumbling out of the nest, I stepped into the huge space that was big enough to fit a dragon comfortably, the ceilings tall. Flickering torches cast shadows on the stone walls. At the far end of the room, light flooded into the … into the cave. Yeah, that was what I was calling it.

My throat dried as I made my way toward the opening, the ground uneven underneath my feet. When I approached the opening, stones tumbled off the edge and disappeared into the abyss of darkness.

Once I grabbed on to the wall, I stared over the edge and swallowed hard. I was hundreds of feet up in the air, above the trees, so high that I couldn't even see the bottom. The forest stretched out as far as I could see, and I'd bet it looked like a sea of green in the morning. But that didn't change the fact that if I fell—or leaped—from here that I would die.

Stepping back from the ledge, I placed a hand on my swollen belly. I had to find a way out, for both of us and for Luciano. Tears pricked the corners of my eyes. Last time I had seen him, he was about to die …

A sob left my mouth, and I dropped my head. He had to be safe. He had to.

I couldn't accept his death. I *needed* him more than anything. He had changed my entire life for the better. He had given me something to live for. He had *saved* me more times than he even knew about.

Maybe Gideon … maybe Gideon had saved him.

That was the only hope that I had left.

After wiping away my tears, I sniffled and scanned the room for an exit. I would be gone by the time that Alvin returned. I didn't care if I had to climb down that ledge and find a vine to slide all the way down to the forest floor.

I refused to let him touch me.

Once I found an exit, I hurried to it, only to make it six inches from my escape, the binds on my ankles keeping me here.

"No, no, no, no, no," I muttered, shaking my head and grabbing a rock. I smacked it against the shackles over and over and over, hoping that I could get it to break. Beads of sweat began rolling down my neck.

Why is it suddenly so hot?!

I slammed the rock into the shackles a couple more times, shaking my head when I couldn't break them. No matter how hard I tried, I wasn't even making a dent in them.

There has to be something here to help me out …

My gaze shifted from the carvings on the walls that depicted dragons in flight, their powerful wings spread wide. Near the back of the cave, I spotted a small chest overflowing with treasure. Among the hoard, a collection of scrolls caught my eye.

What is that?

After glancing over my shoulder, I stood and tiptoed over to it. Maybe this had something to do with my whereabouts and how to get home. Surely, it had to be a map or some secret that I could use against Alvin one day.

I picked up the charred scroll and unrolled it, and my brows furrowed. *What is this?*

The Triad's Bond Curse

By the desire of the gods, let it be known that The One who dares to mate with the Bird of Fire, the Dragon, and the Beast shall be bound by this curse for all eternity:
From the claws of the Beast, may your soul be eternally restless, driven by primal urges and wild instincts. From the flames of the Bird, may your heart forever burn —

Someone snatched the scroll away from me, then wrapped his hand around my throat, pinning me to the stone-cold wall. Alvin smirked down at me, his eyes glowing with colors that I had never seen before.

"You've always been so curious, Little Mouse," he murmured, lifting my chin and drawing a claw up my jaw. "So curious that it has gotten you in more trouble than a soft little girl like you can handle."

CHAPTER
FIFTY-SIX

LUCIANO

YEOSIN SCREAMED my name from high above me, but I couldn't see her. A dragon's claws raked across my rib cage. Pain exploded through my body. I struggled as much as I could, but he was pinning me down with all his might.

"Yeosin!" I shouted.

"Luciano! Help me! Please, help me!"

Fuck, I can't lose her! Not like this. I will do anything.

A burst of fire burned the flesh on my left side, the sudden hiss of the flames making it impossible to hear Yeosin anymore, if she was even close. For all I knew … they had taken her. They had taken my mate!

I turned away as harshly as I could in a measly attempt to escape. "Yeosin!"

From above me, Gideon struck the dragon in the side and knocked him off me. He sank his talons into the dragon's neck. The dragon breathed fire all over him, and Gideon's body burned, but he took no damage.

None.

It almost … made him stronger.

After Gideon ripped out his throat, the dragon collapsed onto the forest floor. I rolled onto my side, attempting to put out my burning flesh while choking on the heavy smoke.

Gideon shifted into his human form. "You should—"

"Get away from me," I spit, stumbling to my feet and clutching my ribs.

He approached. "We need to—"

I weakly shoved him backward. "I said to get away from me. Where's Yeosin?"

"Alvin took her."

Rage rattled every part of my body. I seized him by the throat and slammed him against a tree, my wound so deep that my abilities wouldn't let me heal as quickly as I usually could. "Where were you when Yeosin was taken?!"

Gideon shook his head, but didn't try pushing me away. "I was fighting off dragons myself. We need to stay focused. I'm not your enemy, Luc. We need to work together if we're going to save her."

"Don't call me that," I said. "You lost that privilege when you came back to fucking life."

Still, I couldn't wrap my head around how he was still alive, how he had come back to life. And it surely was convenient that as soon as I was about to show Yeosin his body, the dragons had attacked us.

Once I shoved him back, I turned around and stumbled through the woods, back toward the packhouse that was engulfed in flames. I had no sense about where they had gone off to, where they had taken my mate.

But I had to start somewhere. I had to find her.

"Luciano," Gideon said, following after me, "you need to be healed first."

"No, I need to find her."

"She will be okay," he said to me.

"Okay?!" I snarled, turning on my heel and facing him again. "She'll be okay?!"

"They can't hurt her with fire," he said.

"They could burn her alive!" I shouted. "What the fuck are you on?"

"Luciano, you don't understand."

When he tried to approach me again, I stepped back because I was losing strength to physically fight him right now. I needed to save it so I could ... so I could get my mate and my family back. Now.

"I'm going to find her," I said between my canines. "Don't follow me."

"You need my help, and you know it," Gideon said. "We're stronger together."

I loathed how right he was. I fucking loathed it.

But if I wanted Yeosin back, he could help me. So could the Colossals. Only problem? I didn't trust either of them, and I didn't want to start when Yeosin's life was on the fucking line. How could I?

"I don't trust you," I growled, heading through the forest. "Just don't get in my way."

"I won't," Gideon said, placing a hand on my shoulder and twisting me north. "They went this way. I know where they live. I've been following them for years, gathering intel on them. We'll get Yeosin back, I promise."

FIFTY-SEVEN

GIDEON

I TRUDGED through the dense forest with Luciano a few feet behind me, his glare burning into the back of my head. The dark canopy cast shadows across the overgrown ground. The scent of pine drifted through my nostrils, reminding me of a time long, long ago.

When Luciano and I had run through this forest, first as a playful game of tag, then while we were training to become warriors, then during the night that the dragons attacked us, when he told me to run and never look back.

That night, he couldn't save me.

That night, I died.

That night, I had burned alive.

I peered over my shoulder, and Luciano scowled at me.

"Turn around and keep moving."

After turning back on the path, I let my gaze fall to the ground. Luciano didn't trust me, and I didn't blame him. I wouldn't have trusted me either. There were things that I couldn't explain, secrets burned into me.

"Luciano, I—"

His foot collided with the center of my back, and I hit the ground, belly-first. Still holding his wound closed, he stumbled over to me and kicked me as hard as he could in the ribs.

"I said to keep fucking moving."

"You're acting irrational," I said, taking another swift kick.

He placed his foot against the side of my head, pinning me to the ground. "Where have you been for the past decades? I buried your body. I fucking *buried* you. And now you're back? Now you're alive?!"

"I can explain."

"I gave you enough fucking time to explain, and you couldn't. I'm not following you to my death," Luciano said. "I'm not going to let you fucking kill me too. I'm going to find Yeosin myself, and then we're leaving."

"Leaving for where?" I asked. "The dragons will never allow that."

"I don't give a fuck," Luciano spit, shoving me away and walking in the opposite direction. He had no fucking idea where the dragons' den was, and he would never find it. Not as a beast. "Leave me and my mate alone."

Once he was far enough away to where I knew he wouldn't kick me again, I stood up on shaky legs. "She's my mate too," I called to him.

He tightened his fist, his entire body tensing as he stopped in the middle of the forest.

"How long have you been watching her?" he asked. "*Stalking* her."

"Longer than you."

Luciano whipped back around and glared at me, blood seeping between his fingers. If he didn't get help quickly, then he would pass out, and I'd have to drag his ass all the way to the mountain so the rest of our pack could heal him.

"I don't fucking believe you," he growled.

"Then why'd you ask?"

After a couple more silent moments, Luciano drew his tongue

across his teeth. "What's the orb? The orange one that Mom always knew about. Tell me what it is, and I'll think about trusting you."

I leaned on the closest tree and held my side, biting back a grunt. Luciano might've been wounded, but he was and would always be stronger than me in hand-to-hand combat. I had never met anyone as strong as him, not even the dragons.

"You're not going to believe me," I said honestly.

"Try me."

"Please," I pleaded. "Let me get you help first."

"Fucking useless," Luciano growled, turning around and walking through the woods.

The wind picked up, and I cursed to myself and hurried after him. "The orb is an egg."

Luciano stopped. "A what?"

"An egg."

"Bullshit."

"I told you that you wouldn't believe me."

"What kind of fucking egg is this?" he asked, pulling the orb out of his pocket.

With an orange glow, the sphere rolled around in Luciano's palm. My eyes widened at the sight of it because Mom had told me so much yet so little about it before she died. It was more than just an egg. It was a symbol.

A symbol of the firebird. The phoenix. My father.

"It's …" I started trying to figure out how to explain this all. I'd had decades to figure it out, and I still couldn't. I still had questions that had been left unexplained, questions that I might never find the answers to without Yeosin. "It's a phoenix egg."

His lip curled in disgust. "Liar."

"I swear, Luciano," I said, holding up my arms. "I don't know much. I've been trying to figure it all out for years now, but none of it makes sense. Mom told me that it was a phoenix egg. It's from my father."

"Your father was *my* father," Luciano growled. "Quit making shit up."

"No, he wasn't. Mom … Mom had an affair."

"She wouldn't have done that," he said. "Dad and she were mates."

"You don't get it. Mom was mated to more than one person, just like Yeosin."

YEOSIN

"GET OFF ME," I growled through gritted teeth, trying to shoulder Alvin away.

Alvin shoved me back, and I landed on the ground with a thud in his nest of gold and twigs and souvenirs that he had stolen throughout the years. In the mess of items were several glowing orange orbs, like the ones Luciano had earlier.

"Little Mouse," Alvin murmured, "I'm not letting you out of my sight. Not anymore."

"I hate you," I snarled, more so to myself.

There was no reason to say it aloud. Alvin knew how I felt about him, and it would be a waste of breath to go back and forth with him all night. I needed to find a way out of here even if he did plan on not letting me out of his sight.

I pulled my knees to my chest, the shackles clacking against the hard floor, then averted my glare from Alvin to the orange orbs.

What are those things? I picked one up and rolled it around my hand, letting it burn my skin.

Alvin leaned against the wall, arms crossed. "Curious?"

"Yes," I said. The more information I could get out of him, the better.

"They're eggs from your mother."

"Eggs? My mother?"

A low chuckle escaped his disgusting, shit-talking mouth, and he stalked around the room as if he were a god. I inhaled another whiff of smoke and stifled a cough. I didn't know if I could *believe* anything he said.

"Luciano didn't tell you?" He chuckled. "He probably didn't even know."

"Didn't know what?"

Alvin shook his head. "Weren't you friends with Gideon too?"

"No, Gideon isn't a friend."

Lie. I'd had regular conversations with him, and I *would* have considered him a friend before he started burning me regularly! Still, I didn't know what I thought about him anymore. Was he a friend or foe?

"Don't lie to me, Little Mouse," Alvin murmured, crouching down to my height.

I lifted my gaze to him and glared harder. "Let me out of here. Why are you doing this?"

"I'm doing this because you belong to me, just like your mother did."

"Stop with the lies," I snarled. "All everyone does is tell me half-truths. Either tell me everything or go back laughing with all your friends. It's not like I can escape from here. We're on a fucking cliff, and you've shackled me."

After giving me another shit-eating grin, Alvin turned away. I wasn't sure *how* I had ever liked—never mind *loved*—him. We had been together for a few years, and he had lied and lied and lied to me about everything.

Now he was my captor.

"If you want the truth, Yeosin, I want you to beg for it."

"I'm not going to beg you for anything," I growled.

Before I could say another word, Alvin captured me by my

throat, lifted me into the air, and slammed me against the hard wall made of rock. Something in my spine cracked, the sound echoing through the room. I winced and bit my lip hard to hold back a cry. Tears pricked the corners of my eyes.

What the fuck is wrong with him?!

"Beg. Me."

"No."

Alvin lengthened one of his nails into a large dragon claw and drew it down my chest. I glared at him and kept my mouth shut. I wasn't going to beg him for shit. I didn't need the answers that badly. They wouldn't be true anyway.

"Beg for it."

When I refused again, he sank his claw into the skin above my sternum, slicing so deep that I could feel him touch the bone. I bit back another cry, a thin layer of sweat beginning to cover my lower back.

Fuck, this hurts.

He sliced the talon lower and lower until he reached the top of my belly. Something feral inside me snapped, and I remembered the little pup that I was growing inside me. I couldn't let anything happen to the baby. I would never forgive myself.

"Stop!" I cried. "Please, stop."

"Beg, Little Mouse. Beg."

"Please," I said as his finger moved a millimeter lower. "Please, tell me."

"Make it believable."

"Please!" I cried, sweating and bleeding all over my belly. "Please, I want to know!"

Alvin pulled his talon out of me and dropped me to the ground. I landed with another thud and cradled my belly bump, tears streaming down my cheeks. Inside, I could still feel the faintest of heartbeats.

"Please, tell me," I whimpered. "Please. Please. Please, tell me, Alvin."

Alvin sucked the blood off his finger and walked to the edge of the room, overlooking the forest outside. "Your mother belonged to me. Your mother was *my* prisoner. I had only found out about you after I captured her. She had given you to another family to protect you."

"Why was she your prisoner?" I asked so he wouldn't hurt me again.

"It wasn't just her. I captured all the phoenixes, so the prophecy wouldn't come true."

I stared at my belly and shook my head, brows furrowed. What did he mean by phoenix?

"You're a phoenix," Alvin said. "Born to eliminate the dragon race, and I cannot let that happen. I will do anything to stop that from happening, Yeosin, even if that means capturing you for the rest of eternity, like I have with the others."

"I'm not a phoenix," I said. "It's impossible. I was a human before Luciano bit me."

"That's what I wanted you to think because I didn't want to lock you in the cells with the rest of them," Alvin murmured, moving closer to me once more. He leaned down and placed his hand on my sternum.

I flinched away, expecting him to hurt me further, but instead, he began healing me.

"Wh-what are you doing? Why wouldn't you want to lock me away? That's what you're doing now, isn't it?"

"Now, it is, yes," he murmured. "But I'm not locking you in the cells with the rest of them."

"Why not?"

"Because, Little Mouse, I already told you ..." He pushed some hair off my face. "You're mine."

CHAPTER
FIFTY-NINE

"YOU BIRDS HAVE ALWAYS AMAZED ME," Alvin murmured, tucking some hair behind my ear with his free hand. "Your mom did. Your father. Even Luciano's mother ... I've always wanted a bird of my own."

Luciano's mother? Was Luciano some kind of phoenix too? No, she couldn't have been.

"You are a bird," I growled at him. "You have wings, talons, flight, *fire*."

Alvin brushed his fingers down my open wound. "Not one like you."

I stayed completely silent and eyed the wound, unable to believe that he wasn't trying to hurt me anymore. All this time ... all this freaking time, he had tortured me. Why help me? Why *heal* me after all the pain?

The wound completely closed, leaving no sign of even the faintest of scars.

"You're psychotic," I whispered. "Completely and utterly fucking psychotic, Alvin. Let me out of here. Let me go home. I'll visit whenever you want if that's enough."

"No, it's not enough."

"I'll promise to never hurt you or the dragons," I whispered. "Please."

"It's too late for that," he said. "You're already pregnant. If you don't, she will."

"No, she won't," I tried to reason. "I won't tell her about you."

"It doesn't matter if you tell her about us or not. She'll still find out."

I racked my brain for any memory of weakness that Alvin had shown in the years we were together, for anything that I could use against him, for anything that I could grab to get out of this situation. There had to be something.

"No, she won't," I repeated in an attempt to stall as I thought.

Alvin shook his head and moved closer to me. I shuffled backward and swallowed hard, hoping that he couldn't see how terrified I was that Luciano would never be able to find me up here, that Alvin would keep me as his forever.

"You still don't get it," he murmured. "You're mine. Mine. *Mine.*"

Mine? Why did he keep repeating that word? Why was he so focused on that? If he really cared about me like he claimed he did, then he wouldn't have broken up with me weeks ago. Then he wouldn't have hurt me.

Only Luciano said I was his with such possessiveness.

"I belong to Luciano," I said, holding his harsh stare. "Luciano, not you."

"Is that what he told you? That you were only his?"

"That's what I know. That's what *I* want."

"I don't care what you want, Little Mouse. It doesn't matter what *you* want."

My heart pounded so hard that I could hear it in my ears. I placed a hand on my belly bump to keep my baby safe as his words became more and more harsh, the longer he spoke. I couldn't chance him wounding me again.

"Many prophecies and curses have come true in this world,

not just the phoenix destroying the dragons." Alvin snatched my wrist and brought me over to the scroll I had been reading before he entered the room, and then he unraveled it.

"The Triad's Bond Curse. By the desire of the gods, let it be known that The One who dares to mate with the Bird of Fire, the Dragon, and the Beast shall be bound by this curse for all eternity," he began. *"From the claws of the Beast, may your soul be eternally restless, driven by primal urges and wild instincts. From the flames of the Bird, may your heart forever burn with an indescribable desire. From the scales of the Dragon, may he mark your flesh and bind you with him for eternity. The Triad's Bond Curse shall neutralize any other prophecy and unify them as one species of the forest."*

My mouth dried, and I swallowed to moisten it.

"That's not what it says," I whispered, knowing what this meant.

Alvin held the scroll out for me. "Read it for yourself."

I scanned down the scroll, heart pounding. No ... no ... no!

Gideon was right. Gideon was my mate, alongside Luciano. But not only that ...

So was Alvin.

Or at least, that was what Alvin hoped was true. His ego was big enough to believe that this prophecy talked about him, not any other dragon. Even if this prophecy *was* true and it *did* include Alvin, it wasn't about me, right? It *couldn't* be about me.

No, I refused to believe it.

I refused to believe that I was a phoenix. I refused to believe that I was mated to all three of these animals. And part of me refused to believe that this wasn't all just some sort of made-up dream to help me escape reality.

Soon, I would wake up the day before Alvin broke up with me. Soon, this would all be a distant memory, a dream that ... that I ... a dream that I would miss with my entire heart. A baby I would miss. A mate I would miss.

"You're my mate, Yeosin," Alvin murmured. "And I'm never letting you go."

CHAPTER
SIXTY

YEOSIN

I STARED through the opening at the end of my prison at the dark sky, my eyes becoming heavy. Even if I could get out of these shackles, I wouldn't be able to leap off this cliff and survive, and I wanted to survive for Luciano and our baby.

Alvin was gone, for now, leaving me alone in my chains. My wrists were raw from the metal sinking into my skin. But this pain was nothing compared to what Alvin could do to me, nothing compared to what Luciano would do *for* me.

Pine drifted through my nose, teasing—*no, testing*—me. I needed to get out of here.

But I couldn't escape as a human. If Alvin was being honest about me being a phoenix, then that must've meant that I had powers, right? Maybe I could use magic. Would that work? Though Alvin wouldn't leave me alone if he thought I could use it to escape …

My eyes slowly shut, and I thought back to all those times that Gideon had burned me in my dreams, in my nightmares. Phoenixes burned alive, didn't they? Did Gideon know that I had been a phoenix all this time? Was he one too?

I snapped my eyes open. Maybe he was onto something.

Do I have to burn myself alive to gain my powers?

In the hallway, a lantern flickered against the stone. I stood up from Alvin's filthy nest and moved toward the door, being careful not to make too much noise with my shackles. I didn't want to alert Alvin.

The farther I walked, the more the chains pulled on my wrists and ankles. The lantern was feet away—feet away from my freedom, feet away from me burning alive and burning down this dungeon, freeing all the people Alvin had said he captured, seeing my mate again.

Three feet away, and the chains tugged at my ankles.

Fuck.

No. No. No. No. No. No. Come on! I'm so close.

I strained against my chains, stretching as far as I could, every which way. Nothing. I pulled harder, my muscles screaming at me to stop, but I couldn't. I needed to get out of here before Alvin came back. I had no other choice.

Suddenly, something moved in my peripheral vision. I snapped my gaze to the room across the circular stone hallway and spotted two figures in the shadows. I squinted to make them out. Two young girls—one with eyes that glowed a haunting orange, the other larger in stature with an almost-innocent, youthful face.

The first had to be a dragon; the second looked similar to a Colossal.

"Hey," I whispered, bringing my body back to its normal position. "Can you help me?"

Dragon Girl hesitated, orange eyes widening and pointing toward Colossal. Colossal peered back at her, both not saying a single word. I crouched down and softened my gaze in an attempt not to look like a threat.

"Please," I said. "I won't hurt you. I just need to get out of here."

"We don't have a key," Colossal said. "He keeps them on him."

"I don't need a key. I just need the lantern."

Dragon Girl stepped into the light. "Why do you need the lantern?"

"To escape."

The other girl stepped into the light, next to the dragon, and I noticed they were also bound by chains, but theirs stretched further. Alvin said that all the other prisoners were in a dungeon. Why were their two young girls in the bedrooms?

My stomach twisted, and bile rose in my throat. *I don't want to know.*

"Why should we trust you?" Dragon Girl asked, an unreadable expression on her face.

She didn't trust me, and I understood why if they were prisoners up here too.

I raised my arms to show them that I wasn't someone who wanted to hurt them. "I'm not your enemy. Alvin is keeping me here against my will too. If I escape, I'll free you too. All I need is the lantern."

After sharing another look, they moved toward the lantern, their chains barely brushing against the ground. They must've been here for a long time to perfect walking through the bedroom and hallway without making a sound.

Colossal grabbed the lantern from the hallway and handed it to me.

"Thank you," I whispered, tears pricking my eyes. "I promise I'll get us out of here."

Once I reached into the lantern, I grabbed the candle and pulled it out. Just as I placed the flame near my finger, my baby kicked my stomach. I jerked the candle back and sucked in a sharp breath. The flames ... it was as if the baby was telling me the flames would kill her too.

But what was worse?

Her dying a peaceful death now, or … her living as a slave to Alvin.

What would Luciano want? Would he accept me if I killed both of us to be reborn? Would setting myself on fire even give me another life, give me powers? What if Alvin was wrong? What if I really wasn't a phoenix?

CHAPTER
SIXTY-ONE

THE BABY KICKED AGAIN against my stomach. Tears ran down my cheeks. *How can I do such a thing to her? How can I kill her when this was what Luciano hired me to do? After he told me how he felt?*

"Hurry," Colossal whispered, looking over her shoulder. "He will come back soon."

My stomach twisted into knots, and I backed up farther into my room because I didn't want them to see me burn alive. I didn't want to put them through that torture, to hear my pleas to save me from the pain.

They were right. I didn't have time to waste.

I pushed my finger into the fire and watched as it immediately ignited into flames. The fire crawled up my forefinger, engulfed my hand, and continued up my arm and to my shoulder. I waited and I waited and I waited for the pain.

But it never came. At least not how I'd imagined it.

My baby kicked uncontrollably, the more fire engulfed my body. Tears flowed from my eyes at how cruel I was to do this to her. She didn't even get to experience life, and I would kill her before she could take a single breath.

Enough of my wrist shriveled up or burned off in flakes that I slipped out of one of the four shackles.

Maybe I can do this. Maybe my entire body doesn't need to burn for me to escape out of here!

So, I ignited my other wrist and my two ankles, setting more of myself on fire. Flesh burned off into ash. My tears melted away. I was hot and hot and hot and hot, but it didn't hurt.

What hurt the most was feeling my girl …

Moving. Struggling. Begging me to stop.

But I was close. So, so close.

Vision blurring, I stumbled within the den and fell to my knees. I could barely see straight from the fire's haze, so I closed my eyes and tugged at the chains, desperate to get them off, to slip out of them, to disappear into the night.

"What's that smell?" someone growled, their voice distant.

While I tried my hardest to escape, my strength became weaker and weaker. I gripped the shackles on my legs as hard as I could and tugged away at them. I needed to get out of here right now.

All I could hear was the pounding of footsteps coming up the staircase. I screamed out in agony, not from the pain of the fire, but from the pain that I had done all this … all this and I might still not escape.

Suddenly, I got one of my ankles free.

The fire continued to burn at my body, my insides twisting and shrinking, my baby's strength diminishing as well. I grabbed my other ankle and slipped off the last shackle as someone approached to my left.

"Yeosin, you bitch," Alvin snarled from the other side of the room.

While I still couldn't see, I could feel. His presence. The room. Everything.

I shuffled to my feet and ran as fast as my body would take me toward the cliff. I didn't know why I ran that way. I didn't know how quickly I did. But one second, my feet were on solid ground, and the next, I was floating.

A strange calmness settled over me as my body descended toward the ground, still engulfed in flames. I opened my eyes and physically watched my body fall hundreds, if not thousands, of feet, in what I could only explain was an out-of-body experience.

Down and down and down.

I felt everything and then nothing.

No sound. No light. No sensation.

Nothing. Not even life itself.

CHAPTER
SIXTY-TWO

LUCIANO

MY LUNGS BURNED as blood continued to gush out of my wound. I had lost Gideon miles ago, but continued to follow his directions to where the dragons' den was *supposedly* stationed—on top of some cliffs near the mountain that housed my pack.

Did I believe him? No, but I had no other leads.

Yeosin was gone—*had been* gone for far too long. And her faint scent lingered here.

Someone shouted up ahead, and my gaze locked on to a ball of fire falling from the sky. I furrowed my brows and pushed myself forward. The lower and lower it fell, the stronger Yeosin's scent became. And then I saw it ... her long black hair in flames.

Mate!

I shifted into my beast to run faster and then back into my human, my arms outstretched to catch her before her flaming body smashed into the ground. She collided with me, and we both crashed into the forest floor.

"Yeosin," I shouted, rushing to the nearest lake that I had passed on my way here.

Her flames engulfed my body, burning hotter than anything I

had ever felt before, but the adrenaline rushing through me pushed me further and further toward the lake. Her head was lolled backward, and her bones protruded from parts of her skin.

My hands trembled, and I ran into the water, dunking us both under until the flames died. When I emerged from the lake, I set Yeosin on the dirt beside it and checked for a pulse. Nothing … there was nothing.

"Yeosin …" I whispered, my voice cracking. "Yeosin … no, no, no, no!"

Panic squeezed at my throat. I placed my hands over her chest, made of bones, to start CPR. Tears blurred my vision. I pumped and pumped and pumped in no steady rhythm because I … my mate … our baby …

"Please, come back to me. Please, please, please, come back to me."

Someone grabbed my shoulders and yanked me backward off Yeosin. Flakes of her skin danced in the air, her bones hanging together by tendons and ligaments and a thin layer of skin. I shoved whoever it was off and dropped by her side to continue.

"Luciano!" Gideon shouted behind me, grabbing me again. "Luciano, stop!"

"I will kill those fuckers!" I shouted at the top of my lungs. "Burn them all!"

Gideon shoved me off her. "Calm down. We need to think."

"Think?!" I screamed. "She's fucking dead, Gideon!"

How the fuck could I think at a time like this? My mate was dead. My baby was dead. My life was fucking gone. Every chance I'd had at having a family, at being happy … had been burned by those fucking dragons.

Instead of pulling me back again, Gideon knelt beside me. "I can help."

"No!" I shouted, unable to pull my gaze away from my lifeless mate. "You can't do fucking shit. She's dead!" Tears stung my eyes, yet I was full of rage. "I can't lose her. I can't fucking lose her after everything."

I stood to my feet and turned toward the cliff she had fallen from. Those fuckers were up there. They had to be up there! I shifted into my beast and ran as fast as I could toward the mountain. I would climb the fuck up the edge if I had to.

Once I made it to the mountain, I leaped as far up as I could and latched my claws into the dirt. Gideon grabbed me again and hurled me to the ground, standing between the mountain and me, his eyes blazing.

"You're not going to get yourself killed too," he growled.

"I'm going to kill them."

"They'll kill you!"

"I don't care anymore! I have nothing else to live for. Move the fuck out of my way."

Gideon shoved me back again, this time with so much force that I hit a tree, and suddenly, all the adrenaline that I had been running on for the past few hours evaporated. And a wall of weakness hit me all at once.

"You don't have nothing to live for," Gideon said. "Yeosin isn't gone. Neither is your baby. They're phoenixes, the strongest creatures in this land. They can be tortured, imprisoned, enslaved, but they can never truly die."

CHAPTER
SIXTY-THREE

YEOSIN

BLINDING white light jolted me awake. I sat up from my prone position and shielded my face with my forearm, slowly blinking my eyes open. *Where am I? Dead? Is this the afterlife? Do I even believe* in an afterlife?

When my vision adjusted to the bright light, I fully opened my eyes and stared at the world around me. My body lay to the left of me. Nobody was around, but there were footprints showing me that someone had been here recently.

And everything … was quiet. Too quiet.

I walked to the body and crouched down next to it, my heart pounding inside my chest.

I am in the afterlife. How could I see myself otherwise?

Tears pricked the corners of my eyes, and I reached to brush my fingers against my belly bump in my physical body. As my fingers touched my burned corpse, something kicked inside *my* stomach. My ghostly stomach.

How … how is this possible?

My baby kicked inside my belly, over and over, more active than she had ever been. I placed a hand on my own stomach, the tears stinging my eyes. I wished that my baby had survived so Luciano had someone.

Once I turned back to my body, I cupped my face in my own hands. My tears fell onto the burned and scarred corpse. As my metaphorical tears collided with my real body, an explosion of emotions erupted within me.

I could hear smells, see tastes, smell sounds. The dead world around me exploded into colors, sensations, vibrations. Creatures that hadn't been here before were now walking around me, their bodies so … real.

"What is this place?" I whispered to myself.

The baby did somersaults inside my belly, and I could almost hear her giggling, could almost see her smile right in front of my face, her cheeks chubby, and all that thick hair that she had gotten from Luciano.

A sob escaped my mouth. This world was so cruel for torturing me like this.

I could've had this all if I had lived …

"Lived?" someone asked, taking my hand and pulling me to my feet. "You are alive."

"No. No, no, no, no, no, no," I whispered. "I'm dead."

It was certain. It had to be certain. I had burned alive. I remembered it. I'd *felt* it.

"My dear," she said, lifting my face in her hands. Her eyes were burning the brightest shade of orange, her veins visible through her skin, glowing as brightly as her eyes. "You're alive. I promise you that you're alive."

"I can't be. I felt it."

"Your body might have perished, but your mind is free. Your soul is free. You are a phoenix. You will be reborn and granted another life, one full of power and freedom." She pushed hair out of my face. "But as one of the only phoenixes not enslaved, you have duties."

I shook my head. "No, I … I can't. I can't help anyone."

I hadn't been able to help anyone in my previous life. I had to get those girls to help me because I wasn't capable of escaping by myself. I had gotten so many people killed, put so many people in danger.

This was all … because of me.

"Follow me," the woman murmured, wings extending from her back.

She took my hand and leaped off the ground, beginning to float in the air. And suddenly, I was too. My eyes widened from how easy this was, and I looked behind me to see a set of large orange wings had extended from my back too.

What the hell is—

"They're your wings." She giggled. "You'll get used to them. Trust me."

"Trust you?" I exclaimed. "There are wings in my back!"

She continued to fly upward and toward the dragons' den, where I had just escaped from. "Your baby has them too. She's a phoenix. The first phoenix to be born and reborn at the same time." She placed her hand on my belly and smiled. "I'm so happy for you, Yeosin. You've grown so much."

"You know my name?" I asked, brows furrowed. "How?"

After pausing for a brief moment, she ignored my question and redirected her attention to the cliff I had leaped off of. We touched down on the edge and walked into the empty room.

"It was brave of you to burn yourself. Most phoenixes don't believe in their abilities to be reborn and wait until death."

"Brave?" I mumbled, walking to the stairs and glancing around for the kids who had helped me escape.

The castle, den, whatever it was, it was eerily silent in terms of sounds I was used to. I took a step down the stairs, following a sensation that pulled me downward.

A sensation that ached for me to find it.

The woman moved closely behind, not speaking a word.

I wandered through the den, searching each and every room but finding no physical bodies. The sounds that I could hear, that I could *experience*, were loud yet dull at the same time. Coming from everywhere yet nowhere at once.

"What are these … feelings?" I asked, finding myself at a thick dungeon door.

"A shared consciousness," she said. "All phoenixes gain access when they're reborn."

My baby twirled inside me, as if she could hear and see and feel everything too. I placed a hand over my bump and the other hand on the thick door. Electricity—or more like a jolt of all the pain that'd ever happened within these walls—zipped through my entire body. I yanked my hand back and stared in horror at the door.

"What's beyond here?" I asked. "Surely, you know."

The woman pushed the door open with ease, revealing hundreds, if not thousands, of phoenixes trapped in a dungeon, being tortured by the dragons. My eyes widened further, and I stepped backward.

This was the place Alvin had mentioned …

"You need to save them, Yeosin," the woman said to me. "The fate of the phoenixes depends on you and your child. Help free us from the chains the Dragon Clan has trapped us in. Free your family."

My gaze slowly drifted from the room to her again. "Who are you?"

"One day," she murmured, tucking some hair behind my ear, "I hope to tell you."

And with that, I was suddenly back in the forest, sitting over my body. Alone.

CHAPTER
SIXTY-FOUR

LUCIANO

"WE NEED to finish burning her body," Gideon said.

I stood in front of my mate and stared at my brother, the anger boiling inside me. *How can I allow such a thing? How can he suggest such a thing?*

Yeosin had just burned alive. If she was really a phoenix, she would've been reborn now, wouldn't she?

Gideon tried to sidestep me to get to my mate, but I shoved him back.

"No."

"Yes. It's the only way to bring her back," Gideon said, as calm as ever. "If the dragons hadn't attacked, you would've found my body wasn't in the grave you'd buried me in. Someone dug me up and burned my body until there was nothing but bones left."

"Who?" I snarled, shoving him back again. "Who did that?"

"I don't know," Gideon said.

"Bull-fucking-shit you don't know. You know."

Gideon held his arms up. "I don't. Now, do you want to save her or not?"

My tongue glided across my lengthened canines, and then I

crouched down to Yeosin's corpse. I couldn't accept it. There had to be another way. We couldn't burn the only person to ever matter to me to ashes.

What if she wasn't a phoenix? Then I wouldn't have any part of her left.

I brushed my fingers against her exposed rib cage, then further down to her stomach. Tears stung my eyes. Inside her stomach, nestled around her charred organs, was the smallest corpse that I had ever seen, her bones so frail.

My fingers shook. My throat closed up. I pulled our baby out of Yeosin's stomach, and a sob that I hadn't known I was capable of escaped my throat.

"Our baby," I cried, holding it to my chest. "I'm sorry. I'm sorry. I should've protected you and your mother."

This is my fault. This is all my fucking fault. And I need to fix it.

"I know it's hard," Gideon started, "but this is the only way."

"How can you ask me to do this?" I cried.

"Her death has given us a chance to bring her back," Gideon said. "Let me do it."

"There has to be another way," I whispered, placing our baby back into her stomach and picking up what was left of her. I stood to my feet and scanned the forest, finding a path that led to the mountain where my pack was hiding out. "There has to be a healer who can help us."

I didn't trust Gideon. I wanted to, but I didn't.

"I'm so sorry, my love," I murmured against her forehead, walking through the woods.

"Where are you going?" Gideon asked, following quickly behind me. "We need to burn—"

"Let me try to find another way," I pleaded, feeling the grief in my bones.

When Gideon suddenly stopped, I turned my head to look back at him. I expected him to continue forward with me, continue pestering me about this, continue demanding that we burn her body right here and right now. But he didn't.

Instead, he nodded. "Okay, I will be here when you're ready."

I nodded and turned back toward the mountain, ready to make the journey to bring my mate back to life. I didn't care how long it took, but I knew I needed to get there soon. I knew I needed to bring her back to life as soon as magically possible.

Yeosin's corpse was cold in my arms, yet my body felt warm, like something was holding or *hugging* me from behind. I wanted so desperately to believe that it was Yeosin, but she was dead. Dead and not alive. Not in any timeline.

The forest around me was eerily silent, the only sound the rustle of leaves beneath my feet and the occasional cry that escaped my lips. With every step, my legs became heavier and heavier. So many memories lost. So much time ... lost. So much love ... lost.

Time passed so agonizingly slowly, but I finally found my way to the mountain. My pack—some people who I hadn't seen in years—was crowded at the entrance, as if they had sensed my presence.

"What happened?" one of the elders asked.

Throat tight with emotion, I pressed my lips together and held back my tears, walking through the path of beasts that parted for me. Beasts called for doctors and healers to the front, each bringing magic or devices that could heal my mate.

Nobody here, except Molly and Ella, had met Yeosin, but everyone seemed to know that she meant something to me. I placed Yeosin on a table carved out of rock in the center of the meeting room and collapsed by her side, tears sliding down my cheeks.

"Please, someone, help her," I pleaded. "Please, save her and my child."

Ella appeared before the doctors, her eyes wide and on Yeosin. Her brows quivered, and she looked up at me with tears in her eyes. The last time I had seen her, she had wanted Yeosin dead so she could take Yeosin's place.

"What happened?" she whispered.

"She fell from the Dragon Clan's den in the sky," I said. "Burning alive."

"Luciano ..." Ella said, shaking her head as she approached Yeosin. "There's nothing ..."

"There has to be something you can do!" I exclaimed. "Don't fuck with me, Ella."

Ella opened and closed her mouth a handful of times, gaze dropping to Yeosin's belly, where our baby had burned alive too. Ella slapped a hand over her mouth and let out a sob that mirrored one of mine. "Oh my Goddess ..."

"Gideon said she is a phoenix. He wants to burn her body. I want you to heal her."

"I can't," Ella said. "Nobody here can. She's too far gone."

"No," I whispered, stepping closer. "There has to be a way. Tell me what to do."

"*I* can't do anything," she said. "If she is truly a phoenix, then Gideon is right. You must continue to burn her body, and there is a chance that she will return. It's a phoenix's nature. They must be consumed by the fire to be reborn."

"B-but what if she isn't ... what if I lose her for good? I can't do that."

"If there's any chance of bringing her back, you have to trust in the phoenix's power."

Molly stepped forward and placed a hand on my shoulder. "It's the only way."

"The only way?" I asked myself, staring down at my mate's corpse.

Is this really the only way? Do I have to lose her for her to be reborn? Was Gideon right?

"Okay," I whispered. "Okay, if it's the only way, then let's burn her. I need my mate back."

CHAPTER
SIXTY-FIVE

YEOSIN

MY CORPSE LAY upon a slab of stone within the mountain, covered in flames. I stood beside my mate and clutched him tightly, wishing that he could see and hear me. But nobody in the mountain could, not since I had burned alive and died.

"Don't cry," I whispered into his ear, wrapping my arms around him. "I'm here with you."

To my surprise, Luciano relaxed his body slightly, as if he could feel my touch, hear my words. I knew that it was impossible because he hadn't been able to see me during the entire trek to the mountain. Why would he start now?

I cuddled up next to him from behind, laying my ear against his large, muscular back, and closed my eyes. I hoped that once my body finished burning, I would return in one piece. But just like Luciano, I feared I'd be gone from this world forever.

"It's okay," I murmured. "You're so strong for doing this. So, so strong."

His shoulders jerked forward, and he released a low sob that only I could hear, one that I could *see* after my senses had heightened. It was like a dark mist, filled with lightning and heartbreak and desperation.

My body crackled, the flames eating the last of my skin and organs.

While Luciano's hand was engulfed in flames, he hadn't stopped holding my hand, squeezing the bones, as if … if he did, then I wouldn't completely melt away from him. His body was trembling uncontrollably in front of everyone, except he wasn't making a sound.

A man … filled with anguish but refusing to let anyone see it.

As my chest tightened, a tear slipped down my cheek. How much pain was he holding inside him? How much pain had festered since the first time the Dragon Clan had attacked and taken everyone away from him? When would he show me this pain so I could help him through it?

The scent and the sight of my burning flesh wafted up into my nose. Like his sob, I could *feel* the scent too—orange and red crisps and ashes, the sound like sharp nails scratching at the insides of a coffin.

Luciano fell out of my hold and dropped to his knees. The bones of my hands cracked away from my body and remained in his tight grasp. He clutched on to the stone and tried to stand back up, a sob escaping his mouth.

"Please, stay with me," he murmured. "Please, don't leave me. I need you."

I knelt in front of him and took his face in my hands, kissing his mouth. "I love you."

"I love you too," he whispered.

Just as confused, we looked at each other, his eyes widening more and more and more, filling with trembling tears. He shuffled backward, his gaze all over my body. Murmurs erupted all around the room as everyone stared at me in amazement.

But I could look at nobody other than my mate.

"Yeosin," he whispered, shaking his head as if he didn't believe it. "Yeosin, you're …"

"Alive," I said, breaking out into a choked laugh. "I'm alive. I'm here. Always."

Luciano wrapped me into his embrace and pulled me closer to him, his nose buried into the crook of my neck, right against the mark he had left so long ago. He kissed me over and over and over, as if to make sure that I was real.

Still, I could barely believe it either.

Once Luciano pulled back, tears covered his face. "I'm sorry … our baby …"

I placed his hand over my stomach. "Our baby is still alive. Don't worry."

When she kicked against his hand, Luciano let out another sob, this one like a kick to the gut. He dropped his hand to my belly and rested his forehead against the bump, holding on to it like he had with my skeleton.

I pushed my hand through his thick hair and pulled him closer, hearing and feeling and seeing his heart beat pounding through the air. Nothing could compare to this moment, to the newfound feelings and sensations running through me.

"I love you, Luciano," I started. "But this war isn't over."

After Luciano pulled away from me, I took his hand and looked around at the others. They stared between me and the wings that had formed on my back, ones similar to Gideon's. I stood up in front of Luciano, who remained on his knees.

"We must set the other phoenixes free, and you all need to help. They are trapped in the Dragon Clan's dungeons. I have seen them. They've been held captive, and only after setting them free will you all get to live in your homes again."

The group murmured to themselves, worry etched on their faces.

"We can't," Molly said to my left. "We've already tried once and failed."

"Last time, we didn't have Yeosin," Luciano finally said.

He stood next to me and captured my hand. And for the first

time in a long time, I finally saw the strength return to his eyes. I had thought we had lost it forever.

"Yeosin and Gideon will guide us," he continued.

"Gideon?" the others repeated. "He's dead!"

"He's alive," Luciano said. "Just like Yeosin, he's a phoenix."

"He will aid us, along with the Colossals," I said. "The dragons are powerful, but they will not be able to withstand an attack from all of us. We must free the phoenixes and avenge those the dragons have killed. And we must do it now, before they find us here."

WEAPONS CLINKED TOGETHER as I walked through the cave to where I had left Yeosin—a private sector of the mountain where we could spend time together tonight. Warriors nodded to me while contemplating our battle plans for tomorrow with each other.

"Luciano," Gideon called, standing with the Colossals and chatting with Ruby.

More like *flirting*, but I wasn't complaining. Got them both out of my relationship.

I peered down the cave and grimaced, really wanting to spend more time with Yeosin, but she needed rest. So, I returned my attention to my brother and started his way. He had been right this entire time.

"How's Yeosin?" he asked, brows furrowed.

"Good."

"Come on. That's all you're going to give me?" he asked.

After blowing out a breath, I nodded. "She's doing much better. Thank you for telling me what we had to do in order to bring her back to life. I owe you my life, brother. I wouldn't be here right now if it wasn't for you."

To my surprise, Gideon's expression softened. "You don't owe me anything."

I glanced between him and Ruby. "I see you've met ..."

Ruby stared up at Gideon, her cheeks pink. "A couple minutes ago."

"Does this mean that you and Yeosin ..." I asked Gideon.

"I realized that I am connected with her," Gideon said. "But only because we're both phoenixes. Not because she is my mate. She may be part of the prophecy, but maybe she's not. Maybe that prophecy is just bullshit."

I sure hope so because I won't let Yeosin mate with anyone else.

"The Colossals," I said to Ruby. "How are they?"

Ruby glanced behind her at her friends that I had gotten off on the wrong foot with one too many times. I had thrown so many accusations their way because my mate was in danger, but they didn't deserve it.

Or maybe they did. They'd prove their loyalty tomorrow.

"We have some people stationed around the mountain, keeping watch for the dragons. We all agree that most of us need rest before we attack tomorrow morning. We will defeat them for good this time."

"The dragons won't know what hit them," Gideon said to her, "with your power."

Ruby giggled softly to herself, one hand over her mouth. "You think?"

I raised my brows and took that as my cue to find my way back to my mate. After saying good night to some pack members, I walked through the cave to one of the back rooms, where Yeosin's scent became stronger and stronger.

"There you are," she murmured from the bed. "Everything okay?"

My pack had been living here for years, and one of the

members had given us permission to sleep in their room tonight. He had been a bit too excited to prove himself as a needed beast.

"We're ready for tomorrow," I said, lying down beside her.

She nestled against me. "Then let's enjoy tonight."

I wrapped my arms around her waist and pulled her closer to me, listening to the steady rhythm of her heartbeat.

Tomorrow, we would fight the Dragon Clan with two phoenixes, a group of Colossals, and a pack of beasts.

Tomorrow, we would fight for our future, for our family.

Mouth on her mark, I kissed it softly. Still, I couldn't believe that Yeosin was here with me again, along with our baby. She was alive after I had lost her, not once, but twice. I'd thought she was dead; I'd been willing to kill myself to find her in another life.

I closed my eyes, tears sliding down my cheeks. "When you died … I thought …"

"I know," she whispered, drawing her hands through my hair. "You don't have to relive it."

She took my hand and placed it on her growing belly bump. Somehow, it had grown since she had made it back. I didn't want her to come with us tomorrow, in case the dragons targeted our baby, but I knew we needed her.

Tomorrow, I had to trust her to be strong and smart, and I did.

"She's going to be a phoenix too, isn't she?" I hummed. "Strong like her mama."

"She'll be the first to be born as one." Yeosin beamed.

"How do you know that?"

"When I was dead, someone told me," she said. "Another phoenix trapped in the dungeon of the Dragon Clan. She showed me the horrors that the dragons have put the phoenixes through."

"Who was it?" I asked.

"I'm not sure, but she was"—she smiled softly—"really pretty and sweet."

I kissed her on the forehead. "Just like you."

Like she had when we first met the night at The Breeding

Cave, Yeosin blushed and shuffled in the bed nervously. I tugged her closer to me and pressed my lips to her temple, then her cheek, then her lips.

"We'll free her tomorrow," I said. "We'll free all of them."

CHAPTER
SIXTY-SEVEN

YEOSIN

DAWN LIGHT FLOODED AROUND the trees, creating patterns on the forest floor around me. I stared ahead at the path we'd take—one that we would *forge*—to step into a new life. Soon, the Dragon Clan would be gone. Forever.

Warriors shouted behind me, pumping each other up for the fight. I placed a hand on my belly bump and closed my eyes, hoping to connect to the phoenixes. That woman had said that we had a shared consciousness. But I had been trying *and failing* to activate it all night.

My baby kicked the inside of my stomach over and over, as if she was somersaulting inside of me, as if she was ready, excited even. One of these days, we would have to give her a name. That was, if we made it out alive.

The wind blew heavily around us, blowing the feathers of my wings back. I inhaled the sound of Luciano's footsteps—it was still weird, being able to experience sounds as smells or sight as touch—and moved into the forest.

"It's time to go," I said over my shoulder.

Once the warriors gathered all their weapons, they followed

through the woods. I clenched my fists, talons digging into the skin on my palms. We would win. We had to win. For the pack. For all the families lost. For all the families to come.

"Are you okay?" Luciano asked, capturing my hand.

I released my fist and softly gazed up at him. "Fine."

"That doesn't sound fine."

"I'm nervous," I whispered. "What if we're leading all these people to death?"

Luciano nodded. "We might be."

I smacked him on the shoulder. "That doesn't help!"

"It's the truth," he said honestly. "You haven't been in war before, so you don't know. To be a soldier, you have to be willing to lose everything, even your life. All the warriors behind us know that and accept that. They're fighting for freedom."

"Freedom," I repeated, a sudden pain through my head.

The trees spun around, and I grabbed on to Luciano to steady myself.

"Freedom," I said again.

Another pain split through my brain, and then I had a vision of the phoenixes in that vile prison, those girls that Alvin had locked up, all whispering, "Freedom," alongside me. Their bodies might've been caged, but their minds were free.

In this shared consciousness, they could be and do anything. They were limitless.

"Freedom." The woman from before entered my view. "Freedom." She extended her arm, offering me a soft smile. "Freedom." The word left her mouth, and suddenly, I was back with the group, inside the cages with them.

"Free our bodies," one said, her skin as red as her hair. "We've been waiting."

"Waiting for you," another said. "We're waiting for you to free us."

"Please, come," a male phoenix said. "We will help defeat the dragons together."

I stared around at the phoenixes in cages, my body suddenly on fire, like it used to be inside my dreams, when Gideon was the one igniting my body. But this time ... it couldn't be him. There was no reason for him to burn me anymore now that I was a phoenix.

No, my body was doing this on its own.

"They can't stop all of us," the woman said. "But you have to light the match."

Then a dungeon door hidden underneath vines flashed through my mind.

As quickly as I had entered the shared consciousness, or maybe it was a dream, I woke up and stared around. Luciano was carrying me in his arms, the warriors around him. I fluttered my eyelids open.

"What happened?" I asked.

"You passed out," he said, brows furrowed. "You're not going to fight today."

"Yes, I am," I said, scrambling out of his hold and looking around to take in my surroundings. We were more than halfway to the cliff. We were so close that I could smell the dragon's fire. "I'm fighting with you. I have to."

"You just passed out and were set on fire within your dream," he said, showing me his arms that were covered in burns, his skin charred. "I can't let anything happen to you or the baby. Do you hear me, Yeosin?"

"I didn't pass out, and it wasn't like my other dreams."

Molly shared a look with Luciano. "I think you should sit this one out too."

"No," I exclaimed. "I was talking with the phoenixes. They're going to help us."

"You were hallucinating," Luciano said. "You can't hallucinate during war."

"She's telling the truth," Gideon said. "I saw it too."

"You didn't pass out," Luciano growled at him.

Looks like they are back to hating each other …

"I was just a viewer," Gideon said. "I didn't interact with the others. It would've taken a toll on my body, like it did Yeosin's. She's telling the truth. The other phoenixes will help us. We just have to release them from their cages."

The others marched on, but there was a sudden sensation, a sudden urge for me to stop. Luciano paused, and then the other members followed. I glanced around, something feeling so eerily familiar.

We were going in the correct direction—I was sure of it—but …

I followed the urge further toward the left, like an invisible string was pulling me.

"Yeosin, where are you going?" Brent asked. "The Dragon Clan is this way."

"She is resting," Luciano said. "We will pause here. Molly—"

"I'm not resting," I said, hurrying as the sensation became stronger.

"Yeosin," Luciano growled, following me. "Come back!"

My legs moved quicker and quicker and quicker. Then, suddenly, I found myself stopping in front of a huge tree. I didn't know why. I didn't know for what. But I dropped to my knees and pushed some vines out of the way.

A dungeon entrance glimmered in the dawn light.

"We go through here," I said. "To free the phoenixes."

CHAPTER
SIXTY-EIGHT

YEOSIN

I GRABBED the metal handle and yanked on it with all my might, but it didn't budge. Dirt flew up from the ground, getting in my mouth. After spitting it out, I stood to my feet, grabbed the handle, and pulled on it again.

Still nothing.

Luciano growled under his breath. "Move out of the way."

Once I stepped to the side, he grabbed the handle with one hand, his biceps bulging, and pulled it open with ease. I stared at the veins on it, warmth growing between my thighs, then averted my gaze.

Gods, why is he so ...

"I'll go first," he said, staring down into the darkness.

I grabbed his wrist. "No, you can't go. Only me and Gideon."

"No fucking way," he snarled, eyes blazing a hundred different colors of jealousy and possession. He stood before me, his chiseled jaw clenched and his muscles bulg—

Control yourself, Yeosin!

"You're not going without me."

"We must go alo—"

Before I could finish my sentence, Luciano grabbed Gideon by the throat and slammed him up against a tree, his canines lengthened and dripping with saliva. "What the fuck did you tell her? What lie this time?"

Gideon raised his arms. "I didn't say anything to her."

"Gideon didn't say anything to me. I made this decision on my own."

Luciano glared at Gideon for a couple more moments, then dropped him and turned back toward me, his eyes now hurt. "Why don't you want me to come with you? I'm not letting you put yourself in more danger than you have to."

"Because you can't withstand the fire," I said. "If you or any of your beasts go down into the dungeon with me and the Dragon Clan finds out, then they will burn the mountain to the ground with all of us in it. You will have no chance of survival."

Gideon nodded. "That makes sense."

"No, it doesn't," Luciano growled.

Molly cleared her throat. "She's right. We should stay up here with the Colossals."

"We will wait for the dragons to make an escape, and then we'll catch them," Brent said.

Luciano pursed his lips, nostrils flared, fuming silently to himself. Then he finally released his clenched fists. "You have fifteen minutes, Yeosin. If you're not out by then, then we're coming in."

I stood on my toes and kissed him on the lips. "Deal."

Luciano placed his hands on my hips and squeezed gently. "Don't take any unnecessary risks." He pulled away and looked at Gideon. "Protect her with your life, or I will take yours if she doesn't come back alive."

"I will." Gideon nodded and peered at Ruby. "I'll be back."

What is that? Ruby and Gideon? Good. Gets her out of my mate's life.

Gideon slipped through the dungeon door and started down a ladder. I followed, peering up at Luciano one last time, my heart pounding quickly inside my chest. While I had been collected up until this point, suddenly, everything felt like the night the dragons had taken me away from Luciano.

My chest tightened, and tears pricked the corners of my eyes. Luciano was worried—and for good reason. What if this was the last time we saw each other? What if … they found him and killed him? I couldn't dwell on it.

I stared down the ladder and didn't look back up. We had to do this.

The air grew colder as we descended into the earth. Gideon grunted and hit the ground, grabbing my waist to help me down to the floor, as the ladder stopped a few feet from the bottom. I placed a hand on my belly.

"Which way?" I asked.

"Don't you know?"

"No."

Gideon lit the tip of his finger on fire and illuminated the paths. I stared at each one of them for a few moments, finding the energy that spoke to me the most, the path that was the strongest.

"I think it's this way," Gideon said, nodding toward the right, where I had decided to go.

I followed after him. "It is."

Gideon's breathing was steady, as if he wasn't half as scared as I was. He didn't have a mate like I did. He didn't have a family of his own. It had only been a couple moments without Luciano, but all I could think about was the worst.

Were the dragons in the mountain? Or were they out, searching for us?

The more we ventured through the path, the stronger the energy became until we hit a door. I closed my eyes and pressed my hand to the door, feeling the energy from the phoenixes flowing through me.

The iron was thick and reinforced, and while I was certain this wasn't the door I had seen in that dream, it led to the phoenixes.

They were inside of here, somewhere, somehow. This would lead us right to them.

"Ready?" Gideon whispered.

"Yes."

He pushed on the door, but it didn't budge. I tried it and nothing.

"Pull at the same time," Gideon instructed me.

I placed my hands over his and tugged at the same time as him.

No movement. Not even a creak.

Maybe we do need Luciano.

"What do you think is—"

Before I could finish my sentence, Gideon slapped a hand over my mouth and tugged me toward him. The sound of boisterous men laughing was in the distance, the sound of their voices coming closer and closer and closer.

They were coming from where we had just come from.

Fuck!

"We have to hide," Gideon whispered into my ear from behind.

But there was nowhere to hide. Nowhere at all.

CHAPTER
SIXTY-NINE

YEOSIN

I STOOD in front of Gideon, who had put out the fire on his fingers so we were in total darkness against the wall. My heart pounded heavily inside my chest, and my throat tightened as the voices became louder and louder.

Who is this? Did someone follow us down?

The musty air seemed to get even thicker, the longer we waited in tense silence. When the footsteps sounded like they were close enough for whoever owned them to see us, I pressed up against Gideon, my back against his front.

A moment later, the men stepped into the hallway with us, their torch lit very dimly, but enough to see in front of them. I craned my head up to look at them, their stature at least seven feet tall and several feet wide.

Guards.

I hadn't seen them before while I was here; however, they didn't look human or beast or dragon even. They were an entire other breed of animal, and I wasn't that in tune with the mystical world yet to know what they were.

Gideon pressed his fingers into my upper arms and kept me

close to him. I held my breath, hoping that they wouldn't pick up on the fact that there were two other people in the room with them.

If they found us, then it was over. If they found us, then all the phoenixes would be locked up. Maybe Luciano was right. Maybe he should've come down here with us. He would have been able to take on at least one of these guys.

Gideon couldn't even compete with Luciano, muscle on muscle, strength on strength.

The sound of their heavy boots echoed through the room as they walked to the door we had both just been standing by. When they passed us and their backs were turned, Gideon strummed his fingers against my left arm.

I glanced back at him, seeing him nod at their waist. A key shimmered in the dim light.

One guard grabbed it from the chain and stuck it in the keyhole. When the door opened, my heart leaped out of my chest. I could see hundreds, if not thousands, of phoenixes inside the prison.

"Stay here," Gideon whispered into my ear.

My eyes widened as he gently set me to the side and followed behind the two men.

Where the hell is he going?! And without me?!

I couldn't be left down here alone. I came here to free the phoenixes.

"Gideon!" I screamed inside my head.

To my surprise, Gideon looked back, as if he had heard it.

"I will be right back," he said back.

Then he slipped into the room behind the guard, the door slamming shut behind him. I stared at it for a few moments, wondering why I hadn't gone inside with him. It just … it didn't seem like a good idea for both of us to go.

If we were both trapped inside there with the door completely locked and two large animals with us, then every single one of the phoenixes alive would be imprisoned. Then nobody would be there to save us. Then Luciano would die.

Tears burned my eyes. *Luciano dead? My baby growing up in a prison?*

I would rather actually die than have either of those things happen.

Suddenly, yelling ensued from inside the prison. I hurried to the door, pressing my ear against it to see if I could hear anything.

Was Gideon able to set them free that quickly? Was that happening on the inside? Were we—

"Little Mouse …" someone murmured inside my ear. "Gideon told me you'd be here."

CHAPTER
SEVENTY

LUCIANO

CLAWS EXTENDED, I paced back and forth in front of the dungeon door that Yeosin had disappeared inside of ten minutes ago. Twigs snapped underneath my feet as my heart pounded inside my chest.

Ten minutes of pure torture, and nothing had happened yet.

She hadn't come back. No phoenix had been released. The dragons hadn't shown up.

My stomach twisted into tight knots, a heavy feeling weighing down on my chest. Something wasn't right. I should've never ever let her go in there alone with Gideon. He wasn't strong one bit. Smart maybe, but not strong enough to defeat a dragon.

"We're going in," I said to Molly, Brent, and the others.

"You said you'd give her fifteen minutes," Molly said. "Believe in her."

"I do believe in her."

"If you did, then you wouldn't be demanding we go in," Brent said. "She's strong."

I clenched my fists by my sides, attempting to push down the growing sense of agony gnawing at my insides. Yeosin was strong, capable, and so smart. She had done what I thought was impossible. She could do this, but …

"I believe in her, but I already lost her once," I growled, canines dripping with saliva. "I thought she was dead, and I was ready to sacrifice everything to get her back. She carries the future of this pack. I trust her, but it's my job to protect her."

My job as the alpha, but mostly as her mate.

After stopping on top of the dungeon door, I crouched down and placed my fingertips on the metal. My eyes closed, and I tried to get ahold of myself. I had told Yeosin that I would give her fifteen minutes.

But that was fifteen minutes too long for me and for my beast.

"She should be back by now," I said quietly to myself. "It's almost been fifteen minutes."

"It's been ten at most," Brent said, arms crossed but looking just as uneasy.

We peered at each other for a moment, his eyes shifting through a variety of emotions. Weeks ago, he had hit on Yeosin and even maybe liked her.

Now, I could see that he still cared for her, but as more of a protector, a brother.

He was worried too.

What if something had gone wrong? What if they had gotten caught? What if they couldn't get into the prison to release the phoenixes? Were they stuck in there? What would happen if Alvin found them?

Another moment passed, and I stood back up, shoving my shoulders back. "Prepare."

"But, Luciano," Molly started, "we should—"

"Prepare for battle," I repeated, leaving no room for argument. "We don't know what has happened down there, but nothing has happened out here yet. Half the beasts will enter the mountain through the entrances at the top. The others will follow me down into the dungeon. Brent, take a group. The Colossals will lift you to the entrances at the top. Yeosin mentioned that the highest entrance is Alvin's personal chambers. She doesn't know where the others lead."

Brent nodded. "Will do."

Once Brent led the group of warriors to the Colossals, the Colossals shifted into their giant form and peered into the entrance where Yeosin had fallen from. After making sure it was clear, Brent and the warriors stepped into the Colossal's hand, and she placed them on top.

I turned toward the rest. "Molly, you'll stay out here with a few trackers. I trust you to make quick decisions in case the dragons escape the Colossals when they fly out of the mountain. Track them and leave a trail so we can find you."

Despite the look of apprehension on her face, Molly nodded and scattered throughout the forest with a small group of trackers, hiding in the bushes.

Yeosin flashed through my mind again, and I swore that I heard her scream. Chills ran up and down my spine. She'd had such a fire in her eyes when she said that she could do this all on her own. She was so sure, so confident.

And I ... I had let her go.

I grabbed the dungeon door's handle and blew out a low breath. I couldn't wait.

Behind me, my best warriors—the ones who had survived the dragon attack years ago—moved restlessly, growling and scraping their claws together. Muscles tensing, I yanked the door open.

YEOSIN

ONE MOMENT, I stood in front of Alvin in complete and utter shock, my back turned to him and my feet glued to the ground. The next, he lifted me in the air by the back of my neck, turned me around to face him, and offered me the most menacing of scowls.

"You should've stayed away after you escaped. I wasn't going to come looking for you."

"Bullshit," I spit at him, kicking my legs forward. "Let me go!"

My heart pounded so hard that I could hear it in my ears. Had Gideon really betrayed me? What was he doing in there? What were the beasts and Colossals about to walk in on, especially if the Dragon Clan knew we were attacking?

"Truly, I wasn't going to come after someone who was willing to sacrifice her own life to survive." A low chuckle escaped past his jagged teeth, his eyes glowing hot. "I thought you had died. And I thought that stupid fucker wouldn't have the courage to burn your entire—"

Before he could say another word, I slammed my foot forward, hitting him right in the shin. I might've had access to some of my powers, but I didn't know how to use them yet. I didn't know how to escape or how to get out of this mess.

"Don't call my mate stupid. He's a better and smarter man than you will ever be."

Suddenly, his bones began to break and his skin shifted into rough scales as he transformed into a dragon right in this small, crammed space of the dungeon. The walls broke to pieces from the sudden shift and crumbling down around us.

I saw the scent of the prison before I smelled it. My eyes widened as hundreds, if not thousands, of cages filled with phoenixes surrounded me. Alvin dragged me down the pathways, forcing me to see all the phoenixes he had captured, like they were trophies.

"I was willing to keep you as my own, in my chambers, the ultimate prize," he murmured, continuing to drag me along on the dirt path to a large cage in the back of the prison, one that had bars so thick that I could barely see into it. "But I can't take any chances with you."

After kicking and screaming and trying to summon my powers, I snatched on to his hand and sank my claws into it.

Where are my powers when I need them the most? He can't trap me in here with the rest of them.

Where has Gideon gone?

He wasn't here either.

Alvin snapped open the cage and hurled me inside, stepping in with me. He curled his hand around the front of my neck and pressed his body against mine. "When I finish slaughtering your mate, I will bring you back to that cave and breed you myself."

"No, you won't," I spit at him, hitting him right in the face. My blood boiled, literally burning my skin from the inside out. I grabbed his face and sank my thumbs into his huge eyes. "You're not going to touch me, you fucking bastard!"

"Not going to touch you?" he snarled, slamming the door closed and locking it. He threw me to the ground and stalked toward me once more, one of his eyes bloody from my attack. "You're *my* property now. I will do what I want with you."

I grabbed some dirt and threw it up at him, scurrying out of the way before he could grab me again. Fire burned from his mouth, spewing into the cage around me, the taste choking me. I needed to get out of here now.

But how?

Come on, Yeosin. Think!

When the fire and dirt cleared from the air, I made eye contact with the woman who I had seen in my vision through the bars. I could barely see her, but I remembered her eyes. She had been so hopeful that I could do this, and I had let her down.

"Alvin," I snarled, "I'm not going to let you get away with—"

A sharp pain stabbed through my abdomen, a pain so excruciating that I doubled over onto my knees. At first, I thought he had stabbed me or set fire to my stomach, but when I looked down, there was no wound, no fire, nothing.

What is happening? What's going on? Get up, Yeosin! It can't matter right now.

"Get over here, you bitch," Alvin growled, snatching my hair and slamming me against the wall.

I hit it with a thud, the pain only getting worse. He crawled between my thighs, and I attempted to keep him away as best as I could.

No, I can't let this happen. I need to ... I need to get him away. Right now. Luciano is waiting for me.

"No," I screamed, clutching my stomach, my tears burning my vision. "Get away! I—"

Alvin ripped off my pants, and suddenly, a warm gush of wetness spread down my thighs. My eyes widened, the pain becoming quicker and harder and stronger by the millisecond.

Did my ... did my water just break?! And at a time like this?!

I shoved my hand forward in a weak attempt to keep Alvin back, but he continued to move between my thighs, shoving my knees to the sides and grabbing my waist to pull me closer.

"No, Alvin, stop!" I cried. "Please, stop. You'll kill her. You'll kill my baby if you don't stop."

"Good," he snarled. "Then I can get you pregnant with mine."

CHAPTER
SEVENTY-TWO

YEOSIN

PAIN EXPLODED BETWEEN MY LEGS, and I stumbled back against the wall, grasping at Alvin's chest in an attempt to displace all the agony. My claws dug into his muscle as he continued to move closer to me.

Why?! Why did this have to happen now?

"Stop!" I cried.

My baby might have already died and come back to life, but I didn't want a dragon touching her or touching her through me. What would she think of me if the first thing she saw was her mother being raped?

Alvin advanced, forcing me to spread my legs and touching me anywhere that he could. I had seen this part of him before, the vile animal that came out when I didn't want him inside me.

He had raped me before, but I didn't think that was what it was at the time. I'd brushed it off as something all guys did, but Luciano hadn't dared.

Something creaked to my right, and I peered over in an attempt to look at anything but Alvin. I couldn't bear seeing his face as he raped me. Luciano was right. I shouldn't have come down here alone.

Because I hadn't listened to him, I was about to … about to …

Alvin's mouth met my jaw roughly. I stared through my tears at the vacant cell beside me. Surely, a moment ago, it held a phoenix.

Where … where did she go? Did she leave me? Did Gideon actually help her escape?

That bastard Gideon … he had betrayed me. He wouldn't release any phoenix.

"You're all mine, Yeosin," Alvin snarled. "I don't care what happens to anyone else whe—"

Suddenly, Alvin was hurled off me with power so immense that a wave of air dispersed through the space around me. My body was thrust against the wall even harder, and I dropped to the ground, my legs spread and my vagina aching with indescribable pain.

Rush after rush rattled through my body. My head lolled back, and I sobbed, clutching my vagina. When I pulled my fingers away, they were covered in blood.

Blood? Why are they covered in blood?!

Another indescribable ache, and I found myself on my knees, leaning onto my hands and sobbing. "Please, be alive," I said, feeling her crowning. I dropped down onto one shoulder and spread my legs wider.

I didn't want to give birth in a prison. I wanted to be at home —in a packhouse—with Luciano by my side, him pushing the hair off my sweaty forehead and telling me that I was doing a good job, that everything was going to be okay. But was it? Was it really going to be okay?

I was giving birth to a phoenix in the middle of Alvin's dungeon for phoenixes. I couldn't tell where Alvin had gone, but the room around me was quickly filling with fire.

"Oh my God!" I screamed, pushing as hard as I could. "Fuck!"

Half her head was dangling out of me now. I pushed as hard

as I could again and grabbed what I could of her to guide her out of my vagina.

"Fuck!" I hissed. "It hurts so bad."

After another long, hard push, I completely pushed her out of me.

But I didn't hear her cry.

Babies cry, don't they? Why isn't she?

I cradled her in my arms, placing her against my chest that jerked up and down from my quickened breaths. "Please, please, please, be alive," I cried, tears racing down my cheeks. I could barely open my eyes; the heat from the dragons' fire burned them so badly.

If she dies … if our baby dies … Luciano will never forgive me. I wouldn't forgive me. If only I hadn't gone down here alone with Gideon while I was pregnant. What was I thinking?! How stupid was that?!

"Please, baby," I sobbed, clutching her tightly.

I didn't know when it had started, and at this point, I couldn't remember how, but so much was happening around me—people screaming, beasts growling, dragons igniting the cells on fire, phoenixes burning. But their collective strength seemed to grow by the moment, empowering me to peel my eyes open.

I stared down at the baby—my baby—in my arms, gasping as she stared up at me with Luciano's huge brown eyes that burned a deep, fiery orange in the center.

SEVENTY-THREE

LUCIANO

WHEN I STEPPED through the door of the prison, someone hurled Alvin's body toward me. I didn't have time to react as he collided against my chest and sent me flying back into the dark walkway that we had spent a good ten minutes trying to navigate.

The warriors around me backed up, shifting into their beasts, and I did the same, my nails extending into long talons and my canines dripping with saliva. I ripped my claws into his chest, sending him in the opposite direction.

A flood of screams and fire flowed out from the prison, and Yeosin's scent followed.

Mate. Find mate now.

But I had to take care of this asshole before he could hurt anyone else. Besides, her scent was strongest on him, exploding in waves and waves from his groin. A growl ripped from my mouth, and I lunged at him.

What did he do to her?! Where is she?!

Alvin breathed fire at me, the heat so intense that I could feel it burning through my fur and my skin. But I didn't care. I saw red.

I saw rage. Yeosin's scent was all over him—her scent that only I should know!

More fire exploded through the room, and I breathed it in. If I didn't end this soon, then it would surely kill me and everyone else in the walkway with me. I swiped my claws across his neck, breaking through the thick skin.

"Go! Find Yeosin!" I growled to the others.

Once they disappeared into the chaos, I snapped my hands around Alvin's neck, ducking out of the way so he couldn't hit me with another wall of fire. A roar left his mouth, and he began flapping his massive wings to shake me off him. I held on for dear life, sinking my claws into the flesh.

He lashed his tail out, swinging it from side to side and hitting me in the shin each and every time in an attempt to wear me down, to kick me off. His fire was so hot that my hands began to burn.

It poured from his mouth in bursts, setting the ground ablaze around me. Smoke filled the air, and I held my breath. All this pain ... it fueled me. His fire had destroyed my pack decades ago, and I refused to let that happen again.

We were so close ... *I* was so close to finally being happy, to having a family.

I wouldn't lose that. Not for a second time.

A snarl left my mouth, and I sank my canines into his neck when my hands gave out. I tore through the scales and muscle, the sickening taste of dragon blood filling my mouth. His groan turned into a screech, and he flailed his body around uncontrollably.

"I warned you," I growled. "Yeosin is mine!"

With one swift, vicious motion, I tore into him, ripping through the thick, scaly hide of his neck and reaching his innards. His body convulsed against mine, flames sputtering in his throat before his head lolled forward and his lifeless body fell against me.

Fire dripped from my entire body. I shoved him off me and heaved.

Yeosin. I need to find Yeosin.

I spun around, heart pounding, and sprinted toward the prison door. Inside, fire burned the cages; phoenixes were flying through the air, battling warrior dragons; and beasts were doing what they could on the ground.

"Yeosin!" I shouted through the flames, my body still burning. "Yeosin!"

My beast clawed at my insides, desperate to find her, to make sure she was okay. She had to be. I needed to see her, hold her, feel her against me. She was pregnant, and she had gone down here all alone.

I let her come down here alone.

I scanned the prison, hoping to find her, but locked on to someone else's gaze entirely. My entire body froze, and I could hear the blood pounding in my ears. She stood there, staring back, in the middle of the battleground, untouched by the flames.

"Mom?" I whispered.

CHAPTER
SEVENTY-FOUR

LUCIANO

WHILE CHAOS ENSUED AROUND ME, my world seemed to stop completely. Heat from the flames that burned my skin faded from my existence. My feet were frozen on the ground.

Mom? Alive? Standing in front of me as if I hadn't seen her die decades ago?

What was this? Had Gideon been right about all of it? Had he *known*?

She walked toward me, her features softening the way they had when I was just a boy, when I had come back from playing outside with all my packmates, covered in dirt and mud and grass. I opened and closed my mouth a handful of times, unable to make a sound.

Yeosin. I need to find her.

Yet I couldn't move.

"Luciano," Mom whispered when she reached me.

I swallowed hard because this couldn't be her and stepped back. *No, this can't be her. How is she here? Has she been in this prison for decades? All alone? Trapped? If I had known ... I would have ... I could have ...*

"Luciano," she repeated, taking my face into her hands. She stared up at me with tears heavy in her eyes. "My boy. My baby boy, how I've missed you so much. I knew that you'd find me, that you'd come save all of us."

My throat was dry, my heart pounding inside my chest. I gently placed my hands over hers, feeling her flesh. She was real, not some figment of my imagination, not some trance, not some ghost. Real.

"Mom," I said softly, my gaze scanning her face. "How are you …"

"We don't have time to talk now," she said. "I will explain everything later."

"But—"

She swiped the pad of her thumb across my cheek to wipe away a tear. "Yeosin is fine."

Suddenly, everything seemed to shift back to reality, and I snapped my gaze from my mother, who I had thought was dead, to the chaos around me. Dragons still breathed fire on the phoenixes. Beasts were being thrown around like rag dolls. Yeosin was … nowhere to be found.

"Where is she? I need to find her and our baby."

Mom nodded. "You will, Luciano. She's here. But we have a greater task at hand. Alvin was only part of the Dragon Clan, not the leader of it. From what I've gathered, there are several sections to the clan. The Dragon Clan is vast, and they want more than revenge. They want their empire back. And they can take it if they get their hands on the phoenix eggs."

"Phoenix eggs?" I repeated, gaze still trailing across the prison for my mate.

What did phoenix eggs have to do with this? Mom gave me one to keep at the office.

"With all the eggs, they can easily rise to power again, reclaiming their empire through fire and destruction. You must find them before the rest of the dragons do." She swallowed.

"You've only defeated one section of their forces. More are coming."

More? More? How can we defeat more? We could barely handle this sector.

"Trust me and trust yourself," she said. "We can do this together. The dragons haven't fought a troop of phoenixes like this for over a thousand years. To imprison us, they captured us one by one. We're unstoppable now, especially once we get those eggs."

"Luciano!" Yeosin called, her voice faint. "Luciano, please!"

"Go," Mom urged.

I snapped my head toward the sound, my heart thumping so loud that I could hear it in my ears. My legs started moving before I could process what I was doing, running through the fire, through the flames, through the battlegrounds, where my dead packmates lay, leaving Mom.

"Yeosin!" I shouted, finally spotting her through the haze of smoke.

She was kneeling on the ground in the middle of an open cell with tears running down her cheeks as she clutched something to her chest. My heart raced. She lifted her gaze, meeting mine, and I almost froze a second time.

A baby. *Our* baby.

"Yeosin," I whispered, rushing toward her.

Once I reached the prison cell, I dropped to my knees beside her and pulled her and our baby into my arms with bloody, trembling hands. Our baby ... she was so small. So tiny.

"Luciano," she cried. "Tell me that he's ... that he's dead."

"Alvin is dead," I whispered, placing my forehead against hers. "And you, us—*we* are safe."

For now.

CHAPTER
SEVENTY-FIVE

YEOSIN

FIRE BLAZED ALL AROUND US. I gripped our baby in my arms as Luciano carried me through the chaos. Dragon and beast corpses lay in puddles of blood in the prison around us. I shielded our baby's eyes and squeezed mine shut too, all the sensations too powerful.

"It's going to be okay," Luciano murmured. "Don't worry."

Luciano slipped through the door into the corridor that Gideon and I had hidden in less than an hour ago. The stench of blood and rotting flesh drifted through my nose, and I opened my eyes in time to see us passing Alvin's body.

Chunks of his body were scattered around the dark hallway, and his dragon scales were littered down the pathway. Tears pricked the corners of my eyes because I knew that my mate had done this. My mate had killed Alvin for me. For us.

After weaving through the halls, Luciano finally found a hole in the ceiling above us that led to the outside. He set me down onto my feet, then took the baby from me, cradling her in his large arms. "Can you make it up there?"

"Yes," I said, though I wasn't sure how to use my flight yet.

I stared up at the hole in the ceiling and took a deep breath, trying and trying and trying to summon my wings, like the other phoenixes had. A moment passed, and then I felt Luciano's hand on my hip.

"Don't worry about your powers right now," he said. "Jump, and I'll lift you."

Warmth spread through my chest, and I used all the strength I had left in my legs to leap into the air. Luciano lifted me higher, shoving me as hard as he could. I gripped the edge of the ceiling and pulled myself outside.

The heat from the sun hit my exposed skin, and I looked around to see the outside was just as chaotic as the prison, except out here, the Colossals were fighting the dragons. Fire raged in the trees. We needed to get to safety as soon as we could.

I dropped to my knees and leaned over through the hole, reaching for the baby.

Once Luciano handed her to me, he leaped out with the use of his beast. Then he scooped us into his arms once more and began a trek through the battle, dodging fire and dragons falling from the sky.

"Hold on tightly," Luciano said.

When I gripped on to him as tight as I could, he shifted into his beast. Teeth lengthened into canines. Skin turned into fur. Muscles grew underneath me. And he was off into the daylight, running as fast as he could.

I didn't know how long I held on to him with our baby. Maybe an hour, maybe four.

But he only slowed once the forest became more familiar and The Breeding Cave came into view. He shifted back into his human form and slowed to a stop just out front, finally setting me down and guiding us into the cave.

Memories of our first night here flooded through my mind, and I found myself collapsing onto one of the boulders inside with our baby tight to my chest. So many nights ago, we had been here for the first time.

And now?

Now we were back here, safe, as a family.

"We're safe now," he whispered.

I let out a shaky breath. "We made it."

Luciano leaned on the boulder beside me, wrapping his arm around my shoulders and pulling us close. I rested against him, my head against his chest. All the fear, the fire, the dragons seemed to disappear from my mind.

We were safe. We were really safe.

A tear slipped from my eye, and Luciano was quick to swipe it away.

"Yeosin," he whispered, "we're going to be okay."

"Gideon, he …" I said, my chest suddenly heavy with guilt. "I should've listened to you. Gideon betrayed me, betrayed *us*. He left me alone down there. He … I wouldn't doubt if he alerted the dragons."

"I know," Luciano said, pulling my head onto his chest. "But I think he was the one who let the phoenixes out. Still doesn't mean I like that asshole. Next time I see him, I'm going to kill him. But all that matters now is that you're safe."

"Where is he now?" I asked.

"I don't know," Luciano said. "Gone. But I'll deal with him if he comes back. What's really important is that we find all the phoenix eggs. I saw my mom … she was one of the phoenixes that Alvin had imprisoned. She told me that we need to find the eggs."

"Your mom?" I asked, eyes widening. *Was that the woman I saw in my visions?* "I saw some of the eggs up in Alvin's bedroom. All the way at the top of the mountain. They're in his hoard."

Luciano nodded. "Brent went up there. He'll find them and retrieve them then."

"What if Gideon gets to them first?" Fear rushed through me. "What will happen?"

Luciano paused. "I don't know, but he won't."

"You're so sure of it."

"I trust Brent. Do you?"

I sucked in a breath. "Yes, I do."

"Then all that's left for us to do right now is to go back."

"Back?" I asked. "Back where?"

"To the packhouse. We're going to rebuild our lives, Yeosin. Together."

CHAPTER
SEVENTY-SIX

LUCIANO

WITH OUR BABY in the crook of my left arm and Yeosin holding on to my right, I stared at the packhouse that lay in ashes. Nothing except some foundation was left standing, and the fire from the dragons' attack had burned the trees down around it.

I had never thought that I would be back, never mind with a mate and child.

"When we rebuild it, it can be everything it once was and more," Yeosin whispered.

"You're right," I said softly, wishing that it were rebuilt now, wishing that I would have the chance to raise my daughter in the house that I had been raised in, that my father had been raised in, and his father too. "It'll be more."

But all that I really cared about was that we were all safe.

"I knew you'd be here," someone said behind me.

Yeosin and I looked over our shoulders at Mom as she walked toward me with some other phoenixes following her. Still, I couldn't wrap my mind around how she was here. How hadn't she died? Why hadn't she come to visit me?

I had so many questions that I wasn't sure she could answer.

Mom moved her gaze from me to Yeosin, her smile widening even more. "I see you've met your mate, Luciano. She's stronger than even she knows." Mom pinched Yeosin's cheek gently. "You're going to have your hands full."

"Why didn't you tell me Luciano was your son?" Yeosin asked, rubbing her cheek.

"Because some things are better left unsaid," Mom said, peering back at me. "There are questions I don't have the answers to and answers I can't begin explaining in a believable way. But with time, the truth will be revealed, and everything will make sense."

"How?" I asked. "How are you here?"

"Would you believe me if I said it was magic?" Mom asked, peering down at our baby and tickling her belly with her forefinger. Our baby giggled, her smile wider and brighter than any newborn's that I had ever seen. "You need some clothes for her."

"I don't know what I would believe," I said honestly, taking a small step backward.

I loved my mother, but I didn't trust her completely yet. Gideon had come back from the dead, just like Mom had. He had gained my trust, and then he betrayed me. Or at least that was how it seemed. I hadn't seen him since he had disappeared with Yeosin.

"Things will be hard to explain, Luciano," Mom said, her face remaining unchanged.

"Explain them anyway."

"I'm sure you saw it with Yeosin," Mom said. "Her body died, but she was reborn in it."

"Yeah, but I buried your body," I said. "Just like I buried Gideon's."

"We were dug up," she said. "By Gideon's father."

"Gideon's father?" I asked, venom on my tongue. "The man you cheated on Dad with?"

Mom peered down at her feet. "Luciano, you don't know how I felt ... I can't explain it."

I pursed my lips and nodded because I would never know how cheating on a mate felt. I would never know how betraying the one person who had been made for me felt, how having a child with another felt.

It was disgusting. Vile.

Suddenly, a wave of hushed whispers echoed throughout the forest. I placed our baby in Yeosin's arms and stepped in front of her and my mother, preparing for another dragon to attack. The forest had been too quiet ...

"Hey, hey, hey!" Brent called. "That you?"

I blew out a breath, relaxing only slightly as he and the other warriors came into view. Colossals walked with them, dragging imprisoned dragons after them. Everyone who was still alive seemed to walk upon our old packhouse.

"You made it," I said, gently squeezing his shoulder.

He threw my mate a wink. "You think I wouldn't make it back to see Yeosin?"

She giggled behind me as I let out a low warning growl.

"Did you grab them?"

"Grab what?" Brent asked while the others dispersed and mingled with each other.

Some of the beasts were amazed at the sight of the phoenixes and stared at them like they were the most fascinating beings ever created.

After all, they had been a myth all this time.

"The phoenix eggs," I said. "They were in Alvin's room."

Brent furrowed his brows and shook his head. "After we killed the dragons inside the castle, we searched every inch of that thing. There were no eggs." He peered over at Yeosin. "Are you sure you saw them?"

"Yes," she said, clutching our baby to her chest. "I'm positive."

"Well, they weren't there."

"What the fuck do you mean, they weren't there?" I growled at Brent.

Yeosin froze behind me. "Gideon has them then. I know he does. I can feel it."

With my hands on my hips, I rocked backward. "We can't make decisions on feelings."

"We can make them on *my* feelings," she said.

Yeosin was right. To my understanding of how she explained her feelings and her connection with other phoenixes, we *could* make them based on her feelings. If she felt like Gideon had them, then he probably did.

I had trusted Yeosin once, and she had almost died. But this time, I felt that she was right.

Gideon had the eggs, and we didn't know why.

"Gideon released me from the prison," Mom said, speaking up. "But he apologized right afterward, then disappeared. I don't know why he didn't save the rest of us, only me. I know he saw Yeosin in the cage beside me with Alvin on her."

"He took the eggs," Yeosin said. "It's the only possible explanation."

"Where is he now?" I asked Mom.

She shrugged. "I'm not sure. He didn't say, and I didn't follow him. I was busy releasing the rest of the phoenixes before anyone could capture us all again."

"Fuck," I cursed underneath my breath, running a hand through my hair. "Fuck!"

Yeosin placed her free hand on my chest. "It's okay for now. The phoenixes are free. That's what matters. We'll find the eggs, and when Gideon returns—because he will return—we will deal with him then."

The anger was still bubbling inside me, but I pushed it away. "We'll find him."

"We will," she whispered.

I looked down at my mate and our child, who was safe in her

arms, and I knew we would make it through this. And I would do anything to protect what was mine. No matter the cost.

To read a bonus scene and two epilogues from The Breeding Cave, sign up here.

ALSO BY EMILIA ROSE

Submitting to the Alpha

Come Here, Kitten

My Werewolf Professor

The Twins

Four Masked Wolves

Monster Lover

My Bad Boy Alpha

Alpha Maddox

Summoning Sex Demons

The Breeding Cave

Next Door Incubus

Stepbrother

Poison

The Bad Boy

Detention

My Brother's Best Friend

Science Project

Excite Me

Mafia Boss

Mafia Toy

Mafia Betrayal

Sex Education

Bound By My Father's Best Friend

Pornstar

ABOUT THE AUTHOR

Emilia Rose is a USA Today bestselling author of steamy romance. She loves writing about dirty-talking bad boys who are obsessed with innocent, and sometimes insecure, virgin heroines. She currently lives in a small town in Connecticut USA with her husband and three playful cats.

Join Emilia's newsletter for exclusive giveaways, early chapter releases, and more!

www.ingramcontent.com/pod-product-compliance
Lightning Source LLC
Chambersburg PA
CBHW021136310726
48971CB00002B/351